HIGH OCTANE
UNLEASHED

ASHLINN CRAVEN

author of *High Octane: Ignited* and *Maybe Baby*

CRIMSON
ROMANCE

F+W Media, Inc.

Published by
Crimson Romance
an imprint of F+W Media, Inc.
10151 Carver Road, Suite 200
Blue Ash, OH 45242. U.S.A.
www.crimsonromance.com

ISBN 10: 1-4405-8557-1
ISBN 13: 978-1-4405-8557-9
eISBN 10: 1-4405-8558-X
eISBN 13: 978-1-4405-8558-6

Acknowledgments

I'd like to thank my beta reader and friend, Rachel Cross, and all those in my life who love Formula One—Ulf, Fionn, John, Siobhán, and Caoimhín.

As always, thanks to my wonderful editor, Julie Sturgeon, and also to Stephanie Riva, Tara Gelsomino, and all the great folks at Crimson Romance who helped make this book happen.

Finally, thanks to those dedicated F1 drivers out there whose fascinating and dangerous lives have inspired this story.

Chapter 1

Abu Dhabi

When he heard a warm, female laugh rise like a delicate butterfly above the buzz of masculine noise, Adam Fontaine did a swift scan of the Formula One crowd for its source. Not many girlfriends or wives hung around for this drinks session after the regulations briefing meeting. Given that the bar was jam-packed, loud and sweaty, any women present had to be desperate to please. Or lonely.

But that laugh didn't sound like either; there was nothing artificial about it. Her voice exuded confidence and humor, tempered with restraint—the qualities a woman needed if she were to survive this tramping ground of male egos. He put down his beer that tasted of mass production and chemicals—only a slight improvement on two years ago—and twisted the barstool around to get a visual on her.

There she was, over there with Reece Marlowe. A slender blonde with a severe haircut that showed off a beautiful neck held with ballerina poise. No doubt she'd have a cute little pixie face to go with that hair when she turned around. Bloody Marlowe and his women. Couldn't he have one single night without a conquest?

Adam swiveled back to the bar.

"That's Vivienne McCloud, the new reporter with the Beeb," Bruce, his lead chassis engineer, said, pointing a beer mat to the center of the room.

"Serious?" Adam swung around again to get a better look.

"Yeah I'm serious. And with that cropped hair of hers, she looks like she means business. Just watch what you say around her, mate."

He shot the older man a look.

Bruce laughed. "Yeah, right, no danger of that."

So this British woman got the BBC F1 reporting slot that Peter Dreyson vacated last season. She'd been the girlfriend of fellow drivers Ronan Hawes and then Maddux Bates, an unlikely progression if ever there was one, but each to his own. Thanks to his mashed leg, Adam had missed all the fun and games of last season, held no opinion of her, and that seemed to put him in the minority around here. His view of her was now obscured by a wall of male bodies.

"Don't worry, she'll make it her business to meet you," Bruce said, still grinning.

"And move on swiftly. My life is uninteresting for the readers of gossip rags."

"It's the freaking BBC, not a gossip rag." Bruce rapped Adam's knuckles with the edge of his beer mat. "And be sure she'll want to know all about the Belgian Comeback Kid."

"Good luck to her." Adam shoved the empty beer bottle toward the barman. She'd last about two months. If the attentions of Reece Marlowe and his sort didn't make her want to run screaming, then the politics would.

• • •

Viv extricated herself from her conversation with reigning champion Reece Marlowe to focus on nabbing her next interviewee—his former teammate, Adam Fontaine. In Reece's over-the-top ridicule of the Belgian driver's new team colors, she detected a certain level of contempt for the man inside the radioactive green overalls.

Indeed, team Gatari's trademark colors sparked some good-natured cries of revulsion in the pressrooms across the world, too, but its record in the pre-season testing had everyone on silent tenterhooks. The main source of this awe was the driver standing at the bar just ten feet away.

Her file said the twenty-nine-year-old Belgian had developed an affinity for cars and engines even before he could talk. On his twelfth birthday his parents gave him money and he spent it, unknown to them, on an eighties Chevrolet Camaro IROC-Z that was basically a wreck. He stripped it down, dismantled the engine and rebuilt it piece by piece over the next two years, and by the end of the process knew how cars worked.

He drove that Camaro around the private lanes of their country estate in Wallonia long before it was legal for him to do so. The family moved to the United States when he was fourteen, and two years later, his younger brother died in a quad bike accident. He left home soon afterward to pursue his dream of becoming a driver, proving a severe disappointment to his now-divorced father, who had wanted him to take over the family winery.

Her new boss had warned her in his briefing that Adam was "more taciturn than usual" since he'd crashed in Malaysia two seasons ago and shattered his ankle and lower leg, which explained why she hadn't found any decent coverage on that story. The injury had kept him out of the championship last year.

Thank God, because that meant there was one man in this teeming pit of testosterone who hadn't witnessed her own little saga with her exes in the hotel bars of the world last season. He was clean slate. Sure, she'd seen a few pictures of him—boring crewcut, broad forehead, dark eyes, finely drawn mouth and jaw, sort of the antithesis of shaggy-blond Reece Marlowe. In none of the photos did Adam Fontaine look like he was enjoying life very much.

She kept her phone glued to her ear in fake conversation as she pushed her way through sweating bodies, reaching Fontaine quickly. He was staring ahead at the display of single malts behind the bar. The mid-fifties man sitting beside him must have sensed her presence first because he slid his barstool away from the driver to grant her room.

"Adam," the older man said in a gravelly voice, giving her a wink.

Her interview subject turned around. The intensity of his dark eyes torpedoed out from a face that otherwise exuded serenity. The photos had failed to capture his essence.

She offered her hand, smiling. "Hi, I'm Vivienne McCloud, reporting for BBC Sports this season."

He took her hand, shook it briefly, and then glanced around, presumably for a stool.

"No, it's fine, I'm not staying long," she said. Five minutes tops. This could definitely be done standing.

Still, he slid off his seat and maneuvered it to her using his foot. "I insist. It's yours." Fontaine's voice, with its crisp, staccato North European accentuation, suited his reputation for perfectionism somehow. Scant trace of his fifteen years living in California there.

"Thanks." She propped her handbag on the stool in a show of compromise.

"This is Bruce."

"G'day."

She shook hands with the genial-looking Aussie with oil stains on his fingers and a twinkle in his faded blue eyes.

But the crew technicians weren't on her list. Her assignment was to talk to drivers tonight, twenty-two of them in fact, and she wasn't going to muck up her first official assignment. "I thought I'd introduce myself before my history does the talking for me." She held his gaze to see how this registered. A flash of understanding, perhaps, but no particular interest. Excellent.

"Can I get you a drink?" he asked.

"I'm good, thanks." She raised the lethal Lemon Bomb cocktail Reece had bought her. "So, you're first driver for team Gatari?

That's quite an impressive comeback from your injuries of the season before last with team Supernova."

"I'm first driver, yes." His expression was steady, his body language mimicking hers.

"How does it feel to be back?" Emotions, emotions, emotions, that's what Mack wanted, with an extra dollop of drama.

"The beer tastes better this year. Slightly."

She maintained a smile and waited, but nothing else came out. The lengthening silence whispered the words "blood" and "stone" to her. She beckoned to the label on his beer bottle. "And you being half Belgian would know how to judge that, yes?"

"I'm better judge of wine," he said. "But thanks."

"For what?"

"For not saying 'French', or worse, 'half French.'"

She chuckled. "Well, I do know the difference between Belgian and French. I'm British. We're practically neighbors. So are you a wine snob then?"

"Nobody who's worked in a winery is a wine snob."

"I'll take that as a no." Good thing, too. Fontaine wines were exclusive and highly regarded, and if he were a wine snob, they'd be here all night. It looked like they'd be here all night anyway at the rate she was extracting information from him.

"Is French your mother tongue?"

"He's bilingual," Bruce chimed in. "Speaks Flemish."

"Poorly," Adam added.

"I see. So, you must be looking forward to the Spa-Francorchamps circuit. All those Belgian ... Wallonian fans?"

"It's halfway through the season. Ask me then."

"Oh, I intend to," she said, pen poised for the next question.

Just then, the phone in Adam's pocket buzzed. She got a glimpse of white teeth as he grimaced in apology and slunk away into the crowd, leaving her staring at Bruce. Why Adam, despite the good looks, wasn't another Formula One player was starting to become clear. His charm quotient was sparse. But the appraising manner he had of looking at her suggested he wasn't totally cold-blooded either. Nope, those eyes gave him away whether he liked it or not.

Fifteen minutes later, she shot a doleful look at Bruce. It was way past time to move on, even if Bruce was lovely company, his humorous ways reminding her of her late father. "He's not coming back, is he?"

Bruce shook his gray head.

"What's wrong with him? Why the reticence?"

He patted her hand kindly. "Nothing personal, love. He just doesn't like reporters."

"Has he had a bad experience?"

"I think it's what he's generally trying to avoid."

"Avoid? Why?"

"The thing you need to know about Adam is that he tries to preempt disaster." Bruce rolled his eyes. "He spends most of his waking hours obsessing about what could go wrong—with the car, with the circuit, with the weather—and figuring out how to avoid it. I've only worked with him for a month now, but he's worn me out more than any other driver with his preparations and his questions."

"So, he sees being interviewed as some kind of disaster?"

Bruce shrugged. "Let's just say a risk that he doesn't need to take."

"Is it because of the way the press handled the accident with Reece in Malaysia?"

Bruce prodded the beer mat against the counter. "That didn't help, I suppose." He scanned her face and then seemed to make a snap decision. "Look, in the beginning half of the season, Adam was Supernova's second driver, no problem. But ten races in, he was outperforming Reece consistently in the practice runs and qualifiers—and before Malaysia, Charles, team manager, decided to try Adam out as first driver.

"Reece was furious because his contract now said he should give way to Adam if they found themselves at the lead of a race. No driver wants to be beaten by the one guy who has the same equipment as he does—much less be ordered to give way to him. So in Malaysia, Reece decided he wanted to keep that one for himself.

"They were neck and neck, charged into curve twenty-seven together. Adam assumed Reece would obey the rules and hang back. There was shouting; there was contact. Adam went spinning off and crashed against the barriers, heavy impact, which shattered his leg. Reece went on to win and got Charles to say that he'd still been designated first driver and this was all agreed tactics."

"But how did he get away with it? I mean there are radio recordings, no?"

"Charles's radio message was so cryptic it could have been interpreted both ways. I talked to Charles myself. Eventually the old bastard admitted that he may have covered up a little. What was the alternative? Fire Reece and have no drivers? He wasn't about to do that. The Supernova team won that season. They got a good, obedient replacement driver for Adam for the rest of the races who was happy to be second driver to Reece."

She frowned. "But why didn't Adam say something?"

"It was too late—his word against Reece's. Nobody cared. Reece's contract was changed back before anyone saw it. Charles had a winner on his hands—he sure as hell wasn't going to say anything."

Bruce glanced around and, seeming satisfied they weren't being eavesdropped on, continued, "There were connections too. After Malaysia, Reece introduced Charles to a high-class bartender named Julie"—he shrugged—"who became his mistress."

"Giving Charles another reason to 'forget' he'd made Adam first driver?"

Bruce gave her an appraising look. "No flies on you. Reece was more popular all around, so it didn't play out in Adam's favor. Everyone assumed sour grapes on Adam's part. It fit; it was easier."

"But it's so unfair," she said.

"Drivers ignoring orders to stay behind their teammates or to let them past is nothing new, love. There areplenty others standing around you in this very room."

"Yes, but the cover up?"

"Yeah, that was low."

Bruce had a face you automatically trusted—besides, why would he make this stuff up?

"But listen, don't start writing up any of this stuff I'm telling you. Take it from me—you don't want to mess with Supernova's lawyers."

"Sure. So that's why Adam hates Reece?"

Bruce winced. "He didn't always. They were actually good friends—very good friends—for a while, until it became obvious that Adam wouldn't ever be content as second driver. Drivers can't afford to build true friendships. You know that yourself, love. Hurts their racing."

Viv nodded. In her experience, drivers tolerated nothing and nobody that would hurt their racing. You had to tiptoe around them all the time, produce glamorous smiles in the sunshine, and disappear when the going got rough. "Why are you telling me all this? This isn't common knowledge."

"You care about people, don't you?"

She straightened her posture. "I like to get to the truth of things."

Bruce grinned. "Well, you're going to have fun around here."

•••

"*Oui?*" Adam said warily into his phone when he'd found a quieter, but hotter, corner outside the bar. It was Saskia's number, but Jeff might've hijacked her phone again—

"It's me." His sister's soft tone sounded distant over the line from the States.

He relaxed his shoulders against the gritty wall. "Hey, Sask."

"I'm not interrupting, am I?" These days, she spoke only English to him, and she managed to sound a bit more Californian every time he talked to her. He missed her badly; he hadn't seen enough of her since he'd joined F1which she was fond of reminding him about.

"Not as such."

"Okay, here goes … wait for it … I'm engaged!" she said with a self-conscious giggle afterward. "I mean, Jeff and I are engaged."

"Whoa, Sask … that's … that's news." Adam stared up at the peeling yellow plaster on the ceiling. "Dad's okay about it, is he?"

"Yes, of course he is."

He could picture the vertical line forming between her elfin eyes, matching the peevish tone that had crept into her voice.

"Why wouldn't he be?" she continued. "Jeff's been amazing this past year; he's practically taken over the day-to-day running of the winery."

"I know." In fairness, Saskia had become happier, more settled, less needy, adopting Jeff's relaxed attitude to life and his West Coast accent. God knows, she deserved her happiness, even if it left him even more out in the cold.

But Jeff had turned up conveniently soon after the winery had started to go into profit and he could live off it. Where had he been during the tearful years when Saskia had run things on her own with Dad, in near poverty? What did Jeff have to show for his previous life? Nothing. A ski bum—that's what he was underneath and always would be. "When's the wedding?"

"Don't worry, we're holding on 'til your season's over. December fifth's the date. We're doing it right here in Emily's Hill, in the south vineyard. Won't that be romantic?"

"I guess." Adam wiped beads of sweat from his hairline with the cuff of his overall.

"Maybe we'll have something else to celebrate then, yes?"

"If you mean the championship, count on it."

"*Fantastique*. Then we can have a celebrity wedding, can't we? We'd be B-celebs if you won."

"If you say so." His cool tone was deliberate so she'd wake up any decade now and address the problem here.

"Oh God … you and Dad. Look, I have thought about it. And I have a plan."

"I'm not showing up unless he actually wants to see me. Sorry, but you know how it is. And Sask," Adam paused, "none of your games, okay?"

He hung up.

Turning toward the door of the bar, he deliberated. No, it was time to a call it a night. Little point in going back in there and getting more questions. She'd have moved on by now anyway.

Chapter 2

Next morning, Viv's phone trilled at what felt like an ungodly hour, only it wasn't. It was a boringly normal 8:00 a.m. Emirate time. Day three in Abu Dhabi, and she was still disorientated. She peered at the phone. UK number. Maybe her brother Liam wanting the usual blow-by-blow account of her evening hobnobbing with the drivers? But not his number. And it was the middle of the night in Britain. She pressed the fragranced quilt against her cheek. *Work! Must be work.*

Before she'd fully come to her senses, Mack's booming voice over the line informed her of an interview with a sponsor called Al-Saeed, some big shot whose money decided the fate of the Pantech-Windsor team. Rumors circulated that he was pulling out. It was a matter of strategic importance within F1 circles. Mack wanted the scoop. He wanted it today. This morning.

"One last thing," her boss said, making his first pause in the rapid-fire monologue, "He's in Riyadh."

"Riyadh?" Viv shot up into sitting position. Five hundred miles away.

"Yeah, Riyadh. I've arranged the flight. At noon. You'll arrive there after one, get the interview, be back on circuit before they finish the qualifiers for some interviews with the drivers and the engineers and whoever else you can get your claws on. Oh, and this guy is a traditionalist; you'll need to wear a headscarf and an abaya."

An abaya. Ironically, she'd been this close to bringing the black cloak-like garment that an Iranian friend had suggested, but had decided against it at the last minute to save on suitcase space. Abu Dhabi and Bahrain were not strict enforcers of Sharia law; it sufficed for non-Muslims to cover up limbs and chest. But Riyadh was a whole different ballgame. Abayas and headscarves were non-optional wardrobe items for women of any persuasion.

Wonderful.

"I'd a hard enough time getting Al-Saeed to agree to being interviewed by a woman," Mack grumbled. "It's not like I have a whole sodding team out there to cater to these people's every goddamn whim. So, don't be late. Grab your gear."

Viv tossed the phone on the bed. "Holy Mother, how am I even supposed to get one?" Okay, Yas Viceroy was one of the finest five-star hotels in Abu Dhabi. They must have a five-star solution service on hand for silly Western damsels stranded without their abayas. She dialed reception.

"Yes ma'am?"

"I need to buy an abaya. Do you stock them in the hotel shops?"

"No ma'am. But you can go to the mall, and they have a very good selection, ma'am. We can call a taxi for you. No problem."

"Yes, um," Viv paused, rubbing her forehead. "Maybe later. I'll call you later. Thank you."

Damn. This meant she'd have to go outside the hotel, and all she wanted to do was have a quiet breakfast and lock herself up in her air-conditioned room to prepare for her TV interviews at the qualifiers this afternoon—her first-ever F1 appearance as an official reporter, as opposed to official girlfriend. She glanced around the room desperately … maybe a curtain? A sheet? No. Wrong color.

She was being ridiculous. What kind of world-class journalist was she if she couldn't handle the little hiccups that always accompanied global travelers? She grabbed her purse and marched out her door to the elevators. After a quick breakfast, she'd just zip to the mall on the way to the airport. End of story.

Dashing full speed around the breakfast buffet, she met Reece Marlowe deliberating over some sushi in a glass vitrine. "Always wondered if one should eat sushi for breakfast," he said by way of greeting.

"I wouldn't risk it," she said. "You know what happens when you barf with a helmet on."

Reece's face twisted. "My, you are a charming princess this morning. What's wrong? You fall out of the bed?" He leaned closer. "Get tangled in the sheets? Aha-ha. Who was it this time? Who's lucky number three?"

And there it was. The unspoken question, now very much spoken. She forced a smile. "What makes you think it's only number three?"

That shut him up. She turned to the coffee machine and busied herself making an espresso. It was far too early to be dealing with Reece without caffeine in her system.

"Is that all you're having?" Reece continued, undeterred, as she sat down at the nearest table with the espresso and a croissant.

"I guess."

"I guess you need some help. Come over to our table. We've enough to feed a small army."

"Reece, if you really want to help me, you could find me an abaya. And a hijab."

"Abaya? Hijab?"

"Uh-huh. See what the women are all wearing on their heads, or is that too high up on their bodies for you to have noticed? That's a hijab."

"Ah," he grinned. "So that's what they're called."

"Well?" As she didn't expect him to actually solve this, she wanted him out of her way.

His gaze landed on a young waitress bending over to clean off a table at the far side of the room, and Viv couldn't miss the gleam in his eye. "Here's the deal. If I get you an abaya and a hijab, will you come for a drink with me after the qualifiers tonight? A proper drink, not one where you scoot off to talk to the miserable half of the Gatari team."

"In the next half hour?"

His gaze trailed after the young waitress's curvaceous butt as she entered the kitchen. He shrugged. "Hell, yeah."

"Deal." She tapped her wristwatch to let him know she was already counting down.

He swept his hand across her shoulder as he strutted off. Viv plastered on a confident smile and looked around to check if anyone had noticed Reece's pretend familiarity.

She caught the eye of Adam Fontaine, who was sitting on his own in the dead center of the room, chomping his way through a croissant. He broke off eye contact and seemed to be tracking Reece's departure from the room, his expression blank.

She smiled at him tentatively, but then the two Finns, Hänninen and Voutilainen, plunked down in front of him, blocking her view. Knocking back her espresso in one gulp, she got up to leave.

• • •

Half an hour later, Viv descended from her room ready to hit the road. There wasn't a hope in hell that Reece would come up with the goods, but it was only polite to honor their arrangement to meet at the dining room entrance in thirty minutes. At the forty-minute mark, she picked up her handbag and headed toward reception. Just as she'd called for a taxi, she heard a male voice boom out.

"Viv. Wait."

Reece sauntered up, his sneakers squeaking on the marble floor.

"Any luck?" she asked.

"No." His brows rose in his tanned face. "I can't believe the women here. That cute little waitress looked at me like I was the devil incarnate when I was just trying to make pleasant conversation and do you a favor. I had to scamper before she summoned her menfolk to stone me or—"

"All right, all right," she said. He'd been overconfident in his ability to attract the waitress, centuries of religious tradition notwithstanding. Ten out of ten for arrogance. It must be hard for him, discovering that not everyone swooned at his Formula-One-champion feet. "You did your best."

"So." He clapped his hands. "Still on for that drink tonight?"

"Let's see—later." She turned and made a dash for the front door. Her taxi to take her to the mall was waiting in the already muggy heat. She jumped into the freezing vehicle and grinned at the sight of Reece standing where she'd left him, folding his arms across his chest. Just how easy did he think she was? "To the mall and then on to the airport please," Viv said to the driver, forgetting to avoid eye contact in the rearview mirror. The driver responded with a frown.

She sped through the mall, grabbing the first example of each item she saw in the first traditional clothes shop that presented itself. No haggling involved, which was most certainly a tourist's mistake. Only back in the taxi did she convert from dirham to pounds and discover she'd forked out five hundred quid for the abaya alone—a freaking week's budget.

The material was thick and very black—not her color at all. Several lines of Swarovski crystals garnished the top seam. No wonder it had cost a minor fortune. As the taxi was so cold, she was happy to drape the heavy fabric around herself.

She stared out at the hi-tech Masdar Institute as they zipped along the highway to the airport. You couldn't pull off futuristic in cloudy Britain somehow, but here architectural lines were etched with convincing precision against the deepest of blues.

Just as she was settling into the drive and daring to relax a little, she felt a bump, bump, bump, and assumed it was the tire. Forgetting all propriety, she searched for the driver's reaction in the rearview mirror. His scowl made her flinch. The man, a sinewy twenty-something with a nondescript face half covered by a beard, hopped out of the car, muttering to himself. He circled the vehicle four times. It was obvious he hadn't a clue what was wrong. Viv didn't even pretend she wasn't watching. Five agonizing minutes went by on her wristwatch.

I've had enough of this shit.

The wall of heat nearly knocked her down when she stepped out of the car, but the abaya shielded her from the sun's harsh rays. She circled the car once to establish that indeed it wasn't the tires. She motioned to her phone and then to his, hoping he'd take the hint and call for someone. He shook his head and indicated with agitated gestures that she return to the back seat.

She frowned back at him. Wonderful, a macho man who couldn't ask for help. It was already 11:00 a.m. She could miss her flight, boarding at 11:20 a.m. How the hell did you call for emergency pickup in this desert anyway? The driver was now making a big show of inspecting the engine. Did he know the first thing about cars?

Viv took her phone out of her purse. Of course, she didn't have data roaming to look up taxi numbers. All she could do was call the hotel to send a new car. If she had reception. She stared at the non-existent bars of the signal strength. None. Holy crap. How could this be, surrounded by hi-tech? Unwilling to believe it, she tried dialing anyway, but it was useless. Hopeless. Infuriating.

A plane passed overhead with a lazy roar and a perfect line of white against the blue. She shielded her eyes, watching it. KLM. *Take me with you to Amsterdam.* Mack would crucify her if she didn't get this interview with Al-Saeed, and her failure would prove that she couldn't handle herself on her first real assignment.

She scuttled forward for a peek, ignoring the look of abject terror on the driver's face when he saw her inspecting the engine. He made shooing motions with his hands.

"Look, whether you speak English or not, I have a flight to catch, and no charming old customs are going to make me miss it. Let me have a look. I know what I'm doing. Oh no … I think it's the transmission." Great. No way of fixing that in the short term, certainly not standing here on the side of the road.

The man's eyes were frantic. Sweat trickled into his thick, black beard. Viv peered around—what was he so afraid of? And what was so bloody fascinating? In every single car that passed, people's noses were pressed to the windows as they watched. She swung back to him. "You can't fix it. Call someone or give me the number of another taxi service. Do something!"

He shook his head and returned to his futile inspection of the engine, flinching like a nervous cat every time she took a step closer.

"Oh come on," she pleaded, "use the goddamn phone." At the very least he'd have to drain the transmission fluid—impossible on the side of the road with no tools. He continued poking as if she hadn't spoken. As if she didn't exist.

Stranded on side of road. Only five miles from the airport. Nearly made it. That wasn't a story that Mack was going to appreciate from his newest recruit.

On the verge of giving up and walking back to the hotel just to show the stupid driver that his macho pride had forced this very last and potentially dangerous resort, she heard a car slowing down. A blessed car. At least someone in this country saw fit to help a fellow human being. She waved anxiously.

The silver Audi screeched and came to an abrupt halt on the side of the road behind their taxi. A cloud of dust and sand particles billowed into the air. The driver stepped out. Shielding her eyes to get a better look, she stumbled backward in surprise.

Adam Fontaine.

Swamped with relief, she laughed out loud as he marched up to them. Same black T-shirt as at breakfast, same black jeans on taut, long legs. Her eyes trailed back up over the impeccable torso to his face. She couldn't see what was going on beyond his mirrored, Police sunglasses, and the rest of his face gave nothing away.

"Thanks for stopping; you're very kind." She gestured to the car. "I think it's the—"

Adam held up his palm, turned and strode over to the driver, which she found rather abrupt. Folding her arms, she observed how he signaled to the driver to step away from the engine. The taxi driver underwent a transformation, jabbering away in a stream of Arabic, his big yellow teeth flashing in a wide grin, sounding for all the world like he couldn't believe his luck.

Adam meanwhile fished a handkerchief out of his pocket to avoid scorching himself on the engine. She leaned against the side of the taxi, enjoying the sight of him bending over to check the oil levels. There were some advantages to sitting on the sidelines after all. He replaced the oil gauge and slid gracefully under the car. Whoa, it must be a furnace under there.

After half a minute, Adam eased himself out from under the car and straightened up, shaking the sand from his hair. Color suffused his face. He tried to communicate in hand signals to the taxi driver, who just kept nodding and smiling.

Finally he turned to her. "Need a ride?"

"Yes, I'm going to Riyadh—"

"Riyadh?" He whipped off his glasses and wiped his forehead with the back of his wrist.

"No, no, I mean to the airport to fly to Riyadh. That was the idea. Would you drive me there? To the airport? Please? I'm sorry, but my flight's in … fifty minutes, boarding in ten, and I really, really have to get this—"

"Come on." He cocked his head toward the Audi. The glasses went on again, and he clapped the taxi driver on the back. Viv grabbed her bag from the taxi, still reeling from this good fortune.

When she looked at them again, the taxi driver was holding a pen in his hand, thrusting a sheaf of paper under Adam's nose.

Adam scribbled something and made hand signals toward his Audi. The taxi driver held up his camera to take a photo. She shook her head in disbelief. Hopefully the surly Arab would get over himself and use the phone to call for help as well.

She flung herself into the Audi, sinking back in relief against the cool leather seat.

"Which terminal?" Adam asked as he started the engine.

"No clue. Domestic flight." She rummaged in her bag for the tickets so she could check. "Look—thanks a million. I can't even begin to tell you how much I appreciate this."

"Don't mention it."

She waited until they'd secured some distance from that hateful taxi before asking, "What about the driver? Should we have just left him there?"

"He'll be okay."

"You think so? He didn't seem capable of anything, not even calling for help, and people around here don't seem to want to stop."

"That's because you were there." Adam's eyes never left the road.

"Come again?"

"Not too many drivers here will stop when they see a woman parading about on the side of the road, an abaya on upside down, and cropped, blond hair shining out like a beacon."

She sat in stunned silence.

"No offense," he added.

Heat rose up along her already sweaty neck. She wanted to let off steam. "So I should've stayed inside the taxi, out of sight, is that what you're saying?"

"That might have been an option."

"Sitting quietly while this useless, misogynistic driver poked around at an engine like a complete Barbie doll?"

"Would making a fuss have solved the issue?" He turned to her, and all she could see in his mirror glasses was the duplicate image of her flustered face.

"Damn right it would," she said. "I'm not such a bad mechanic—"

He swerved between two cars, and her heart lurched. She gripped the side handle tighter. Ronan and Maddux used to drive like this, too. She'd never gotten used to it.

"Sorry," he muttered. "You were saying?"

Viv forced her eyes away from the speedometer and exhaled as though nonchalantly smoking a cigarette. "I would've told him what was wrong if he'd only let me."

"Is that so?" Adam's voice seemed to hold a challenge.

"That is so." She couldn't resist mimicking his staccato accent.

"All right. Tell me." He pressed his back further into the seat as if settling to hear a great story.

"Well, from what I could feel, it was a faulty transmission."

"Incorrect."

"It was torque convertor lockup caused by flushing with the wrong transmission fluid or the heat. I was talking about the effect, not the root cause. So, yes, the transmission."

He said nothing. She was tempted to add, "I'm right, aren't I?" like she was sixteen again, trying to get one up on her smartass, younger brother.

"What's happening in Riyadh?" he asked. Unlike his driving, his method of changing the subject was clunky to say the least.

"Interview with Al-Saeed. He's pulling out."

"I know. And they're sending you?"

"So it would appear, yes." Holy Mother, had all mankind turned misogynistic overnight?

"Tough assignment."

"Thanks for the confidence vote."

"Look, nobody knows why he's bailing, so he's chosen to keep it secret. Sending a journalist over there—especially a female one—is hardly going to make him talk."

"I have ways and means."

"I bet you do." His eyebrows lifted behind the glasses. She imagined she saw a tug on his cheek muscles, too.

Then she felt the car decelerate as they entered the airport. How in the heck had they gotten there so fast? The car eased to a halt outside the terminal building.

Inertia rooted her to the seat for a moment. She clasped her bag, her hijab and her abaya to her chest with one hand and opened the door with the other. "How can I repay you?"

"What makes you think you have to?" He lifted the glasses above his chiseled hairline and scanned her face for a brief moment with his solemn, anthracite eyes.

"Well then, thanks." The purple hijab slipped off and onto the floor.

He swooped down and placed it back on top of the abaya. "Do you know how to put this on?"

She shrugged. What? Was he some kind of hijab-draping expert as well as everything else? "No, but I'll get an air steward to help me."

"Good. Well, take care out there."

She nodded, and before she could entertain the unlikely fantasy of his fingers patting and tucking material around her newly shorn head, she dashed into the terminal building.

As she fumbled with the boarding pass machine, the belated questions assailed her. Where was he going? What was he doing away from the circuit at all when they had practice runs this morning and qualifiers this afternoon?

What kind of journalist was she anyway if she couldn't even do that right?

Chapter 3

Adam made it back to the Gatari garage just before eleven thirty. A blockade of taxis at the airport had slowed him down after dropping off Vivienne McCloud, making him seethe with frustration. He'd hated to do it, but he'd violated at least six local traffic rules to get out of there.

Bruce came charging up as fast as his untrained legs could carry him, his face puce and bathed in sweat. "Where the bloody hell have you been?" He jabbed his wristwatch. "You've only ten minutes to get geared up. This is so unlike you."

"I'm on it." He wriggled into his overalls.

"Where were you? I wanted to go over the seat adjustments one more time. Now we'll just have to take our chances."

"The seat's fine. I haven't grown since yesterday."

"But where were you?"

"I had to help someone." He hunkered down and ran his hands over the surface of his new drive, the Honda GTX with its direct injection, turbocharged V6 engine and revolutionary energy recovery system.

"Help someone? Who, in the name of God?"

"Doesn't matter. Nobody."

"One of these days your little habit of driving around between practice and qualifiers is going to get you into real trouble, you know? And I won't be around to see it because I'll have died of a heart attack. Don't you know the death rate on the roads here? It's astronomical."

Adam ignored him and continued his inspection of the car's wing.

"Don't touch that, the paint's wet."

He ran his fingers along the patch anyway.

"Murphy's ninth law of technology," Bruce grunted, handing him an oily rag to wipe his fingers.

"What?"

"Tell a man there are three hundred million stars in the universe, and he'll believe you. Tell him a car has wet paint on it, and he'll have to touch to be sure."

"That's nice, Bruce."

"Yeah. We've ten executives upstairs wanking off on the power produced by this baby, so don't let us down."

"I'll do my job."

"Right." Bruce set down a spanner on the bench and wiped his brow. "God, it's hotter here than Melbourne in January. Sure you don't want the GT? You were a tiny bit slower this morning."

"No, let Albany have it. Have some faith. Besides—" He jumped into the cockpit and ran his hands along the interior of the chassis. "She feels good. I haven't felt this way about a car since my Ferrari in Montreal."

"Where you'd a five-second lead on Bates. In the pissing rain. Can you repeat that?"

"Ask me when this is over." He pulled on his helmet and started the ignition, listening for the unique sound of the engine. Always a thrilling moment.

With a thumbs up to Bruce, he drove the GTX slowly out of the garage and onto the circuit. The sun above was as high and as hot as it got. Merciless. Great wine-growing weather, not that you could grow anything in this desert sand.

Of all the days to lose his head and do something really stupid. If he messed up these first qualifiers he'd never, ever forgive himself.

•••

"Good on ya," Bruce said, as Adam whipped off his helmet in the garage. "Nice driving. I thought you'd make pole after those first sessions. But you lost a little time there in the finals."

"It's oversteering." Adam forced the words out through vocal cords stiff with exhaustion.

"It can't be."

"But it is," he hissed. Twenty million dollars on research and development, and they couldn't get this right.

There was a horrible silence.

Bruce scratched his head and consulted the three other engineers who'd gathered around him, their faces creased with concern. "It was fine yesterday, right?"

Adam nodded and flung his sweat-sodden helmet onto the bench. "We're under parc fermé now. That's it—nothing can be done." Under the watchful eye of the FIA Technical Delegate and race scrutineers, they could add fuel to the cars, change tires, and bleed brakes. Minor front wing adjustments were also allowed, but little else. Certainly not enough to fix this problem before the race tomorrow.

"We checked everything," Bruce said. "It was perfect, as you know. We've been working around the clock since we got here to make sure of it."

"Well it's not perfect now. And it sure as hell won't be tomorrow."

"Adam—" a junior engineer called.

"Don't want to hear it," he cut him off, shoving his way through the group to storm through the exit. Outside the garage, the dead heat assailed his unprotected face. So hot he could smell burning tar, burning rubber; even the plastic coating of his overall smelled like it was burning. The oppressive sun high above seemed to mock his shadowless figure on the dusty circuit.

His time had been okay—enough to get him in fifth, but for this crucial first race he'd desperately wanted an outright pole position, and had been sure he could get it. But who got it? Yeah, Reece, of course.

He flung around as someone called his name. Bruce was half running toward him. Adam slowed to let him catch up—last thing he needed was his chassis engineer having a heart attack.

Bruce gasped as he drew close. "We're sorry, mate."

"Bruce, stop." Adam held up his hand. "Just … go back."

"No, you listen up. The engineers, they've been busting themselves fixing up the GTX. In this heat. You have to remember, they're regular guys at the end of the day. It's more than a job for them, it's a passion … but they're only human."

He hesitated, unsure how to respond. Of course Bruce had to defend his team, but surely trying to eliminate the sources of the problem was more important right now? Of course, he should have checked it himself, but the team manager told him he was first driver now and shouldn't spend so much time in the garage. Like a fool, he'd listened.

Bruce was still gasping for air. "You're one of the best drivers I've had the privilege to work with, and you have an uncanny knack with engines. You understand engines like—well, like some men understand women."

"Your point being?"

"Sometimes things go wrong no matter how much you check them. And when it comes down to it, I'm going to side with my engineers. I'll say this to any driver I work with: Sometimes you have to care about the people aspect, too, you know? Treat people nice, right? Especially my team."

"Okay. Point taken," Adam said, more to end the conversation than anything. He wasn't about to apologize for wanting a perfect car when he was one being strapped into it.

He strode on toward the main circuit building. And voilà, there was the very thing he didn't want to see—the unmistakable figure of Reece with his red overalls and yellow, shaggy mane lounging in the concrete shade of the building's porch. Even fifty meters away,

Adam could smell the smoke of his disgusting Petroff cigarillos. Who did he think he was? Clint Eastwood?

Ignoring him would be worth a try at least.

"Hold up," Reece said, sliding his boot in front of the large aluminum door. Just two syllables of his hateful London accent set Adam's nerves on edge.

"What do you want?"

"What's wrong with it?" Reece beckoned toward the Gatari garage.

"Nothing."

"Nothing, huh? What's got you looking so mad then?"

"Out of my way, Reece."

"Just one thing."

"What?"

"Have you seen Viv?"

"Who?"

"Vivienne McCloud. Blonde BBC reporter? *Total* babe. She's supposed to be here. You know, interviewing drivers?" He smirked. "Interesting ones. Sociable ones."

"Meaning you, I suppose."

"For example." Reece exhaled a long plume of smoke. Adam itched to cough the poison out while Reece pretend cuffed him on the shoulder. "Do you know something?"

Adam turned his attention to the door handle. Reece never asked idle questions, so why was he asking this? "Don't make me kick your foot away."

Reece's blue eyes studied him through the smoke. "Do you have another facial expression? Because that one doesn't come across too well on TV."

Adam clenched his teeth. Reece had done a pretty good job himself of masking his megalomaniac tendencies two years ago when they'd been friends.

"You might want to work on that." Reece chuckled. "As well as your steering, of course."

"Anything else?"

"No, apart from that, you're fucking perfect. But if you do come across Viv, tell her I'll be in the Infinity Lounge, third floor." He removed his foot, which was just as well because Adam was about to do it for him.

"Tell her"—the Englishman's voice turned even slimier than usual—"tell her that her favorite driver will be waiting for her."

"Sure," he said. If he encountered Vivienne again, he'd do her a big favor and direct her as far away as possible from the Infinity Lounge. If she made it back in one piece from Riyadh, she wouldn't want the likes of Reece breathing down her neck. She seemed too smart to be taken in by him.

Then again, she'd dated Maddux Bates.

• • •

Viv never wanted to go to Riyadh again.

After a long, insect-infested wait in a corridor in the palace Al-Saeed called home and a stilted interview with the sheik himself, she hadn't squeezed a drop out of him that she hadn't known already. Five minutes in, it became apparent that the surly sheik sitting before her wrapped in his pristine white dishdash wasn't going to divulge anything and she was wasting her time.

From observing him at F1 events last year, she'd pegged Al-Saeed as a mild-mannered individual, nothing like this belligerent, monosyllabic ogre. There was something wrong.

Curious, she hung around for a bit in the leafy shade, watching black chickens cluster around a trough of scraps in the courtyard. She struck up a conversation with a junior clerk standing outside smoking. He had on the traditional robe too, but he seemed very interested in all things modern, especially Formula One. After an animated debate on the prospects of the German team this year, he opened up and admitted he was in disgrace for messing up one of Al-Saeed's appointments.

She offered her sympathy. The young Arab waved her off. "He's not happy," he whispered. "Daughter missing."

"Missing?"

"Yeah, two weeks."

"Really? How awful."

"She's seventeen," he added as if this explained everything. Without another word he buried the cigarette butt beneath a tangle of pink flowers and strolled off through the long corridor of arches, his sandals slapping against the stone tile.

She knew that in this strict society it was unlikely the daughter ran away, and this could mean a kidnapping—especially when coupled with a potentially large transaction of money. Did Al-Saeed need his F1 money to pay a ransom?

The poor sheik—he must be so worried about his daughter. No wonder he didn't want anyone to know why. It could ruin his daughter.

She wasn't going to be that journalist.

Instinct told her not to tell her boss. Mack was curt on the phone when she got back to Abu Dhabi, but he accepted her story that Al-Saeed was a bad-tempered despot who'd changed his mind on the sport. He conceded that a few seconds of footage from the interview would suffice to prove they'd talked to him first, so it didn't matter how the grumpy sheik had conducted himself. Mack forgave her less for the plane being delayed and not managing to interview any drivers down at the qualifiers.

"Marlowe got pole position as expected," he said.

"Fontaine?" Viv asked.

"Fifth. Not happy."

"Fifth doesn't sound too bad."

"Hah, you don't know Fontaine. He'll be pacing around now. He'd been telling people he had a winner of a ride. Cocksure of himself he was. Now he's back in his den howling at the moon or whatever it is he does at night."

She chuckled. "Now there's an interview I'd like to get."

Mack's laugh boomed loud. "Girl, keep talking like that, and you and me are going to get along just fine."

Chapter 4

The next morning, Sunday, Viv found herself sitting in the spot she'd coveted for a long time—the cream leather couch in the all-glass BBC Abu Dhabi studio above the starting line. She had a perfect view from here, better than from the jam-packed stands. Unlike the conditions borne by the mere mortals sweltering outside in the mid-afternoon heat, this studio was air-conditioned.

The preparation, the speculation, and the posturing all came down to one crucial two-hour slot starting in five minutes. Excitement crackled in the air, making the hairs on her neck stand on end. She hadn't managed a bite of breakfast.

Her job was to chat during the race whenever there was a break in the blow-by-blow commentary, to keep a nice back-and-forth going between the main commentator, Rick Everett, and herself. She'd be the yin to his yang. She'd bring up the backstories, speculate on why things were happening and on how the gladiators were feeling in their cockpits zipping around the circuit at ungodly speeds per hour.

"You'll have notes, but once you're on camera you'll be ad-libbing your little heart out. Whatever happens, just remember to look relaxed, okay?" a red-haired waif of a technician called Sarah briefed her as Viv was getting her makeup done.

"I've been on camera before." Viv waved off the makeup artist who was trying to apply blusher. "I'm looking forward to it." Well, she'd done some stints as a local TV journalist in Edinburgh after graduation, but nothing like this. Nothing like five hundred million viewers.

"Have you practiced the Finnish names?" Sarah asked.

"Hänninen, Voutilainen."

"Lord, you're good. And Greek guy?"

"Papastathopoulos."

"You'll be fine."

The race started without hiccups. Rick's commentary fizzed with excitement, and she marveled at the energy he infused into his voice. Then again, the man was a rabid fan. Beside him, it wouldn't be too hard to come across as the voice of reason and calm and deep inner reflection.

The starting lights flashed on, and a scream of tires and engines cut the air. Reece in pole position had pulled off first, as expected, and most drivers retained their starting grid positions for the first five laps.

"Gonna be a boring one," Sarah said in Viv's headphones, which was surprising, since talking on air was verboten. Sarah raised her mug of tea in rebel salute.

She nodded back, glad to have an ally in this strange new world of live F1 reporting. And a predictable race would be a nice, gentle way to start the season. In many ways, this was the first day of her real career.

"No ... wait!" Rick yelled. Viv flapped down her notes and stared at the screen. "He's leapfrogging Hawes and now Anderson ... this is incredible! Fontaine is gaining on Reece and Bates. After starting in fifth, Fontaine has managed to make up ground in a truly spectacular way."

She watched the green streak of lightning zoom into third place, just behind Maddux. "How did he do that?" she wondered aloud.

Rick's voice had calmed down after a lap, and he gave the thumbs up, a cue for some chitchat. "Indeed, Viv, how did Adam Fontaine do that? That's the question we're all asking."

"Well, this is the new Honda GTX we've been speculating about," she said, heart thumping with the pressure of having to deliver intelligent, rapid-fire commentary. "Built in the garages in Tokyo and shipped to Gatari's HQ in Atlanta, it's been a closely kept secret for over a year. But, Rick, it looks like they've got something here. The magic of Japanese engineering. Or is it the driving panache of Adam Fontaine?"

Rick laughed. "I don't know, Viv, but panache is a word that certainly springs to mind. See how he overtook Anderson on the straight? I didn't even think that was possible. The speed of the thing. Question is, will those soft tires hold out until the end?"

"Yes," she agreed, "that's something he'll have to watch. An extra pit stop for tires will lose him those precious seconds he's now gained on Reece Marlowe and Maddux Bates." It felt weird referring to her ex, Maddux, like this. She knew her voice shook a little at times, but with any luck her audience would put it down to the general excitement of the race.

"He's trying to overtake again! Adam Fontaine's trying to overtake," Rick yelled.

She watched, fascinated, forgetting to comment, as Adam's green car sailed past Maddux, then, going into the curve, settled into second behind Reece.

• • •

Adam stared at Reece's tail end. He bit down on his bottom lip and thought a silent prayer, the same one as every time.

Are you watching up there, little brother? Help me out here.

He glanced at his battered old watch that was stuck at one minute to four, as it had been ever since he'd taken it from Eddie's cold wrist.

"Adam, your settings are fine. Remember to go to fuel mixture 5 and revs 7," Bruce's voice crackled through his headphones. "No, make it revs 8 please, revs 8."

"Got it."

Reece kept blocking him in four successive turns, but Adam lost no ground.

"Beautiful mate, beautiful," Bruce crooned.

Several minutes later he said, "There's a yellow flag up somewhere, uh, I'll let you know where."

Who is it?

"There's a Pantech-Windsor off somewhere, there may be debris on the track. We don't know where yet ... uh, wait. It's in turn 14, turn 14. Be careful."

"Okay." Pantech-Windsor; either poor Hawes again, or Papastathopoulos.

The next laps passed without incident, and Adam got into the zone where velocity, time and gravity obeyed different laws than in normal life.

"All right mate, Maddux is in P3 right behind ya. Race order is MAR, FON, BAT, AND, VOU.Nice job of keeping the rear pressures high, keep it up."

Then, "Adam, tell me about the car. How is it?" Bruce's anxious voice sounded in his ears, halfway around lap twenty.

"It's got poor grip; I've oversteer again."

"Revs 7 and push, push Reece down the straight," Bruce replied. "Let's build a cushion for the pit stop."

Adam's pit stop went without a hitch, and he joined the race again ahead of Maddux, but he needed every ounce of concentration with the damn GTX oversteering.

"Revs 7, please, Adam." Bruce again. "Keep pushing; this is looking good. It's still really, really tight to Reece."

On lap forty-six, it was Chad Teague, his team manager, shouting excitedly in his headset. "Reece has just pitted, you need to push, come on!"

Like he needed to be told. This was his window of hope to gain time over the Englishman. Adam willed the GTX to warp speed. But as he continued to circulate toward his planned stop on lap fifty-five, he began to catch lapped traffic. He cursed under his breath.

"Okay, mate, we're on it already," Bruce said.

"I'll arrive in the traffic soon!"

"I know, mate. We're going target plus 5 now, that should be okay for us."

On lap fifty-four, one lap earlier than planned, the team called Adam into the pits. "Where's Reece, where is he?" Adam yelled.

"Only three seconds ahead. And Maddux is eight behind—stuck behind Pete."

Adam grinned. It was just he and Reece now. And then on lap sixty-three, he finally saw it: a chance to pass.

"Last lap?" he called.

"Yeah, mate, last lap."

Adam blinked the sweat from his eyes. He'd need to overtake Reece in one of the curves of death between now and the finish … not something he liked to do, ever, and with the car oversteering like it was, it was far too risky. He sped over the line in second position, very close on Reece. Close, but not close enough.

"Well done, mate," Bruce said, breathing heavily into the microphone.

Adam tried to swallow his disappointment as he addressed his team of engineers. "Thank you, guys. *Merci, merci à tous*." Then he whipped off the headphones in irritation and steered the car back to base.

• • •

Viv tried to clear her head of dizziness. She'd watched the same pattern repeat itself. Adam was nail-bitingly close to overtaking Reece on the straights, but once a bend came, he seemed to pull back. By the end of the race, everyone in the studio was exhausted from his repeated attempts on the first position. The end positions were Reece Marlowe, Adam Fontaine and Maddux Bates.

"By leapfrogging Hawes and Anderson, Fontaine managed to make up ground in a truly spectacular way, but it just wasn't enough. And so, folks, an electrifying race has drawn to a close," Rick concluded in his plummy Sussex accent. "A fight between equals. Now over to Viv for a word."

The camera zoomed in on her, the studio lighting glaring into her retinas. "Yes, Rick, I can't believe it, but despite all the attempts on his lead, the reigning champ has managed to keep a grip on it. He'll be a happy man tonight." Determined to infuse some personality into this, she added, "I hear Marlowe is quite the party man."

Rick chuckled. "Yes, Marlowe may be tenacious, but he's always realized there are other things in life than motor racing, such as partying. I'll bet he sinks a few beers tonight. So what about Fontaine, Viv?"

"Um, well, he definitely deserves a few beers as well."

"Yes, he must be frustrated after that. I mean, eighteen points are eighteen points, not to be scoffed at, but still ... so close and yet so far."

"I agree ..." She faltered. *Think, Viv, think.* "I noticed that he very nearly overtook Marlowe on the second to last straight I believe if the straight had been two hundred meters longer, he might have made it."

Rick nodded sagely and looked straight into the camera. "I believe if the entire race had been on a straight he'd have won it, too."

"Yes, he seemed to be guarded in curves." She warmed to the topic. "It may be connected to the race two years ago when he tried to overtake Marlowe in a bend in Malaysia and spun out of control, shattering his ankle. I think overtaking in curves is his Achilles heel."

"Heel or ankle?" Rick quipped, eliciting groans from the cameramen.

She forced a chuckle. "Well, he'll have to get beyond it if he's to beat Marlowe this year. They have special therapists for overcoming phobias. In fact, some drivers have been known to do hypnosis to aid in this, so they can free up their minds for driving."

"And there you have it, folks, from a woman with degrees in journalism and psychology," Rick said, beaming at her. From behind the cameras, the program director made the chopping signal, which meant five seconds until the break.

With the cameras off, Viv removed her microphone and stared into space for a moment.

"You were great, darlin'; you were just great," Rick enthused. He seemed to be as excitable and likable off-screen as on—which was not always the case, as Viv well knew.

"Thanks." She felt herself blushing out of happiness and sheer relief. The toughest job was done for the day. They'd get someone else on now to do the postmortem analysis of the race. She was expected to go down and get some opinions for the website articles, so saying bye to the crew, she packed her bag and left the studio.

She placed herself strategically near the podium so she could grab a winning driver or two to talk to when they stepped off. But she soon discovered the naiveté of that idea. The place was mobbed with too many reporters pushing, grasping for a piece of them.

Reece Marlowe was surrounded by fans and journalists alike and thrived on the attention. Adam Fontaine looked like he was charging through the enemy line on a battlefield, looking neither left nor right. Third-place Maddux Bates was lapping it up, waving magnanimously as if he'd won first place. There was no way of approaching any of the trio without getting crushed.

From her position, she kept her eye on Adam. He navigated to the edge of the crowd and disappeared into the VIP hospitality tent. Viv pulled out her press pass and scuttled over to the tent, microphone in hand.

Inside the stifling VIP tent, the BBC's race coverage was being replayed on a huge plasma screen, and the racing community was glued to it. Two air-conditioning units whirred away uselessly in the middle of the tent. She grabbed a vodka and tonic to celebrate her first real TV exposure in her job.

Seeing herself up there on the big screen was unsettling. Hearing herself speak was even weirder—she sounded breathless, high pitched. And, in this last part they were now showing, she was coming across as some kind of self-styled, psychoanalytical guru on the mind of a motorsports driver.

"It's great, Viv," a Pantech-Windsor replacement driver said, standing beside her.

"Thanks," she said, and plunked herself down at their table for some insider analysis of the race.

After getting the full spectrum of Pantech-Windsor opinions, she rose to get water from the bar at the back of the tent. She was glad of the semi-darkness after all the bright lights. As she stood at the bar, she rested her head on her forearms. Her brain was spinning from the day's exertions. And she'd only been *watching* the race.

If she didn't toughen up, she'd never pull this off week after week for the next nine months of season. Stamina was important to a journalist, to an F1 journalist, doubly so. Maybe she should start going to the gym every morning, like they all did?

"What was all that?" a staccato voice resonated in her ear. She whipped her head up and drank in the sight of Adam Fontaine in his green overalls, their luridness less obvious in the gloom, his neat, dark hair even blacker with sweat, his sharp cheekbones protruding from the shadows.

He didn't look happy.

"All what?" she asked.

"The pseudo-psychology. This—this fear-of-curves bullshit."

"I just thought—"

"No, you didn't."

Viv held her chin high. "Excuse me?"

"You didn't *think*." Adam's dark eyes narrowed. "After yesterday, I thought you had a brain. But no, you're just like the rest of them. You'll say anything if you think it's entertaining."

"Well." She slapped her palm against her throat. "If anything I said is untrue, I'm sure you'll be able to correct me and let the audience in on the real facts of the matter." She pulled out her microphone and waggled it under his chin, tempted to whack him with it.

Before she even registered movement, her wrist was enclosed between his thumb and index finger. She felt callouses where his fingers joined his palm. He guided her arm and the microphone downward, gently but firmly. It forced her to step forward, closer to him. He caught her gaze for a long, strange moment. His eyes, when he wasn't averting them, were quite beautiful—dark, engaging and haunted. His rigid jawline seemed to soften. She couldn't move, speak or think while he looked down at her like this, at such close quarters. Something deep inside of her did a cartwheel … and then a backflip. She forgot to breathe until he looked away again.

Oh no, she thought. *Oh no, oh no, oh no.*

Chapter 5

Adam had to force himself to release her smooth wrist. The sensation of her skin lingered on in his palm and sent a shiver of awareness through his fingers and up his arm. His anger dissipated. He stepped backward. He hadn't meant to violate her personal space. It had just happened. Now her hazel eyes were drilling into his soul, and she looked beautiful with her flushed face tilted upward.

He cleared his throat. "I drove carefully in the corners; it would have been suicide otherwise."

"I'm still allowed to have an opinion on that," she said, rubbing the wrist he'd held. He hadn't hurt her, had he?

"And that's your opinion?" he asked. "Fear?"

"Well, if it's not fear, then what is it?"

"It's oversteer, plain and simple."

Her forehead creased. "Oversteer?"

"Yes."

"Oh. It was slipping out, was it?"

"Yes. I had to correct it with steering and throttle to stop it spinning mid-corner. It ruined my lap times and my tires. When it's like that, it's difficult enough to exit safely, let alone while overtaking. I couldn't take that risk no matter how much I wanted to. I don't mind an oversteer-ychassisto a certain extent, but that was ridiculous." He brushed a hand over his jaw—why the hell couldn't he shut up?

"Is it that bad?" she asked.

"We'll fix it."

"Oh. Well. There goes my fear theory. Puff of smoke." Her eyes wandered around his face. "Look, I didn't mean to psychoanalyze you." She sighed, and he heard the uncertainty in it.

"I want to know why you do this," he said.

"Do what?"

"This." He gestured to the scene in the tent. "Why waste your time trying to make something entertaining that's clearly not?"

"Because it's my job? I'm a journalist, remember? But also because I've loved this sport since I was a little girl watching with my dad and my brother, as do millions of others, okay?"

Adam fingered his watch. How ironic that the sport that had brought her closer to the men in her family had torn him apart from his. "Well, I'm glad you derive some pleasure from it."

"What's that supposed to mean?" she demanded.

"It takes a certain sense of the absurd to come back here as a journalist considering how the media followed you around with Hawes and Bates."

Her nostrils flared. "Yes, call me absurd. I know everyone's thinking it and worse, so I should at least be grateful you're saying it to my face."

"That's generally how I say things."

"Well, well, well, looky who's here, skulking in the dark." Reece swaggered up to them, the archetypal victor with the spoils, grinning from ear to ear. He had a champagne bottle grasped in one hand, two flutes in the other, and a harem of grid girls in tow. His zipped-down driving suit revealed tufts of grimy looking chest hair. "Surely not a lover's tiff?"

Adam searched Vivienne's face for her reaction. Her face was professionally blank.

"Hey, doll, is this guy boring you?" Reece said with full on lascivious grin. "Why don't you talk to me instead?" This, despite the fact that he had several women hanging off him. Reece was, after all, the king of irony.

"I would," Vivienne said smoothly. "Except," she beckoned toward Adam, "I find this one kinda interesting."

A microbe of warmth expanded within his chest. Few women could put Reece down like that, and none with such flair.

"Interesting?" Reece shook off his girls and made a show of scanning Adam up and down. "Not the first adjective that springs to mind."

They were the same height. They used to laugh about this when they'd been friends. About how difficult it was for tall men to sit in cramped cars for more than an hour. About their struggles with a team manager who'd wanted to squeeze out all their free time from their contracts. That friendship was gone, replaced by rivalry and a sense of repulsion. Any closeness had vaporized after the collision in Malaysia—the collision that shouldn't ever have happened between teammates. He seldom misjudged people, but he'd grossly misjudged Reece's character.

"What adjective springs to mind?" he asked, with a note of warning that he knew Reece would understand. They may be the same height, but there the similarity ended. If it came to blows, Reece didn't stand a chance and he well knew it. He was too undisciplined to work out properly, and his lifestyle was wreaking havoc on his body. His ability to withstand the g-forces of acceleration and deceleration was nothing short of a miracle, and it wouldn't last forever.

Reece shrugged and backed off into his bevy of girls. "Before you die of boredom, Viv, come meet us at the Pool Bar party. Fifteenth floor." He winked at her.

The privileged, London accent reverberated in Adam's ears for several angry heartbeats after the playboy departed. "He throws a good party," he said, watching the direction Reece had gone to make sure he wasn't coming back for another go at her, which wouldn't be at all unusual.

"So I hear," she said. Her mouth was curled into a wry grin as if she'd drawn this conclusion herself from experience.

"Don't let me stop you."

"Was that your cue for me to leave?" she asked.

"No." Adam stepped closer. Where had that precious moment gone? He wanted to ask her about Riyadh, but she was all business again now, reporter-like. That was Reece's fault. "Just acknowledging the competition."

"The competition for what?"

"For your attention."

"Don't worry, you've got it, as a reporter."

"Good. But don't expect me to be entertaining."

Her forehead crinkled. "Look, it's a sport, and a dangerous one at that. Having been involved with those drivers and friends with so many others, I can't ever forget that. Just like I can't forget the images of your accident in Malaysia. I may be looking for entertaining, yes, but I'm not blind to the sport's serious side. I'm not out to trivialize this it. Give me some credit here."

She didn't sound like other reporters. She sounded genuine.

"Think I'll head over to that party to talk to some people—you know—on the record."

He found his voice again. "Vivienne—wait."

She turned with an expectant cock of her eyebrow.

"Don't mention the car. You mustn't mention the oversteer. Please."

She smiled, but it didn't reach her eyes. It didn't even reach her cheeks. "I won't."

He watched her disappear into the crowd. Why couldn't he say the right thing at the right time around her? Why did she always seem to want to get the hell away from him?

• • •

Viv left the VIP tent and climbed into a stand to watch the crowds begin to break up and progress towards the exits. The tension receded from her body. Of course, she had zero intentions of going to Reece's private party—she'd only said that to get a rise out of Adam. His inability to distinguish a female journalist from a party girl reeked of the lazy sort of association everybody seemed to draw about her. Was it a hazard of the media profession, or was it some kind of universal rule that a female sports journalist in a male-dominated sport was always going to be a joke?

There was nothing wrong with trying to make his sport more accessible in a sensitive, intelligent way. And him? God, he could do with a spoonful of sugar.

Make that a bucketful.

She pursed her lips and looked around the circuit. The crowd had dwindled. Here in Abu Dhabi, the US fan contingent was feeble, but those that did brave the trip were die-hards. A few Star-Spangled Banners fluttered in the warm afternoon breeze, competing with the Union Jacks. She wondered what Adam's fans thought about him. Surely they had a more favorable opinion. She approached the nearest US flag bearers.

"Where are you from, ma'am?" she asked the forty-something woman in a glamorous white trouser suit, a schoolboy of about ten years old in tow. Viv could smell the woman's Chanel No. 5 vaporizing in the heat.

"New York."

"And who are you here to cheer for?"

"Well, we like a good race no matter where they're from."

Viv nodded, smiling encouragingly. "Given that two US drivers are racing, are you hoping one of them wins this year? After all, they've both had such a great start here—in second and third place."

"Well, we're going for Maddux Bates." The woman nodded to her son who wore the Supernova orange T-shirt emblazoned with the name Bates and sunglasses to match. "Huge fan."

"Yes, I can see that. What about Adam Fontaine?"

The woman screwed up her face in thought. "No … not really. I mean, he drives well and everything, but he—"

"—doesn't do fun ads," the boy said. "Maddux has a great beer ad."

"Shhh," the mother said, nudging him. "Anyway, he's not really American, is he? They're a Belgian family. He was born over there. Just because they have a winery in California doesn't make them American."

"He's Mr. Spock, yo," the boy said.

"Why do you call him that?" Viv asked.

"That's his nickname."

"Well, why do you think that is?"

The woman shrugged. "He doesn't smile?" The boy also shrugged.

"Would you like him better if he smiled?" He thought about it and nodded. His mother was nodding, too, eager to get away, no doubt.

Viv thanked them and let them go. She scribbled up a few notes on her notepad as they walked away. They'd got that much right; she'd never seen him smile either. God knows it might dent that perfect jawline of his.

She wandered over to a group of youths smoking by the barricade to the pits to ask them the same question. It had barely registered with them that Adam even was a US driver; they were mad about Maddux, they said in a half-drunken chorus. He was a good guy, they said. On being asked to elaborate, they held forth on his driving tactics. One of them mumbled about a charity organization he thought Maddux might support, but couldn't name it or anything.

She was glad none of them recognized her as the ex-girlfriend of their hero. Though ex-girlfriend was an exaggeration. Despite all the press hype, she'd never been physically involved with Maddux, just good friends. He was handy to have around after she and Ronan had split up. The typical rebound friendship. Neither she nor Maddux had felt inclined to debate the truth of the matter with the media.

The public perception of drivers could change overnight, given the right positive—or negative—press. Public spats or beer ads or kindness—a well-placed photo with a child, or even better, a handicapped child, could alter a driver's image just like that. It had happened with Maddux, and even to a lesser extent, Ronan. Of course, with a character like Adam, there was no telling whether he'd cooperate enough to allow it to happen. She pitied his PR people, whoever the miserable creatures were.

But his relative invisibility was exciting from an academic, journalistic point of view—a tabula rasa—a real chance, if she handled it properly. None of the other journalists seemed to be paying much heed to him yet. But two years ago, he'd driven faster than Reece during the second half of the championship. So he could do it again. She had to keep her head cool and scoop a good story on him. Because she'd bet her Swarovski-studded abaya there was some juicy story he was keeping all to his lonely self.

• • •

Adam exited the VIP tent after another beer and returned to the peace and quiet of his hotel room. He had to get a grip on his anger over Reece, or it would distract him and affect his performance, which was, of course, precisely what Reece wanted. The fact that Reece was chasing Vivienne McCloud didn't help matters. It shouldn't bother him, because Reece chased every half-decent looking woman he set eyes on. But for some reason, it did.

Saskia had called him again, so after a quick bath, he lay on the bed and returned the call.

"I asked Dad how he'd feel about the whole family getting together in December for the ceremony," she said, "with full emphasis on 'whole' so he couldn't willfully misinterpret."

Adam sat up. "What did he say?"

"He said the family's never going to be whole, with an emphasis on 'whole' so *I* couldn't willfully misinterpret." Saskia sighed.

"Did he say anything else?" He felt the knife of hurt and guilt twisting in his gut.

"No, he went off on one of his usual tirades about, well, the same old shit I've been listening to for the past ten years."

"It's how he sees it."

"I don't care. You're not the one who's had to grow up with this. You ran away, remember?"

"This is not a helpful conversation." He traced the outline of his watch with his index finger.

"I'll tell you what's not helpful. It's not helpful that he can't just relax for a moment and let us celebrate as a family, or what's left of it. You know … for once." Her voice was tearful. "I mean, he wouldn't even have to talk to you, would he? I could keep you at separate tables. Oh, Adam, if you couldn't come, it wouldn't feel like I was getting married properly. It wouldn't feel real."

The desperate silence made him clutch at straws. He should've given this wedding business more thought, but he'd been too wrapped up in the car problems, too immersed in his own world as his sister often accused him of, and rightly so.

"You could get married twice," he suggested. "You know, have a second little ceremony, you and Jeff and me and some close friends."

"That's not funny, Adam. It's not funny that my brother and my father still don't speak to each other. I didn't just lose a brother … thanks to you and Dad, I lost everything. And trying to play peacemaker these last twelve years—well, what can I say; it hasn't been at all easy. So, it's the least you could do."

"Reconciliation can't be one-sided, Saskia. You know how Dad is. It's easier for him to lump what happened onto my shoulders than to accept the blame himself. So be it."

Another silence. He could almost hear her brain switching gears, changing track.

"Well, I'm not doing two weddings. Never. A girl wants one wedding, not a patchwork. That's silly."

"I was only trying to help."

"You're not very romantic, are you?"

"I'm not even slightly romantic," Adam agreed.

"Well then. Couldn't you sneak in the back of the church after everyone's been seated? Just for the ceremony itself? I could keep you hidden after that. He doesn't even have to know."

"You're asking me to sneak into a church? How about I wear a disguise?"

"Adam—"

"Sask, I love you, but what you're asking is impossible. I'm not going to sneak around, hoping he doesn't notice me."

"Oooh, you're as stubborn as he is. Do you realize what it must be like from his point of view—to have one son killed while driving and the other making it his livelihood?"

"Drop it, Saskia."

Her tone turned plaintive. "You could set up a garage or help us tend the winery. We're always hiring people."

"I have a job. This one. Does that mean nothing to you?"

"But Adam, at what cost?"

He said goodbye and hung up. He had to race. He had to win. Whatever it cost. He'd chosen his career over his family business, hell and isolation over his family, because it had been a choice forced on him by his grieving father half a lifetime ago. And that was supposed to change just because Saskia was marrying? The last twelve years of fighting through the barriers were all about this moment, this season, this chance.

Eddie would have understood perfectly.

Chapter 6

A week later, the frenzy of the Abu Dhabi Grand Prix had died down. The whole circus was moving on to just-as-hot and just-as-sandy Bahrain. Viv was clearing out her desk when Mack's unwelcome, stocky figure strutted by. He'd flown in from London to join them for the second race, and his sudden, oppressive presence reminded her of exactly how little she enjoyed being micromanaged.

"Good to get the two desert races over with in one go," he said, red-faced, plunking his load of packing boxes by her feet. He straightened up, puffing with exertion. "Then you can move on and shake the sand out of your knickers."

"Quite." Was she being overly sensitive or was the discussion of knickers bad form with your boss? She'd explore that philosophical question in more detail when her probation period was over in six weeks. And what was she supposed to do with Mack's boxes in the meantime?

"I liked your interview with Reece. Fun guy."

"Yes." And it had been fun battling off his advances afterward, too.

Mack exhaled noisily. "I'm missing some coverage on Fontaine. It's a gap. I know he's reclusive, but in my books, he's first driver for Gatari and a serious contender for the championship title this year. If he makes the podium again in Bahrain, we'll need an in-depth interview with him straight afterward. That clear?"

"As crystal. I don't think he's as anti-social as some of the gossip columns are making him out to be. I mean, he did give me that lift to the airport."

As soon as she said the words, her stomach plummeted. That was *the* worst thing she could possibly have let slip.

Mack leaned his forehead closer to her face, his blubbery lips moving but the words failing to come out, hampered by growing incredulity. "Are you telling me, you sat in the same *car* as this guy?"

If smoke could come out of Mack's hairy ears, it would be spewing out in large plumes.

"Yes," she squeaked.

"And you didn't find out anything … anything *at all* about him?"

Part of her wished that the power would blow and thrust them into darkness so she could scarper out the door. "I was panicking, Mack … the taxi broke down, the stupid driver, he could do nothing, and then Adam picked me up, and it was the middle of the day, you can imagine how hot it was …" She broke off, realizing how unprofessional she sounded.

Mack shook his head in resignation. "I thought hiring a woman was a smart move. You seem intent on proving me wrong."

She looked down so he couldn't see this getting to her. Swallowing quickly, she looked up again. "I can't speak for every woman—or man—but I can prove that hiring me was a smart move."

He strutted off.

God, she'd prove him wrong, arrogant old fart that he was. If she didn't—if she had to start back at square one again of the journalism ladder—she'd kill herself. Her whole adult life had been spent flitting from one thing to the next—psychology, then marketing, then journalism with stints in between as a waitress, barmaid and content manager to fund all the college courses and distance learning at night.

She'd flitted from one person to another, changing boyfriends as often as she'd changed jobs. It had taken her a long time to figure out that you have to be happy with your own life before you could be happy with another person in it. And she'd yet to feel happy about her own life.

Her childhood had been the complete opposite. None of this jack-of-all-trades stuff. She'd been dedicated to school and, from age seven, to ballet. She had choreographed simple routines to pretty much every song she'd heard. The competition had been fierce, her muscles had ached every night, she hadn't been able to wear sandals in public, her summer holidays had been swallowed up by training, but it'd all been worth it when she'd executed a perfect triple pirouette before everyone else in her class. It had given her life structure. And it had balanced out her tomboyish tendencies resulting from Liam and Dad's influence and their love of cars.

At fifteen her father had died, and six months later, just after her sixteenth birthday, she'd taken stock of the depth of her desire, the level of her technique, the reality of how likely a professional ballet contract was, and had decided she'd prefer to direct her attention to something she had more control over—a career as a psychologist, or maybe a journalist, or maybe, both. Her bereaved mother told her it was all okay.

She hadn't even had a real physical reason to give up ballet like many other dancers who'd suffered strained hips, warped feet, twisted spines. It was all in her mind. It had seemed like the right decision, and the only decision, at the time. But she'd never felt as grounded since she'd given up the rigors of the dance.

Mack may be the bane of her existence right now, but the way he pushed her was a good thing, something she'd perhaps be grateful for later. Besides, she'd had worse bosses before, paying lower salaries. This was a test she was going pass, with flying colors.

•••

Viv left the hotel after dinner and went for a long walk by the garages, on the lookout for some engineers, or anyone, to interview for her latest BBC website article, "The Men Behind the Machines." She was determined to come up with a piece to knock Mack sideways.

Most of the garages were still lit approaching 10:00 p.m. Some doors were open, letting in the cooler night breeze. Her footsteps slowed as she approached the Gatari garage. Her last-ditch, stupid hope, which she could barely even admit to herself, was that she'd catch Adam Fontaine in a rare talkative mood. Maybe in the week since she'd seen him, he'd strayed to the BBC website and seen her articles on other drivers and realized she wasn't illiterate, brainless, or out to ruin him in some way.

She peeped in through the open door. To her surprise, the place was crowded. To her even greater surprise, the male-female ratio hovered suspiciously around the fifty-fifty mark. Precious little work was being done. And there was no sign of Adam.

A buxom blonde draped her tattooed leg around the engineer nearest the door with his back to Viv. The blonde caught Viv's eye with a speculative look as if to say, "come join the fun." The engineer paused in his beer drinking and twisted around with an indulgent grin plastered across his features. His face dropped when he saw Viv.

She looked away hurriedly, turning her attention to another engineer, a young Japanese man she remembered from the pit stops during the race, now leaning into the GTX's cockpit. Judging by his repetitive hand motions, she reckoned he was using a screwdriver, until he moved position and she saw it was a giggling woman sitting in the cockpit that he'd been working on.

Viv was poised to leave when someone slid up from behind and tapped her on the shoulder. She yelped and whipped around. Reece stood there, gripping a bottle of pink vodka, grinning down at her. "Whoops, where are you off to?" he asked.

"I'm—I was going to interview the Gatari engineering team, but looks like I've come at a bad time."

"This is a splendid time to come"—Reece waved his hand at the amorous scene—"as it were." At least four engineers were paired off from where Viv was standing, and they were getting raunchier by the second.

He edged closer. "In fact, I'm feeling kind of left out here."

She recognized one of the grid girls she'd seen him with after the race. "You brought these women here, didn't you?"

"They came of their own accord."

"But this isn't your garage."

"I know, but these boys deserve some fun, too. You see, there we were, strolling by, and we looked in here and saw the crew slaving away. These wonderful, caring women felt all sorry for them. What could I do? They tore themselves away from me and ran to them, like Florence Nightingales to wounded soldiers on the battlefield."

"When Adam sees what they're up to, I fear they will be wounded," she muttered.

"Are you still talking about him?" He came close enough for her to smell his vodka breath, and he caressed her cheek. She fought not to flinch. "What is this unhealthy fascination with him? You deserve so much better."

"It's my job to be fascinated ... with all kinds—for better or worse."

Reece flicked a damp lock of hair off his forehead. "Come on, babe, let me show you what a massage in a Jacuzzi can do to a tense body." His arm slid between her shoulder blades where, in fact, she was rather tense, and his big paw there was multiplying the tension. "I guarantee you'll find it fascinating."

A svelte brunette in a tight, leather miniskirt and matching purple eye shadow and lipstick slid up to them and ran her fingers along Reece's arm. She gave Viv a sultry look.

"Take Florence here instead," Viv said.

She turned and walked into the darkness, speeding up as she went. She glanced back to see whether she was safe. The scene in the garage unsettled her—it amounted to a twisted form of sabotage. The last thing a Formula One driver needed was a team of engineers with emotional issues, or with slow reactions. Reece definitely wasn't supposed to be there. And Adam needed to know.

...

The odor of sweat greeted Adam as he entered the hotel gym next morning at seven, the place already teeming with drivers and their trainers. He'd normally arrive earlier, when it was cool and empty, but a long session discussing the GTX's load balancing with Bruce last night had set him back an hour or two.

He warmed up for twenty minutes on the treadmill and made his way over to the weights. He'd concentrate on the deltoid muscles today.

To his irritation, Reece hovered around near the shoulder press machines he wanted to use. His former teammate wasn't in the habit of hitting the gym until well after breakfast.

"You're early," Adam said, sitting down at the machine, setting the weight to 50 kilos and grabbing the side handles. He didn't want to start a conversation, but the Supernova driver being silent and moody was even more unnerving than him just being his normal, irritating self.

Reece took the identical machine right beside him and adopted a starting pose in silence. Adam stole a glance. Reece had set his machine to 50 kilos as well.

So he was going to play that game, was he? Adam increased his own setting to 60 kilos. Never mind that his limit was 55.

Reece slid him a look and did the same.

Adam braced his shoulders and regulated his breathing, trying to find inner peace. He'd need it for 60. And Jedi-like strength. *Focus.*

"I had a hot date last night," Reece announced loudly.

Damn, his concentration was broken. "Well there's a surprise." Whatever made Reece think he might actually be interested? He exhaled, extending his arms, pushing up the incredibly resistant handles, his jaw clenching with effort, knuckles whitening, triceps screaming. Quarter way … halfway …

"With Viv McCloud."

Adam's arm muscles slackened, he slumped forward, and the weight plummeted down with an almighty clang.

Reece laughed. "What's wrong, *mon frère*? She told me last night that you didn't even want to talk to her."

"She said that?" He tightened his grip around the handles again, let out a grunt and pressed the weight up halfway, then fully. It hurt like hell, and he almost blacked out with the effort. The weight came crashing down again. But he'd done it. He grabbed his towel and buried his pumping head in it.

When he looked up, Reece was still eyeing him. "Yeah. She did. And I said, 'Why Viv, that sounds very much in character, why don't you come out with me and I'll talk to you,' and she did. Simple as that." Reece's mocking grin widened, and he extended his arms halfway. The veins in his forehead protruded with the effort, and he let the weight slam down to base. "Holy fuck."

Adam sat back, folding his aching arms. "What's wrong, Reece? Can't get it up?"

Reece panted a few breaths. "Oh, ha, ha, Fontaine. How I miss your razor-sharp wit. At least I know where to put it when it's up." He took a slurp of water, wiped his mouth with the back of his wrist, and shot Adam a smug, challenging look.

Adam answered by walking off to a different machine. Goddamn it, did she sleep with him after all? It was getting harder these days to tell when Reece was bluffing. It wasn't yet half past seven and his day was totally ruined.

Chapter 7

He'd won. His first Grand Prix. By four seconds. Adam stood bewildered on the podium, hardly able to remember the events that had brought him here, Maddux Bates on his left, Dave Anderson on his right, Reece nowhere to be seen. The relief this win brought was a mighty burden lifted from his shoulders. He felt lightheaded. He lifted the bottle high.

Eddie—can you see this?

Crowds stormed around them, faces, arms, cameras, microphones and smartphones all pointing toward him, all wanting a piece. Crazy. But all that mattered were those blessed twenty-five points.

He squirted champagne over the others, and they reciprocated. His father used to say that champagne had no other uses—better dripping in it than drinking it, since it was only red wine that counted. Specifically, his red wine, the Fontaine Cabernet. *Well, here's to you, Dad.*

"Smile!" shouted a platinum blond reporter, grabbing his attention with a low-cut T-shirt. You didn't see much of that in Bahrain—most women possessed at least a modicum of cultural sensitivity. He raised the bottle again in a salute to her. She'd better cover up or risk a host of men gawking after her.

"Fontaine, where's your party tonight?" Maddux Bates asked as they stepped down from the podium. Security personnel made their path through the crowds possible. The Texan wiped the French bubbles from his chin stubble. "Man, we haven't talked in ages."

"It'll be low key. Flying to the States tomorrow. It's my chance to see my sister."

"Yeah, it sure will be great to be back. I'm going to hang around another day or two here though, before I head back to Texas."

"How's Brynn?" Adam asked, referring to Bates's woman.

"Pretty good." A contented look traversed the Texan's face. "Her new gig's going well. We're happy." He shot Adam the look—the what-about-you look—which Adam ignored.

"So, small, little, microscopic party, huh?"

He nodded. "Yeah."

Bates clapped him on the back. "Fontaine, if you don't party now, when are you gonna party?"

"Monte Carlo. Final race. Consider yourself invited."

Adam broke away from the crowd under the cover of a bunch of security guys and made a beeline for the hospitality tent. Halfway there he was surrounded by his team of jubilant engineers.

"Nice work," Bruce said, clapping him on the shoulder and removing the champagne bottle from his hand. His face grew serious. "Reece is stirring up some shit—claiming our car's illegal. He's got nothing though. Charles is talking to the race scrutineers as we speak."

"What? You're joking."

"'Fraid not. But we're okay. It's a bluff. Chad's up there fighting our case."

"Reece is unbelievable."

An American reporter came up and shoved a microphone under Adam's nose. "Thoughts on Reece's challenge to your win?"

Bruce tried to wave the reporter aside.

"No, I got this." Adam leaned into the microphone and paused to find the most eloquent way of expressing how he felt about this. "Reece is talking through his ass. Our car conforms to all regulations. To the letter."

"But the Supernova team is saying you deploy front-to-rear suspension that violates the regulation on moveable aerodynamic devices." The reporter's voice hummed with excitement.

"Yes, and I know Supernova is not running it this race, but that doesn't make ours illegal," he said. "If and when the rules change, we'll adapt. In the meantime, Reece Marlowe should look more carefully at the rules and less at our car."

The reporter started to ask another question, but Adam held up his arms to ward him off.

He strode on, Bruce shuffling beside him. Up on the big screens, the brief interview was being played back at full stadium-level volume, and some enterprising producer thought it hilarious to put the words "Reece is talking through his ass" on a repeat loop. The rest of the interview was, of course, forgotten.

"You told 'em," Bruce said. "But I sure don't like the look of that crowd."

Adam didn't like the look of them either, crammed into the nearest grandstand he'd have to pass to get to the exit. Brits mainly. A high quotient of British ex-pats lived here in Bahrain, many of them F1 supporters. And today their golden boy, Reece, had been beaten, pushed off his first place position on the table, and they weren't taking too kindly to it. They were bad losers just like their poster boy.

They waved their Union Jacks in a choppy sea of protest against his win, as if he were to blame for Reece's inferior driving today. The crowd cast garbage items, empty lunch sacks, beer cans, all aimed at Adam, most of them landing just beyond the wire fence at the front of the stand. "It's the bad old seventies all over again," Bruce said.

"Who do they think is going to clear that mess up?" Adam stopped walking and turned to the offending grandstand. He was still being followed on camera, and his face appeared up on all nearby screens. The Reece supporters went into a frenzy of rage.

Bruce tugged on his arm. "Fuck's sake, mate. Either smile or keep your head down—don't ... stare."

"What? You want me to look intimidated by—?"

Then something hard—something fast—smashed into the side of Adam's head, and blackness took over his vision. He stumbled, reaching forward. His knees buckled, and he lurched through space, the ground flying up toward him. The suit cushioned the blow for most of his body, but his head whacked against hard concrete.

The impact left him motionless for a second, and all he could think was *my eyes, my eyes!*

Through a series of painful stabs he heard crowd noises— jeering, hissing, booing. He raised his head inch by inch, and felt a surge of relief as his vision cleared. He could see well enough to watch his green helmet roll away a few feet in front of him and come to a wobbling halt in a puddle of brown oil. He reached out for it but missed.

"Adam, mate?" He felt Bruce's arms tugging under his armpits.

He wriggled away in protest. "Cameras, Bruce! I'm okay. Let me … let me stand up myself. Cameras. Block them."

He could only see the world through a dark and sticky substance. His vision was okay though. Nothing that would impair his driving. He looked down at the smear of dark red on his fingers. Blood.

"Mate, it's pumping out. You need medical help. I'm calling them. Hang on … they're coming over. Stay still, would you?"

The crowd's jeering quieted as he rose to his feet. Flags and other banners jiggled up and down in a blur. Another object was thrown but landed wide of its mark. It filled him with a grim satisfaction.

Medics came over and fussed about, dabbing his forehead with cotton as they led him away. Adam could feel the sting rip across his temples down to his cheekbone.

"You got lucky," declared a medic with a heavy Saudi accent and kind face when they were into the medic tent. "Missed your eye by millimeters, but you'll need more than a couple of stitches on that."

Adam groaned. "They sure know how to put on a welcome party."

The medic pressed a bandage against the cut. "What did you to do provoke them?"

"Nothing."

The medic raised his bushy eyebrows. "This is an emotional sport. You have to take the rough with the smooth."

"Oh, come on," Adam bit out. "They're hooligans. If I get injured it should be on the circuit, not off it."

Why did his achievement only stir up the wrong kind of emotion? He'd won fair and square.

• • •

Viv trudged grumpily back up to the studio after a failed attempt to find Adam in the VIP tent. With any luck she'd nab him this time. He'd been stuck in the garages ever since he'd arrived in Bahrain. Nobody had seen him with his helmet off. But now that he'd won, it could be a whole different story.

This was one of the thrills of it all—interviewing the victors, all drenched in champagne and adrenalin. And with Adam Fontaine there was the extra thrill of it being his first time. Now surely he'd have a little smile for her?

Sarah, the technician, accosted her. "Did you hear the news? Fontaine got hit by a glass bottle thrown by a British fan!"

"No way! Is he all right?"

"Yeah, yeah, he's fine. Here, watch." Sarah beckoned to her screen where a confusion of medics milled around the driver sitting on the ground. "No wait, lemme go back to the start."

Viv watched the replay of the incident in horrified fascination, unable to believe it. An inch closer and his eye could have been taken out. She couldn't breathe when the camera closed in on his face and she saw the blood trickling down his jaw. Now it was real. For someone so clean-cut, so controlled, it felt *wrong* to see him like this.

"Something to do with Marlowe claiming he's cheating," Sarah said. "Lord, they're catfighting."

"Has Marlowe a case?"

Sarah shrugged.

She was playing the clip again when Mack walked by and rapped Sarah's monitor with his pen. "We want to know what he does, what he loves, what he hates, whom he fucks and what he has for breakfast next day. This is the potential Formula One champ we're talking about. Forget Marlowe for the moment, get on Fontaine."

Yeah, this would be funny if her career didn't suddenly hang in the balance.

"I'm talking live TV. In our US studio. We've a slot on April fifth, the day before the Austin race."

Her heart hammered. Live TV? US-style? Talk about the deep end. This could obliterate the guy's persona, not unlike using a sandblaster to reveal a Renaissance fresco. "What if he's a little, um, camera shy?"

"I don't *care*. I want his backside on that leather couch come April fifth. Otherwise you can consider your own backside taking a different route."

Mack wandered off to bully someone else.

"Oh my God," she said to Sarah, who touched her arm in sympathy. Viv had liked her from day one.

"Where did the BBC find that dragon anyway?" Viv asked under her breath.

"Well, he was like that with some other sports reporters, too, in the beginning. Martin Tanner for golf and equestrian can tell you that. Mack's very much a believer in 'when the going gets tough.'"

"How about when the going gets pretty bloody impossible?"

Sarah shrugged. "That's too fine a distinction for him."

"I mean, what am I supposed to do? Go knocking on Fontaine's bedroom door for an interview?"

Instead of protesting at such a ludicrous suggestion, Sarah simply pulled a thoughtful face.

She groaned. "Okay, okay, I get it. Privacy be damned, I go knocking."

Chapter 8

Adam sat up in his armchair, a headache drilling into his temples. A dozen stitches and a long thin scar they said. He raised the eighteen-year-old single malt to his lips. Medicinal purposes. "What *was* it anyway?"

"Glass bottle. Supernova energy drink. Keep your motor running," Bruce said, mimicking the narrator on the famous TV ads. "I'm told it's already at three hundred thousand hits on YouTube, and sales have doubled in an afternoon. Nice work."

He groaned at the irony.

"You're damn lucky it didn't crack open against your thick skull and do some serious facial surgery."

"Guess I must have a guardian angel."

"Well, that guardian angel might be on a lunch break next time you decide to stop and stare down a crowd of Reece fans on the rampage. So watch it, mate."

"I'll keep my helmet on."

"And Reece's bluff came to nothing. What a bastard. I mean, our suspension is on the very limit, sure, but how the hell did he know that?"

"A lucky bluff?"

"I don't know, Adam. How was it out there today, other than that? Give me the full version."

"The GTX is as perfect as a car can be now," he enthused. "It went with me. Every time. And starting in second position, we could make tactics and stick to them. What a contrast to Abu Dhabi."

"Yeah." Bruce took a sip of his whiskey. "And you never got yourself in a position where you had to overtake in a corner."

"No, thank God."

A rap sounded on the door.

"Room service." Adam sighed and rose. "They never leave me alone since this happened." He pointed to his bandage. "Ice, chocolate, extra pillows, you name it. That's it. I'm staying in a three-star next time."

The knock came again as he was a few paces from the door.

"Adam—" Bruce began.

He opened up to find Vivienne McCloud standing there in hip-hugging jeans and a silk print blouse that covered up everything in a way that made her even sexier. His breath caught in his throat. "Vivienne?" He held the door open and took a step backward.

"Hi, Adam. I heard about … Are you okay?" Her clear, hazel gaze, wide with anxiety, roamed his face and then narrowed in disgust. "Ooh, it's bruising."

"I'm fine," he said, gruffer than intended.

She nodded and turned her attention beyond his shoulder. "Am I disturbing you?" Her fingers twitched and she wasn't carrying any writing pad or microphone. Intriguing.

"No. Please, come in." He waved to the armchair. "You've met Bruce before."

Bruce grinned his ruddy face off at her. His chief engineer definitely had a soft spot. "Ms. McCloud." His Australian accent thickened. "Come join us in a whiskey. A beaut. I'm guessing you're Scottish from your surname and will appreciate the finer things in life." He threw himself down on the bed and patted the space beside him.

Vivienne smiled big at Bruce. Adam folded his arms, watching her settle snugly beside the engineer, on his bed, shoulders touching. Neither of them asked him to sit down.

"Indeed," she said, "McCloud originates from Mc L-e-o-d, a Scottish clan. My father was Scottish. He's dead now though. Passed away when I was fifteen My mum's a Lancashire lass, and that's where I grew up. There, and Edinburgh, if you can count six years of university as formative years."

"There you go, Adam." Bruce finished pouring her glass and smirked. "I got the whole family history already, and I bet you never knew any of that."

She laughed, a soft, measured kind of laugh, like she was on her guard. Adam leaned his throbbing head against the bathroom doorframe. "I could have guessed it from her accent."

"See, you never actually have to *tell* Adam anything." Bruce handed Vivienne her whiskey with a ceremonial flourish. "He just knows everything instinctively."

She looked straight at Adam, but he refused to hold her gaze. What was wrong with this picture? A stunning woman in his bedroom who'd come to him, who was sitting on his bed, drinking high-percentage alcohol, and then his bloody engineer making fun of him? It was obvious what was wrong.

"Vivienne, did you want me for something?" he asked, emphasizing "me."

Her eyes glowed in the ambient light. "Well, now that you mention it, Adam, I was rather hoping you'd do an interview with me ... with us, the BBC. Now that you've won."

She fingered her little, silver earring and made big doe eyes at him. "We'd love to have you in our studio. Or anywhere of your choice. Preferably around the April fifth time frame, if that would suit."

Bruce put down his glass on the bedside locker and shot him a look of sympathy.

Adam swallowed in his dry throat. Her delicate features tilted upward, questioning him ... her perfect body perched on his bed in her flimsy blouse that clung to her in all the right places, begging to be torn off, her tight jeans showing off elegant curves ... it was all too much, and too little. The whiskey in his veins ... he'd had three or more ... warming him, warping his mind ... but she'd already managed to do that well before this moment. What if … what if he'd been here on his own? What then? What if she'd walked in on him then and used this begging tone with him? Yes, he'd like to do something with her—

"Adam?" she asked, her eyes wide. God, he loved that Scottish-Lancashire lilt.

But what she was asking was not good.

"I don't do interviews."

Her face collapsed into a determined sort of pout, one that he recognized from his sister as meaning this wasn't the end of it. Not by a long shot.

Bruce sighed, emptied his glass and slapped his thighs. "Well I'll be off to bed then. First flight out to Atlanta tomorrow."

Yes, thanks, Bruce, go. Adam held the door wide for him to exit. As he passed, Bruce muttered under his breath, "Be nice."

"When am I not?" he murmured back.

Bruce laughed all the way down the corridor.

She shifted her ass on the bed as if she could read his deepest, predatory thoughts, avoiding him now that he'd shut the door. He should say something to put her at her ease, but damned if he knew what.

It was clear from the way she was drinking the whiskey that she didn't normally. "You don't have to drink it," he said. "The minibar has other drinks."

"You're right." She smiled and cradled the glass in her lap. "But I do like the smell; it reminds me of my father."

"That's a good thing?"

"Oh yes." She looked at him with curiosity. "I guess your father's more of a wine drinker?"

He fingered his jaw. "Yeah."

She nodded, eyes wide. The silence lengthened.

"How was Riyadh?" he asked.

"Oh yes, we haven't spoken since then. Well, not properly. Riyadh was—" She stopped.

He cocked his head, waiting.

"—an experience."

"Did someone give you trouble?" he asked sharply.

"No, no, not really. Al-Saeed, he's not in a good place right now. But I think he wants his privacy."

"Yes."

"And he's entitled to it."

"Of course." Adam found he was in the middle of the room now. He could either sit on the bed beside her or on the chair by the desk. Indecision held him frozen in place. Without another word, she took her sweet ass off his bed and walked around him to the window, wringing her hands.

He stared at the perfect indentation she'd made on the quilt and sat in the same position with his back to her. He studied the faint trace of her lipstick on her whiskey glass and then twisted his head around to see if they matched her lips.

The silence seemed to creep in around them.

"God, that crowd though," she said suddenly, "How horrible were they, throwing a bottle at you?"

He looked down again at his bare feet. "A partisan crowd, of no consequence."

"Oh but they are. Doesn't it affect you … all that booing and hissing?

"No."

"Adam," she implored. "You need to do something about this."

He refused to look at her lest she think he actually agreed with this. Pandering to the fans came way, way down in his list of priorities. "What do you suggest? Exercise mind control? They're Reece fans. Of course they hate me."

"They don't hate Maddux. Not in the same way. And he's American, too."

"British connections though. He launched his career in the United Kingdom "

"Well, take any of them. But you're an easy target. Adam, look at you. You could be popular. I'm serious. You need to hire a decent PR team. You need to seriously revamp your image."

"I don't care about it." This conversation was much easier with his back to her.

"But everybody else does. It's becoming a problem."

"Not for me, it's not. You shouldn't care about it either, Vivienne."

"But I see how it affects you. It affects everything about your career, your sponsorships, your interviews, the press conferences. Even your personal safety, Adam. Don't you see it yourself? I can't believe you entered Formula One without an inkling of how it works."

"Really?"

"Yes, really. You may not accept it, but the proof is out there. I'm just trying to help you."

"My job is to drive a car around a circuit and to follow team orders. No help necessary."

"It's not that simple, but there's no talking to you." She sighed heavily. "I know you used to be friends with Reece and everything, but there's something you should know."

Was this the point where she told him she was sleeping with Reece? "I think he's a distraction," she said.

"For you, or for me?"

"For your engineers."

Adam bolted up and faced her. "What do you mean?"

"He's been down there. In your garage. He had a troop of girls there a couple of nights ago. Look, maybe you already knew about this, but I thought you should know."

"What were they doing exactly? What was Reece doing? What do you know?"

"Having fun. Drinking, partying. You know how Reece is."

Too right he knew how that jerk operated. A kick in the nuts would be too mild a response to his ex-friend's backhanded ways, but that's what he had coming to him.

Vivienne drew a sharp breath and pressed her back into the window. Without realizing it, he'd started toward her. Her gaze darted over his shoulder to the door and then came back to him. He caught a flash of something—fear?

He closed his eyes. Christ, what was he thinking? She was a woman alone in a room with a man twice her weight, reeking of whiskey no doubt, and he was cornering her? He backed up a step. "Don't be afraid of me. Please, not that."

Her laugh came shakily. "I guess I could say the same thing to you."

Slowly, he examined the contour of her lips, the slope of her neck, the parabolic curve of her eyelashes, knowing they'd all resurface in his dreams. Her hazel eyes had taken on less of a deer-in-headlights quality and more of a sultry vixen. Or was that just the whiskey talking?

"Thank you for this information," he said.

"No problem." Vivienne marched past him and didn't stop until she'd reached the door. She paused before leaving. "Adam, I wasn't partying down there with him. I just saw them, okay?"

He nodded. What was there to say? He sank back down on the bed and knocked back the whiskey from her glass. How had Ronan and Maddux managed to get through to her the way they had? Charm? But she didn't seem to be someone who fell for charm alone.

Which was why he still held out hope that she might, one day, feel something stronger than professional interest toward him.

Chapter 9

As it was her last evening, and she was pretty sure the next hotel the BBC occupied in Austin wouldn't be half as luxurious, Viv decided to check out the hotel spa. What was the point of staying in a Bahraini five-star if you never took advantage of the facilities? She could do with a bit of pampering to coax the tensions out of her body.

Fifteen minutes later, she leaned back against the mosaic tiles of the hamman, feeling the rush of steam in her nostrils, her muscles already unclenching in the damp heat. This felt wonderful. She closed her eyes and concentrated on clearing her head of all its debris. All her doubts about her choice of profession and her choice of men in the past began to fizzle away in the steam.

She just had to stick to her guns and not let them get to her. Any of them. When she was a famous journalist reporting from war-torn northern Iraq or Kyrgyzstan or wherever, she'd smile in memory of these strange beginnings. And they'd all still be sitting in their cars spinning around circuits that cost the GDP of a small country, trying to find the meaning of it all.

The glass door opened, bringing in a gush of cold air and a tall male. She peered through the steam at the hazy figure. Adam Fontaine. Naked except for swimming shorts, his sculpted upper body revealed in all its hard, sinewy glory.

Holy Mother.

He cleared his throat and looked like he was going to exit again, but then he sat opposite her, as far away as possible in this tiny space.

A new batch of steam plumed upward from the vent in the center. It burned her face for a moment and obscured her view of him completely.

"Is it hot in here or is it just me?" his voice penetrated the plume of steam.

She snorted involuntarily. Was that a sense of humor trying to claw its way out of his robotic intelligence subsystem? She blinked water from her eyes. "It's very hot and very moist. Sure you can handle it?"

"Let's see who gives up first."

The air cleared a little, and she saw him better. He sucked in his lips a few times and raised his chin in a show of examining the pretty mosaic pattern of the arched ceiling. His expression was pained. Maybe steam baths weren't his thing? Had he followed her in here?

Well, it was time to see him sweat.

"Adam," she said, breaking the silence. "What really happened in Malaysia two years ago between you and Reece?"

"What did you hear?"

"Just a rumor. I heard you were first driver and that Reece crashed into you and then claimed he'd been first driver all along and you were trying to usurp him. Is that true?"

"That's a very specific rumor," his reply came. "I suppose it's from a very reliable source?"

"Very reliable."

"Bruce."

She didn't bother denying it.

"It would be better to stick to the official version and forget about it, Vivienne. Digging that up won't help your career. Or mine."

"It's not about my career. I just want to know."

There was silence except for the steam machine bubbling away cheerfully, spurting out new clouds of vapor as if trying to compensate for their lack of conversation. Her face was streaming with condensation and sweat. No doubt she looked a total mess. Normally she'd stay a maximum ten minutes in a steam room, but she wanted to use this opportunity if it killed her. She'd lost her cool in his bedroom and wasted that chance.

"Are you involved with him?" Adam asked suddenly.

"Who?"

"Reece," he hissed.

"No. Why do you ask?"

"He bluffs about a lot of things." When he raised his head again, Viv imagined she saw a tilt in his upper lip. A trickle of water slid in a curve down his perfect cheekbone and rested in the corner of his mouth. She had a sudden crazy urge to go over there and lick it off.

She shook her head. "Oh yes, I heard about his attempt to disqualify you. But your car's within the legal limits, isn't it? That suspension's okay?"

He nodded. "Yes, and thanks to you, I know how he knew we'd adjusted it, and which engineers I can trust and which I can't."

"Glad to be of service."

His gaze latched onto hers, intense and calculating. She didn't know where to look—at those eyes, or his sensitive mouth, or the intricate muscle and bone of his shoulders, or his perfect, contoured torso, all screaming out to be touched, caressed, kissed … Did he have a woman hidden away somewhere?

She shut her eyes, and the heat within her grew more intense, matching the heat of the steam. And if he didn't have a woman, did he do quick, no-strings-attached shags? No, of course he didn't. He didn't even do slow relationships, according to the files, and she'd scoured them all for precisely this information. Either he was very good at stealth, or he really was half Vulcan.

The quick shag was a dumb idea anyway. No way was she going down that road again.

Not that he was asking or anything.

When she opened her eyes, he was looking right at her with an unguarded expression of interest, piercing through the steam. She dragged her toes against the rough mosaic surface but kept the eye contact. She needed an interview with him. That was *all* she needed from him. But she'd have to work up to it. Gently.

"You should take that watch off," she said conversationally. "It'll break in the heat."

His fingers clutched the rather tarnished-looking watch. The only shabby thing he ever wore, in fact. He didn't answer.

Great, back to the stony silences. Maybe she could remark on the weather ? Hot and sunny. Hot and sunny. Hot and sunny ...

"I'm frying up here," he said. "Please tell me you're ready to give up, too."

"How long you can hold out in a steam room is not a test of your manhood."

"In that case," Adam rose, "you'll find me at the water machine drinking copiously."

"Sure," she said with a nonchalant wave. Water machine sounded like a good place for an interview. Nice and casual. So casual he wouldn't even know it was happening.

A blast of delicious cool air enveloped her as he stepped out. Her throat constricted at the sight of his wet swimming trunks clinging to firm buttocks, tracing a convex outline across firm muscle.

Alone, she stared into the steam, calculating the last time she'd had sex. Right now it was impossible not to think about it; she might as well give in to the thought. Okay, seven months. Liam had set her up with a banker on a blind date that had developed into something. Kieran, the Liverpudlian of the ubiquitous gray suits, yellow ties, and Joop! after-shave, who'd had to decide between a job in New York and her. He'd chosen the Big Apple. In secret, she'd been relieved that they had been able to pin their incompatibilities on that external reason.

She'd give this steam torture a minute more, so it wouldn't look like she was chasing after Adam.

Pushing the door open with a squelch, she released her roasting body into the coolness of the spa's lobby. Adam was stuck in what appeared to be a serious conversation with his second driver, Pete Albany, engrossing him. He didn't look like he was going to move any time soon.

The last thing she was going to do was hang around, waiting for him, looking like a tomato, sweating like a pig. She threw her towel around her neck and headed for the changing room. She'd catch him later in the hotel bar. It was a driver tradition to meet on the last night of any continent.

But Adam wasn't at the rooftop 20 minutes later, only Reece's and Ronan Hawes's groups standing in two tight little circles on either side of a grand piano. She chose Reece's group, as there was little new she could learn about Ronan, and she was determined to get something out of Reece by asking him the same question she'd asked Adam.

She managed to maneuver Reece to beyond hearing distance of the rest of his group and launched into her attack without preamble. "So, were you surprised when your erstwhile teammate came back to launch a challenge on your title this year?"

He stopped chewing his greasy chicken leg, took a swig of wine, and rubbed his eyebrow to clear a sudden frown before answering. "Frankly, I hadn't given him any thought until he won on Sunday."

"Really? So now you do give him thought?"

"Only when I have to." Reece swung his fork. "When he's in my way, in other words."

"But you used to be such friends."

He mopped his mouth with a napkin. "Did he say that?"

"No. It was all over the press from two years ago. You went on day trips together. He never partied much, but you did some hikes together in Germany and Austria, did you not?"

He pulled a sheepish face. "Things were better then, I'll give you that. But Fontaine completely lost it in Malaysia, you know? He just couldn't hack being second driver and backing down when he was supposed to. For the sake of the team."

Her internal lie detector was beeping loudly. "But wasn't he nominated first driver before Malaysia?" she asked innocently.

Reece's blue eyes turned frosty as he scanned her face. "Oh you'll hear a lot of different theories out there depending on whom you talk to. Be careful you can back up whatever you're planning on writing down. Because I would hate to see the BBC embroiled in an ugly legal case."

Jackpot. She regarded him through narrowed eyes. Here was the real Reece at last. One expected a degree of self-absorption and arrogance from F1 drivers, but this guy was more sociopath than narcissist.

"Hey." Reece moved his hand to cover hers on the table. She flinched but didn't withdraw. "You have to understand that Adam looked up to me. He got very attached to me, let's just say. That was his first year of F1, and he didn't have many friends, except me. He took everything so personally. As he still does."

He leaned forward. "The thing is—he got cocky after he won a few qualifiers." Reece's eyes shone with utter conviction on this point. He sighed and took a drink.

"He'd worked on this car he had. Himself, you know? Tuning this, adjusting that, the obsessive stuff he does. And got it to go really fast. Faster than my car, which was supposed to be better. And then he beat me in the qualifiers for Japan. Well, it was like a switch had been flipped on, or off—hell, I don't know which— but he changed that day, for the worse. No longer content with being second to my first. No, he became a single-minded, arrogant asshole.

"See, not to get all Freudian on you and ruin your gin and tonic, but he saw me as some kind of brother replacement before that, which made it all the harder for him to adapt to the realities of competitive racing."

"Brother replacement?" She whipped her fingers away. "Oh come on, his brother is long dead." She calculated. "Twelve years. It would have been ten years at that stage. Why would he see you as a brother replacement?"

Reece raised his eyebrows in silent answer.

"You were that close?" she pressed, puzzled.

"How close would that be exactly?"

"You tell me, Reece. You're the one making all the claims of brotherly closeness here." Her reporter instincts flared up, demanding more. What did she know about the brother? What did she *need* to know about the brother?

"Don't you see? That's why he took it so hard when we accidentally rubbed wheels in Malaysia. For all I know he was re-enacting … oh, Viv, you're the psychoanalyst here. You figure it out. I'm done with him and his problems. Can't we just relax and enjoy our drinks? Please?"

Re-enacting what? She glanced at Reece, but his attention was absorbed by the exquisite décolletage of the waitress topping off his wine glass.

She felt a bit lost. How deep would she have to dig to uproot the real Adam Fontaine?

• • •

Next day, Viv bumped into Mack before she could get her second coffee.

"Get that interview sorted yet?" he asked sharply. "April fifth is around the corner."

"No, but I'm working on it. I've noticed he's not as popular as he could be. I'm thinking we could play our part in redefining his role. I mean, we could humanize him."

"Humanize him? Not part of the job description."

"No, but an interview at this stage isn't going to achieve much either. People will switch over to another channel if you let him sit him there saying nothing. He'll twist it all back to something impersonal or just … sit there. I know him; he could do it. He does it all the time. It'll make for dismal TV."

"If you know him so well, why can't you get one goddamn interview?" Mack shook his smartphone under her nose. "We've had enough studio interviews with Maddux and Reece to host our own fan shows for a decade."

"Working on it," she repeated.

"Did you use your," he paused and lowered his eyelids, and his voice dropped an octave, "charm? Come on, you have an advantage over Channel 4 and Sky and the rest of them—they're all male."

"He's not like that."

"Of course he's like that, all men are like that."

"Well, I still think we can take a different angle."

"Spit it out then."

"I think … I think we need to contextualize him, build up a story around him. Explain to the public why he is the way he is. We build up a story—a story about how weak his fan base is. How he could be earning more fans, more adulation, more money, if he … played the game, lightened up a bit, put on more of a show, acted more like a fallible human than a machine. Acted more like the other drivers. That's what the fans have been telling me. He's Mr. Spock, and they want Captain Kirk."

Mack harrumphed. "Wouldn't be the first time in F1." He looked like he was going to move on. Viv crossed her fingers behind her back.

Mack frowned and retraced a step. "This angle of yours. That's the beginning. What's the middle, what's the end? Come on, come on, run it by me."

"Well, we kind of take ownership for his transformation. We start off with the usual footage where he's looking blank, avoiding everyone. We try to explain why this is. Then we introduce a photo where he's smiling. It can replace that sour one we keep pulling up when there's a profile of him on some news item—"

"You ever seen a photo where he's smiling? 'Cause I sure as hell haven't."

"No," she admitted, "but maybe we can catch him on camera while he's watching a funny show, or someone's telling a joke … or I … don't know … I haven't worked out the finer details, but how hard can it be?"

"I notice your grand plan doesn't include a live studio interview."

"Yes, but—"

"You're making it very complicated when it could be so simple. If he wants to be a grumpy bastard, let him. Paranoid android Fontaine versus playboy Reece Marlowe works fine in my books."

"I'll work out the details, Mack. I will. You just have to trust me on this."

"I want to. I really do. Look, everyone knows the facts: the rich wine-making family, the arduous rise through Formula Renault, F3, F2, blah, blah, blah. But I've heard from a reliable source that it wasn't Daddy's money that got him there. No, his first sponsor was Tony Villiers, a friend—and the whole privileged family story doesn't add up. We've records of Fontaine working as an impoverished mechanic for a couple of years in a sketchy part of L.A. Something fishy there, Viv, so reel it in, filet it and grill it."

"Consider it done. Could you give me those records?"

"Already have. Check your mailbox, you ninny."

"Yes, Mack, I'm on it. Anything else I should know?"

He glanced at his watch. "You tell me."

"Do you approve my travel request to go to California?"

"Are you kidding? You call, or you Skype."

She couldn't press it. She was still in probation period. But her journalistic instincts told her there was something in the Fontaine winery that held the clue to unraveling the man. If she had the private funds, she'd go there herself. But she didn't. All she could do was call on this Villiers guy.

Chapter 10

Austin, Texas

"Read the attachment I sent to your mail before you go off to California," Chad Teague said on the other end of phone. "I want all team members to know the new regulations by heart and that includes you drivers. We can't afford any misunderstandings what with Reece's antics last week."

"Sure thing," Adam agreed. "Anything else?"

"No. Well, have fun."

"Yeah." Adam clicked off the call. He opened up his email and frowned. When was the last time he'd checked his mail? A month ago? Before Abu Dhabi? He had an entire screen here, which meant fifty unread emails. And he didn't recognize a single sender. What kind of new virus was this?

He glanced at the bottom of the screen and his breath caught. This was the first screen of *sixty-seven* screens of new emails. Three thousand three hundred and fifty messages? Just what he needed. A virus on kryptonite.

He searched for Chad's mail among them, found it and sent it to reception to print out. That done, he scanned the unopened mail subjects again to find a pattern in the scam. He shouldn't open any; that was rule number one. But the names looked genuine, real sender names, not randomized characters.

Curiosity overcame him. Hell, sometimes rules were too boring even for him. He clicked on one that seemed to have a legitimate address and even a personalized title: "Adam Fontaine—we love you!" Well, this was a virus on kryptonite with a sense of humor.

It was an email from a fan club in Slovenia, sent back in March. Adam frowned in surprise.

Dear Adam,

We wanted to let you know that we joined your fan club (FontaineFans. com website—you have one at last—and we are the Slovenian branch!! We're travelling to see you in Hungaroring. Don't let us down!! Don't let Reece-Bighead-Marlowe get the title this year!!!
If you want to write us back, we will be ultra happy.
Yrs,

Anton Vracnik & Anton Lovrencic

Who'd have thought it? A Slovenian fan club composed of two Antons? He closed the email and went on to the next one.

A lady from Brussels wrote in French, saying that she admired what he'd done for the sport. *Why? What have I done for the sport?* She didn't elaborate, but the tone was polite and very friendly. Too friendly. Then he clicked on the attached JPG, and the lady turned out to be a teenager with a skimpy T-shirt stretched over huge breasts emblazoned with the words "Team Adam"… one word for each breast. She'd left her phone number with a final line in English: Call me when you get to Spa-Francorchamps x Bettina.

"Sorry girl, not interested," he murmured and went onto the next one.

Really, why did people write to him like this? Had they no lives of their own? It was clear where they'd got the address though— from FontaineFans.com.

He went to the website to check it out, knowing he'd regret it. He got sidetracked looking at the pages in pink and green. So this is what a fan site looked like.

The landing page displayed a big photo of him holding up the champagne in Bahrain. It was quite flattering, especially with Maddux and Anderson standing in obvious second and third on either side of him, drenched in champagne. And no Reece to spoil it. Eddie would get a real kick out of this. He'd write back to the fans.

There were some photos of himself that he'd never seen before. "Latest News," "Bio," "Links," "Contact."

He didn't see any names under "Contact," so he opened a command prompt window and entered the WHOIS command to find out the site's registration. It was Dreyfuss Lane in London under the name of a certain Liam McCloud.

McCloud. How very strange. How many of them could there be in London?

• • •

Adam flew from Fort Worth to LAX to the Santa Barbara airport and rented a car to drive to Santa Ynez. It was a long trip from the circuit in Dallas, and he knew Bruce and Chad considered him crazy for spending his free time doing yet more travel, but he had to check in with Saskia while he was in the country. No question. Even if he had to travel sixteen hours to see her for two.

Saskia had been a complete angel and managed to get Dad out of the house to visit his friend down in San José this weekend; she'd texted to say the coast was clear.

He drove over the national forest pass, past the Cold Spring Tavern on the old stagecoach trail. Once he got to Oxnard, he relaxed and let his mind drift. Winning Bahrain had allowed him to dare hope. To hope for something beyond the madness. The hope of making a step that he couldn't articulate even to himself, but it had all to do with fulfilling Eddie's dream. And it had a lot to do with showing Dad that a father had no right to dictate a son's career choice, especially after what Dad had done.

As he neared the place his sister called home, the heavy feel of dread didn't weigh down his chest as much as it usually did on this road.

Beautiful, luscious, spring growth all around urged him to get out of the car for a moment and smell the fragrant foliage. If he'd had a whole week off, he could have made a leisurely road trip out of it. But there was only one holiday in the F1 calendar, and that was in July, not April.

At the turnoff to the winery, he slowed the Audi to a walking pace to gaze at the façade of the family home perched on the dry brown, grassy ridge, flanked by flowering vines and plants—bougainvillea, morning glory. Lights blazed in the living room and the top-left bedroom. Saskia and Jeff must both be home.

He swerved off on a dirt track toward the big stone barn that housed the farm equipment, where he'd arranged to meet Saskia, well out of sight of the house, just in case Dad refused to go at the last minute. They kept the rendezvous location for the sheer hell of it because they'd loved this barn as teenagers. He eased open the squeaky, wooden door.

"Adam!" With a high-pitched screech, his sister leapt out of the shadows. Dust motes sparkled in the amber, dusk light as his eyes adjusted to the gloom of the machine-filled area. His sister's frizzy hair blazed a deep auburn as she ran up to him. Her thick lumberjack shirt failed to disguise she'd gotten thinner in the last six months.

He squeezed her tightly into his chest, the bittersweet joy of being near her filling him. "Thanks for coming, Sask."

Saskia pulled back and scrutinized him with her piercing green eyes. "Don't worry, he's not here. I told you. Jeff is, though."

"Say hi," Adam said, hurriedly, lest she'd any notions of instigating a cozy get together with his future brother-in-law who would poach the precious two hours he had. "I haven't got long, but I had to see you."

"I'm thrilled. And thrilled for your win!"

"Thanks. Anyway, show me this engagement ring of yours."

"Oh you don't seriously want to see that."

"True. But you're going to show me anyway."

She wiggled her ring finger under his nose. He had to agree that the ruby stone was unusual and pretty damn gorgeous in the golden dusk.

"You or Jeff?"

"Oh, I chose it. But he has good taste."

"Good taste in women?"

"Impeccable." She poked him in the ribs. "So how long you hanging around for? Dad's not back 'til Sunday."

"Just this evening. I've to get back to the hotel tonight at Santa Barbara. I'm heading back to LAX tomorrow first thing to fly to Dallas. Practice."

"Right. I won't be able to watch it live on Sunday. Father Dearest's been grumpy—all this avoidance of Formula One you know—it's a full-time job and it takes a lot out of him *and* us."

"Sorry you're caught in the middle there."

She snorted. "Anyway it'll be heaps better when Jeff and I move out after the wedding. Dad won't be able to dictate what we watch on TV then."

"He does that?"

"Have you any idea how frustrating it is to have your brother racing live and not being able to watch, especially when he wins? My phone was hopping with friends and neighbors congratulating me before I even knew you'd done it in Bahrain."

"I'll let you know in advance next time."

"You winning Texas?"

"Bet on it."

"Maybe I will. Interest picking up here since Bahrain, you know? Local press is full of it." She shot him a worried look. "Not just the racing."

"What do you mean?"

"People called Fontaine Fans are coming to ... well to do wine tasting, only they don't know a pinot from a merlot, and they ask about you. They talk about a fan site called FontaineFans.com where they meet up. We've had, like, two such groups in the last two days."

God, FontaineFans.com. He'd forgotten about the stupid site. He still had 3,348 unread mails sitting in his mailbox. Probably more. He should have asked Vivienne McCloud if she'd any involvement there, and if she had, to put a stop to the nonsense. Only he hadn't seen her since that hot encounter in the steam room. God, she looked gorgeous in a bikini.

Saskia rubbed her forehead in agitation. "Adam? They asked about Eddie. They called the house on Monday after your win. Luckily it was me who answered and not you-know-who. At least I could fob them off—"

"Christ, no." Adam clenched his eyes shut. Worst-case scenario—Dad being confronted about Eddie's death by a group of racing fans. "He'd take a pitchfork to them."

Saskia eyes widened as her head bobbed up and down in agreement.

Images swirled in Adam's mind of Eddie's broken body lying against the rock in Henson's field, his neck twisted at an impossible angle, his fine, blond hair matted with blood and clay. The gap between the rocks was only wide enough for one quad bike. Eddie knew that, he'd known it; they'd done it many times before. Eddie would have braked last minute if he'd been able to. Adam took a shuddering breath.

Of course, Dad couldn't see to it that Eddie's brakes worked properly. Dad was too like Eddie—a big picture person, not interested in the details—the details of running a winery profitably, the details of maintaining an engine properly, the details of ensuring functioning brake pads. No, he had run on hope. Hope that had extinguished once his dearest, blond son had been crushed and then his brokenhearted wife had divorced him within the year.

Adam swallowed. Particles of sawdust agitated his throat. "How did they ask? Did they ask like they knew I was there? Were they fishing around? Or was it just idle curiosity?"

"How should I know?" She kicked the sawdust over the tracks she'd made with the tip of her shoe and then sniffed in the dust. "But these were two female fans and they seemed to … well, *like* you."

"What did you say about Eddie?"

"Nothing, of course! What do you take me for? Dad's the only one who talked to the police that day. Sergeant Wade's dead years now. Nobody has to know you were there unless you want them to know, Adam. Jeff has sworn to secrecy, and I trust him with my life. But you do have to make your story, and you have to stick to it. Decide it and let me know—now. If a question like that ever gets asked live, how will you cope?"

"I don't do live interviews. Not personal ones anyway."

"You can't be at your level and *not* get interviewed. It's going to happen whether you like it or not. You managed to avoid it two years ago by having that accident when you got famous … which you know some people might interpret as being something you actually wanted."

"Sask," he warned. God, another woman with ridiculous psychological theories about him.

He strode over to the red truck that had been bothering him in the corner of the barn. The truck looked like it hadn't been driven in several months. "What's wrong with this?"

"Bad rear axle. Gear system broken, too." She sighed. "Jeff tried to—"

"Christ no, let me look. Is my toolset still under the window bench?"

"Yeah, I'll get it."

Adam rolled up his sleeves, laid out his tools on a large black towel and started fixing the truck. She sat on the floor watching him, as if they were fifteen and twelve again, with Eddie skipping around the place, telling dumb jokes and making them laugh.

It hurt to picture that. Charming, funny Eddie at age fourteen, the oldest he'd ever get. But the repetitive motion of twisting off the oil-slicked bolts, the quiet buzz of flies, the soothing presence of his sister, all conspired to reduce the old hurt to a smooth, delicate kind of melancholy, like a fine Pinot.

"How are the wedding preparations coming along?" he asked after a while.

"Well, fine. Apart from an obvious gap in the invitee list. Mum'll be there with Harry. She's got no issue being in the same room as Dad. Just you missing."

He remained silent.

"You should talk to him. It's been twelve years now."

"I'll think about it." But it was funny how every year of non-communication got easier. If it weren't for this wedding there'd be no issue at all.

"And if you do come, should I book you in for one or two people?" She had a mischievous glint in her eye.

"Let's not get ahead of ourselves here."

"Hey, I'm not the only one around here who can propagate the Fontaine genes. You're going to be thirty soon."

"Don't worry about me."

"Oh I *don't* worry about you"—she huffed—"I want the pressure lifted off *me* a little bit, you know?"

"One of these days, Sask. I promise. It will get easier. Sooner rather than later."

"Well, you don't make promises lightly, so I'll have to believe you. Come on to the house now and say hi to my fiancé."

Adam nodded and wiped a spanner clean on an oily rag. He'd managed to get the truck going with a satisfying roar.

"What'll I tell Dad when he comes back?" Saskia asked, locking the barn door behind them. "Miraculous recovery?"

"Tell him Jeff fixed it. No one will dispute it. Least of all Jeff."

Saskia laughed and slapped his arm. "Oh, go back to Texas and your fancy cars, would you?"

Chapter 11

When Adam sped over the finish line in Austin in first place again the following day, Viv squeezed her fists under the desk in glee. On air, she and Rick debated about the man in green's championship chances. She offset her furtive hopes by predicting that Reece would win.

Off-air, Mack was on a rampage through the studio. There was no escape. Sarah made hand signals behind his back, but Viv wasn't in the mood.

"You were supposed to have an interview yesterday, and now he wins on home soil!" he thundered. "What's the point?"

She held her chin high. "Look, I asked him a week ago, and he said no, and he's been in California with his family since then. I wrote up a piece for the website, and I talked to the son of his former sponsor, Villiers, on the phone, who confirmed that yes, the money came from him and not from the Fontaine family. I've succeeded in building up an aura of mystery around him, and the comments on the website have been numerous. Over two hundred. That's not nothing, Mack."

She didn't mention her own secret fan club website, FontaineFans.com, she'd started in her spare time in the evenings. She'd even recruited her computer whiz brother to help design the templates and set it up with an Internet provider.

Mack tensed his fingers in front of her as if crushing an invisible skull—hers. "We have the current Formula One leader here, and we haven't got a solitary interview with him. This is your responsibility. This is not what I call world-class journalism!"

His voice rang out, penetrating every cable-strewn corner, every paper-littered alcove of that studio. Other employees turned around in theoretical sympathy for her before swiveling back to whatever they had been doing.

Viv propped her chin onto her fingers, willing her heartbeat to return to normal. *So fire me.* She couldn't bear this confrontation. Nobody else had managed a live interview either, so why all the theatrics?

"Honestly, I don't know why I pay you," Mack continued. "We'll have to pick up with someone else in Hungary who can actually get an interview with the front-runner. Someone with a bit more nerve."

Yeah, good luck with that. Now every news outlet in the world wanted to know who this guy was. The Belgian stations had claimed Adam back as one of their own, and he'd answered some post-race questions in French. She'd watched that one three times because he'd sounded so sexy.

Reece was on the main studio TV screen being interviewed at the FIA post-race press conference, his confident voice booming out. "One more, one more and I could have given it a good go. I wasn't close enough, but next lap I would've. But unfortunately that was it." He flashed his trademark lady-killer grin right into the camera. "So, a bit gutted, but still, second place, still close to the championship, and many more races to go."

The screen switched to Adam being asked the secret of his success. "No secrets; it's been hard work, really constructive work." She turned to watch closely. His face was flushed, the dark stubble on his jaw glistening with sweat, or champagne. Even through her present misery she felt a massive throb of attraction. "We stumbled in the beginning. We fell, we built it again, and the team has been building and building. It's remarkable, the actual car itself; the downforce is excellent. It's the best engine this garage has created."

Mack waved this off. "Blah blah blah. Bullshit. This is the guy who was shouting at the engineers only this morning. Come on, I want to know why." He gestured toward her laptop screen as if the truth was somehow lurking in there.

She escaped to the canteen with Sarah. Sarah dumped three packets of sugar in succession into her latte foam and stirred. "Are you okay, Viv?"

"I've had a few pushy bosses in my time. It'd take more than this to get me down."

"No one's managed to land a studio interview with Fontaine. Not now, not two years ago either, when he won a few qualifiers. So why's Mack giving you such a hard time about it?"

"My guess? He thinks I should be able to sleep with Fontaine—me being the famous F1 slut and all—and get him to reveal his darkest soul to me."

Sarah looked at her in dismay.

"It's all right, Sarah. This *is* why he hired me—not for my journalistic qualities, but because I'd already slept with two of them. Foot in the door. Who cares? It's what I make of the opportunity that matters."

"Yes, you're right. But I thought you—with your master's degree and everything—wouldn't have to stoop to that."

"Ah yes. Journalism-slash-psychology. That'll get me a lovely web content editor job in some pharmaceutical conglomerate where I wax lyrical about drug trials."

"You've done that?"

"And several others like it—soul destroying. Back then I was just working to live, and party and have fun in London. But, hey, looks as though my dream job isn't exactly coming up roses either." She tried to smile.

Sarah peered into her latte. "Then this is probably not the best time to tell you, but …"

"What?"

Her friend winced. "I saw the roster for the next five. After Budapest?" She sucked in breath through her teeth. "You're not on it."

Blood pounded in Viv's ears. "Are you sure about that?"

"No, but there's a big TBD with three question marks where your name should be. I mean it could mean nothing. I'm sure it's nothing, Viv; don't read too much into it. But do go have a talk with Mack."

Viv's heart plummeted. He'd *already* decided? Was it time to start searching for job number thirteen? Damn Mack anyway.

Chapter 12

Adam watched the TV in disgust, but he couldn't make himself switch it off. It was his one free day in Montreal before the qualifiers started, and he lay on the hotel bed, catching up on the BBC omnibus edition on F1. After the Texas race coverage from Sunday, there were interviews with all the drivers. Reece, Maddux, David Anderson, and yes, himself. He'd done okay in the press conferences and the quick interviews at the podium, concentrating on the facts, on the race itself. He'd not come across as a complete robot, as far as he could tell.

But what was this stuff? Reece in some kind of glitzy BBC sports personalities chat show with the audience hanging off his every word? Someone must be holding up signs telling the studio audience when to laugh, because he wasn't funny. He was flirting with Vivienne McCloud.

The worst part? They looked good together—Aryan twins— Reece in his tight white T-shirt, yellow leather jacket—*who the hell wears yellow leather?*—and tight, gray jeans, and Vivienne in her crisp white, body-hugging dress and light yellow scarf. Like they'd color coordinated beforehand. Maybe they had. Adam pushed mute so he could watch her without Reece's irritating voice ruining it for him.

Except now her body language became even more apparent beneath the poise and the elegance—touching her neck, behind her ears—flirting, subconsciously telling the audience Reece was hers? God, it was so obvious. And no wonder—wasn't Reece the twin of her ex, Ronan? Didn't he have the same swagger, the same easy way with the ladies? The same bucketload of British charm? She was falling for it, like all women did, or she'd already fallen.

When the interview switched to the commercial break, he switched off the TV and turned on the laptop. The Pantech-Windsor guys had mentioned some article just published on him on the BBC website. Normally he'd ignore it, but they said it was written by Vivienne McCloud. What could she have to say about him?

Damn. She'd gotten in touch with Villiers. Jacques—the son. He speed-read the entirety of the article. The report pointed out that his sponsorship money had come from Villiers and not from his father as previously supposed, and that his family had wanted him to pursue a career in winemaking rather than driving. All civilized and polite. Not a word of Eddie, thank God. The tone, in fact, was favorable.

But it wouldn't take long for someone else to interview Villiers and then to start attacking Saskia or his father with questions about that awful day and why he'd left home so suddenly. And that someone could either be a professional or an amateur from that ridiculous fan site. Vivienne McCloud had single-handedly released a flock of vultures on Saskia and Dad. Someone had to tell her to stop.

• • •

After the live chat show, Viv showered and made her way a few blocks from the serviceable press hotel to the drivers' swanky hotel. She took an armchair in the lobby with a view of the main revolving doors. Her plan was to sit tight until Adam Fontaine walked by. Then she was going to throw herself at him, figuratively speaking, and tell him that she was his best hope of getting a fair, sympathetic interview. If that didn't work, she'd play the pity card: it was either that or she'd lose her job.

A long forty-five minutes later, having brushed off four polite staff inquiries, she was starting to feel pathetic. Even a social recluse couldn't stay in his room all day, could he? Or did he manage to sneak out some back way? She wouldn't be surprised if there were a secret VIP exit for the F1 elite somewhere on the executive level. Was he even there last night? Maybe he kept a hot girlfriend under the radar and they were—

Then she saw him. Instead of the usual black, he had on a red-checkered lumberjack shirt that made him look tons more approachable. After discussing something at reception, he donned a red baseball cap and his Police glasses. She wouldn't have recognized him if she hadn't been watching the whole time. Well, except for the lean legs and the perfect ass in the snug jeans She *might* have recognized those.

She got up to intercept him, but he was heading in the wrong direction—not the taxi rank out front, but the garage. Shit.

A crowd of tourists had entered reception and blocked her path, but she wriggled through and rushed to the door of the garage. A dusty draft assailed her, making her cough as she took the concrete steps down.

Had he parked in level zero or level minus one? Peering in through the door of level zero she could hear nothing. She scrambled down to minus one. She opened that door in time to see the taillights of a Cadillac disappearing up the ramp. Shit again.

She raced back up the two flights of steps and bounded out the door, almost tripping over a suitcase one of the tourists had abandoned in the middle of the floor. Panting, she got to the head of the empty taxi queue outside and clambered into the front of the first taxi.

The driver was a woman of about her own age.

"Go around the corner first," Viv said, panting, "to the guest parking garage exit."

The woman gave her a jaded look but said, "All right," and shoved into gear.

Viv watched as Adam leaned out of his car to slide his ticket into the machine, and the barrier to the parking garage went up.

"Okay, follow that Cadillac. The red one."

"Yeah, I've seen this movie," the taxi driver muttered.

With the slow traffic, it wasn't difficult to follow him into the center, and she began to calm down a little. She'd loved Montreal when she'd first come here with Ronan—it was like a rich blend of French Canada and Europe. Montreal didn't bombard the senses with advertising and marketing, so the city served as a gentle introduction to North America for someone coming over from Europe.

"Who's in the car?" the taxi driver asked at the next red traffic lights. "Your ex-boyfriend or something?"

Viv laughed. "No. Adam Fontaine."

"And who's he?"

"He's a driver."

"Yeah, well, I can see that."

"No, I mean a Formula One driver."

"A Formula One driver? Stuck in this traffic, poor boy."

"Be glad we're not on the freeway."

The cabbie laughed. "No match for me."

Two traffic lights later, his car slowed down and entered a parking garage in the Latin Quarter. Viv paid the driver and jumped out.

"Good luck," she said. "Hope you get your autograph."

"Me, too."

Viv followed him as he walked down Rue Saint-Denis, with its trendy shops, charming restaurants spilling onto the street, myriad bars and theatres. Pedestrians milled around attractive windows displaying secondhand LPs and new age clothing. There was a cool bike-jumping event happening in the street. Adam walked at a brisk pace through it all, and she had to concentrate to keep up.

At one point, he stopped and glanced around. She ducked behind a woman walking a poodle.

At the intersection of Sainte-Catherine and Saint-Denis, he turned down a parallel side alleyway. She followed at a distance of thirty feet or so. Halfway down, he disappeared. She searched all directions frantically, but he was nowhere to be seen. He must have gone into one of the buildings. She sped up to the position where he'd disappeared.

She reached a doorway of a café called Le Chat Noir. *Here?* She stepped into the dimly lit café porch. Something grabbed her elbow from the shadows and pulled her to the left. She gave a yelp as she landed smack against something hard and unyielding. Adam Fontaine stared down at her, and, as usual, he didn't look too happy.

Chapter 13

Adam knew she'd been following him ever since he'd pulled out of the hotel garage. Did she not know drivers were trained to see things in their peripheral vision that normal people didn't? Did she not realize he was driving purposely slowly so her taxi wouldn't lose him? And honest to God, she'd never make a paparazzi journalist the way she trailed people so conspicuously down a sidewalk.

"Hey." She tried to wrench her elbow from his grasp. "Let go."

"Explain." He let her go.

"Well, um, I … I followed you." At least she had the grace to look abashed. A pink glow suffused her cheeks.

"I see that. I suppose the question is why."

"I needed to talk to you."

"Well I need to talk to you, too, so it might as well be right here."

"You do?"

"Yeah." He stepped forward, and she shrank back against the wall. "What's with the Fontaine Fans website? Who's Liam McCloud?"

Her arms folded, she adopted a defensive pose. "That's my brother. I asked him to do it for me."

"Why?"

"Why not? You should be happy, Adam. It's a fan site. You didn't have a proper one as far as I could tell. There can't be any harm in that, can there?"

"I told you, I don't need one."

"Did you?"

"I'm telling you now. It's a stupid waste of *your* time. And it's creepy. I thought you were a serious journalist."

She straightened up. "I *am* a serious journalist. I just wanted to contextualize you. Humanize you—"

"Humanize me? I didn't realize I was a monster."

"Not a monster. A robot. A zombie. Going through the motions. Where's the joy? Where's the love for the sport?"

He stepped away from her—he'd more than violated her personal space. He headed to the door, saw the pedestrians marching by with their shopping bags, trying to dodge the rain that had just started, and turned back to her.

She winced as if in sympathy with him for something, and that bothered him most.

"It's important how people perceive you," she said.

"I don't subscribe to that philosophy. I am who I am, not who you or they perceive me to be. Next question. Why do you need to talk to me?"

"It's very simple. The thing is, I need an interview with you. My job's on the line. And yes, I followed you to ask you. Again. That's how bad it is."

Adam took off his cap and wrung it in his hands, avoiding her doe-eyed look. It had been hard enough to refuse the last time.

But she waited, her eyes never leaving his face—hope and determination written plain across her features, and yet something else underneath, too. What was it? It looked a little like fear … desperation?

"Why is your job on the line?" he asked.

"It's Mack, my boss." She gulped. "Says I'm no good as a journalist if I can't get an interview with you."

"That's insane."

Her eyes flashed in sudden anger. "Yeah, well, that's the way it is over at the BBC, Adam. And pretty much anywhere else, too!" She heaved a few breaths.

"You're in distress." He took a step closer and put his hands on her shoulders. She didn't flinch. Her face was just inches below him now. What would those pink lips feel like if he were to grasp the back of her head and pull her toward him as he so wanted to? She'd probably knee him in the groin if he tried.

"I'm not in distress," she said, raising her gaze to meet his. Teardrops glazed her eyes until she blinked them away rapidly. His chest grew heavy, and something hard in his core melted. He squeezed her shoulders.

"Explain this interview business," he said. If he didn't keep her talking, then something else might happen.

She sighed. "My boss wants more coverage on you. And I haven't got anything. We've truckloads of stuff on Reece—every day I wake up, he's done something—or someone—new. Why can't you be more scandalous? It would make my life easier."

"I don't have the time for it." He let go of her shoulders.

"I'm sorry; I wasn't serious about you creating scandal." She looked up again, professional smile intact. "I think the world has enough of that. But I could reveal the real you, the mysterious driver that people know so little about. You're the current leader, but they don't have a feeling for who the guy is under the green helmet. More and more of them want to know."

"They want a persona. Make it up. There. You have my permission. Humanize me."

"What?"

"That's what you'll do anyway, to fill in the gaps, right? You journalists hate gaps. That's what sent you talking to Villiers and talking to Bruce. That's the game."

"It's no game. It's my job."

"You think the image that Reece projects out there is real?"

"Well, yes. Somewhat." She frowned. "Isn't it?"

"No, it's bullshit. It's a fake persona. The real personality comes out when he's sitting behind that wheel, fighting for his life, trying to decide whether the next maneuver in the rain is worth the risk of crashing—of potentially dying—or not. He doesn't care about anything else at that moment."

She shrugged.

"And after it's over, his sights are on the next race, the points table, the gaps he has to close, the spurious advantage the latest change in his car might have over the next team's car, the margin of possibility at the fringe of the guidelines, numbers, numbers and more numbers. Everything else—the show they put on for you—is fake, surface-level trivia only. Our differences are miniscule compared to our similarities, but some feel inclined to put on a bit of a show. It's product marketing. Branding. You know this."

"Wow." She looked skeptical. "So what's your brand then?"

"I didn't get one."

"Ultimately it is up to you, but F1 as an organization will fight against a blank persona. They like drivers to be interactive with the fans—on Facebook, Twitter and even on their own blogs. It's part of your job description, really. It will guarantee you more interviews, more—"

"More interviews? Just what I need. Look, I have my sponsorships on driving merit. That's good enough for me."

"Yes, but you also need to draw them in with your popularity and your personality. You know, the part that gets you into the best cars? You need branding to have a career; this has been true of the sport since the seventies. What are your PR people doing? Come on, Adam, why do you think kids get interested in this sport in the first place? It's not just the cars—it's you, the drivers. You're heroes. I mean, why did you get into it?"

Her challenge hung there as some people came clattering in the door of the café and lingered in the porch, perusing a menu on the wall. The older ladies looked at them in indignation, as if they were a couple making out in the dark, which, he supposed, they must look like, but at least they didn't recognize him. Wrong demographic.

One of them stood and snorted in distaste as if to say, "get a room."

Meanwhile, Vivienne's eyes shone with the same amusement he was feeling.

"Heroes, huh?" he muttered.

The group of ladies bustled through the inner door to the café, shaking out their umbrellas. A warm blast of pastry smells filled the cold porch. He felt a pang of hunger. He remembered his baseball cap and tugged it back on. "Anyway, I keep away from PR types. I like my private life to be kept private."

"So I've noticed," she said smoothly. "But I'm just saying there are more pleasant ways of achieving the same goal. By having more fans. By having people say nice things about you behind your back. There are countless ways people will cooperate with an international racing star if he seems to be a nice guy."

And there were countless ways a journalist could trip him up on live TV, asking questions about why *exactly* he left home at seventeen, what *exactly* happened to Eddie. Even an innocent question about his motivation to drive F1 could turn into a semi-therapy session. He'd seen this type of interview before with newbie drivers ... where the slightest hesitation in front of the camera spoke volumes, egged on by the laughter of a live audience and the constant pressing by a journalist. You couldn't undo interviews. Ever.

What Vivienne with her optimistic world view failed to realize was that in the absence of a sparkling, witty personality to wow the crowds, the world would pin his identity on past events— on whatever he let slip about his focused, goal-driven life to date. His image would get worse, not better. Why give them the ammunition?

"And you know what?" she continued, "If you do appear to be a nice guy, the press will back off. Because nice is less exciting than mysterious."

That caught his attention. Would they—back off? If he was ever going to find a journalist to help him come across as human, as *nice,* it was Vivienne. Could he—with her help—pull this off? She'd get her interview, and he'd get it out of the way. If ever there was a reason to give interview, it was this.

"How about that interview?" she asked.

"We could do it after the race Sunday."

Her face, which had been poised for further argument, relaxed into a sudden incredulous smile. It was almost worth it just to see that raw emotion. "How about before?"

"Don't push it, McCloud."

"Okay," she said, still grinning. "After then. On camera."

"No cameras."

"There have to be cameras."

"Says who?"

"Mack. My boss. Seriously Adam, it's this, or I get the boot."

"This is emotional blackmail," he grumbled. "Do I have to wear a suit?"

"You can wear anything you want." She gave him a saucy look.

"All right, you got yourself a victim."

"Sounds great." Viv's hands trembled as she fished out her business card. "Here's my number. Call me when you're ready."

"Right." Something in his periphery bothered him. People outside—the way they were looking in. He pulled the card from her grasp, but let his fingers linger on hers for a moment. So delicate. His thumb trailed over her knuckles, and he heard her breath catching. Her hazel eyes darkened. The upward tilt of her jaw and the tiny parting between her lips made him nauseous with desire. He leaned even closer to murmur in her ear. "Listen, the people coming in … they recognize me. I'm out of here."

She twisted around to see what he meant. "Adam," she said, her voice deeper and sterner. "You're staying right here. Remember, nice is less exciting than mysterious."

He tucked his hands into his jeans pockets. Damn it, he couldn't say no to her.

A chattering group of college-age Canadians stood by the entrance, dithering. A skinny, acne-infested, twenty-something guy came up him. "Are you Adam Fontaine?"

"I am."

"Wow, I knew it!" He jostled his mates. "Hey, can I get your autograph? My brother's a huge fan. He's going to kill himself for not coming out with us!"

Adam stole a look at Vivienne, who was grinning widely, ripping a page out of a notebook she'd produced from her bag and handing it along with a pen to him.

"What's his name?"

"Peter."

Adam wrote down "Greetings Peter, from Adam Fontaine" and the date after it. "There."

The guy scrunched up his nose in disgust. "God, your writing's so neat."

"Easy to forge if you need extras."

The guy looked puzzled and then laughed. "Good point. Hey, I can swap this for Metallica's latest album. Thank you." The youths clattered through the café door.

"*A bientôt,*" Adam called after them before handing her the pen.

"Metallica's latest," she said.

"Could be worse." Adam folded his arms so he wouldn't reach out and touch her again. Underneath the friendliness, she was giving off that definite I'm-a-professional-reporter-don't-mess-with-me vibe again.

"See? You've already made a difference in a young rocker's life."

"Or Metallica has sold one fewer albums."

"Mmm, that too."

He wanted to get her back to flirty Vivienne, to that fun and somewhat vulnerable creature she'd been a few moments ago. "So, Vivienne, do you need a lift back or do you prefer a car chase? I'll give you a head start."

She grinned. "I'll hold you to the car chase, but for now I'd love a lift back, yes."

Good, more time alone with her without any microphones.

•••

It was Viv's second time in a car with him and the third time in an enclosed space. Every move he made registered keenly with her; the way he twisted his head toward her when he thought she wasn't looking made her want to hold him in her arms and ask what was going through that handsome head of his.

"Why'd you come into town anyway?" she asked as he pulled up to a traffic light.

"I needed to pick up something … a ticket."

"Ticket? Like for a show?"

"Yeah."

"Metallica playing tonight?"

"Not exactly. It's a ballet."

"Ballet? No way!" She could hear her voice had risen an octave. "Which one?"

"Carmina Burana—they're innovative."

"Wow. Of course, Les Grands Ballets."

"Not what you were expecting?"

"God, no, but I'm … wow, that's great. You actually like ballet then?"

"I actually do," he said. "I find it … relaxing."

"Relaxing?" She laughed. "That's the last thing I'd call it. I used to do ballet, you know."

"I guessed."

"Oh you did, did you? How?"

"Posture, your bearing. I've even seen you standing with your feet turned out. I guess you did it for many years."

"Yes." She wrung her hands. Yes, she had done it for many years, eleven years to be precise. What else was he guessing correctly about her? "Are you serious about the feet? I don't do that, do I?"

"Well, I only saw it once." He looked over. "It may have been my imagination."

"Why were you looking at my feet anyway?"

"I like looking at every part of you."

Her body grew warm at his audacity and his deadpan tone. She fumbled for a comeback, but none was forthcoming. Her throat had constricted anyway, making swallowing hard, let alone talking.

"When did you stop?" he asked quietly.

"At sixteen."

"Why?"

"You know, I'm not even sure. I devoted so much of my life to it until then, it's not even funny. At the end of the day it's a hyper-competitive sport and often harmful. Not unlike racing, I suppose. I just … gave it all up. I had to shake myself up and go for A-levels to scrape into university, or else I'd have ended up drifting even more than I am now."

"That must've been hard. Did you have someone to help you, to push you?"

"No. My parents were always easygoing. Then Dad died when I was fifteen. Surprise heart attack—he was only fifty. As long as I behaved and was polite to people, Mum pretty much didn't demand much else of me. That was my way of rebelling—trying to be something."

"Well, I don't see you as someone who's drifting," he said, after a pause. "You were made for TV, and you're good at sussing people out. Too good, sometimes."

There was a silence. For someone who was supposed to be robotic, his attention to her was more stirring than anyone's, making her feel warm and fluffy and not at all like the hardened journalist she was striving to be. "I'll take that as a compliment," she said in a small voice.

He looked over at her. "Why don't you come, too?"

"To the ballet? Oh no, no, no."

"Ah," he said. "Painful memories?"

"No it's not that. Well, yes. I don't know, Adam, I haven't been in almost fifteen years. That's all behind me. I haven't even watched a ballet since, not live, not on TV. I couldn't bring myself to see others doing … oh, I'm being ridiculous."

"Not at all," he said softly. "I know what it's like to want to be doing, not watching others doing. I watched heaps of F1 in the hospital last year. It wasn't fun to see Reece getting the checkered flag while the doctors told me I might have problems walking again."

"Yes, but you made it. You persevered."

"And so did you. Maybe not with ballet, but you have other talents, and you're using them. And you're in a good place, Vivienne. If you were a ballerina, you'd be almost in retirement now."

"Yeah, that's an encouraging way of looking at it." Nobody had put it quite this way before. "Ballet's not for the old, that's for sure."

"Neither's racing."

She shot him a look this time. What did he mean by that? At twenty-nine he could have another ten years at least. "But you're not old."

"Thirty next March."

"Well, spare a thought … I'm January."

"Any plans to celebrate?" He caught her eye.

"No. I hadn't planned on telling anyone either, so why I've let it slip to you I have no idea."

Adam's cheek muscle did that twitching thing again.

"But you're not thinking of retiring, are you?" she pressed.

"Not before I win."

"And when's that?"

"November."

"I see." She knew there was no other reasonable answer to that one.

He sighed and focused on the traffic ahead. At the ticket office, he got out without a word.

Their trip back to the hotel was filled with long silences and trite remarks about the city; the exhilarating atmosphere of before had thinned out to a wispy kind of tension. She tried to think about her own job instead of the effect he was having on her. She'd do well to pull herself up another greasy rung of the journalism ladder before she made a complete laughingstock of herself.

● ● ●

Mack sat behind his desk at the Montreal studio and folded his meaty forearms. "What?"

"Yes, it's true," Viv insisted.

He scratched the side of his ear, and his eyes took on a pleading quality, the look of someone who wanted to believe what he was hearing, but was having immense difficulties overcoming the last hurdle of doubt. "He just agreed?"

"Yes. An hour ago."

Mack blew out a noisy breath. "Not bad, not bad at all. Day of the race, you say?" He scrambled to enter the date on his iPad calendar. "Okay, the studio's free."

"No, no. I think we'll have to do it on his terms," she said. "His location."

"Which is?"

"Um, he didn't really say."

"You didn't really ask," Mack grumbled. "Who else is he talking to?"

"Pretty sure it's just me."

"What makes you so sure?"

"I don't know!" Viv said, louder than she'd intended. Startled colleagues' faces swung around to gawk, and not all the glances were friendly. Yes, she'd achieved what some of them hadn't managed in two years. She'd have preferred for Mack to be a little more discreet about her success.

Mack's phone rang. He waved her dismissal. "All right. Nice work, don't screw it up."

"Don't worry, I won't," she said, turning on her heel, suppressing a whoop of triumph.

She caught Sarah's eye, and the technician gave her the thumbs up signal. The studio was in full operating mode, getting ready for the qualifiers. All of a sudden, life seemed a whole lot easier.

She passed a group of journalists lounging by the exit, inspecting an inventory list. She sensed an undercurrent of something as she passed.

"Hey, Viv. Did I hear that right—about Fontaine giving you an interview?" a thirty-something, rather plastic-looking blonde asked her. Catherine Price, an anchor for the daytime program.

"Yes." Viv smiled and reached for the door handle.

"Not bad," another woman added, a Catherine look-alike even though they weren't at all related. The wonders of modern cosmetic surgery.

"Thanks," Viv said, pulling the door open and striding out. Before the door closed behind her, Catherine's crystal-clear, BBC-worthy voice rang out. "Well, here's guessing what she had to do to get that."

"Ho, ho," said the other. "I guess Mack's little gamble paid off after all."

The door closed on their laughter. Yeah, yeah, the F1 slut—could they be any more original? Some PR on her own image wouldn't go amiss, if that's all they could say about her.

And that image didn't include traipsing after yet another Formula One driver, getting caught on camera stepping out of the Montreal Ballet house, for example. Adam had seemed taken aback at her refusal to join him, and it had been a knee-jerk reaction on her part, but surely he understood the sacrifice she'd make to give in to such temptation? She'd be paying for it with her reputation and her job, possibly for the rest of her life. Dating a *third* Formula One driver would look to all the world like a pathetic addiction.

Chapter 14

Adam sat in the cockpit and counted down the seconds. Engineers still milled around the cars. "Remember the fifteen-second rule," Chad intoned over the headphones. "No mechanics can touch the car less than fifteen before the start."

There followed an eerie silence except for a low static as the engineers all rushed away from the grid. Adam felt grateful for this moment of calm. Soon there'd be a cacophony of voices in his ears, telling him what to do.

Bruce's voice hummed, slow and steady. "Twenty seconds … fifteen seconds … ten seconds …"

The lights were off. He pushed down hard. Tires screeched and engines wailed their high-pitched screams of resistance. The air filled with thick fumes. No mishaps. Good sign. He placed second in the qualifiers, three-hundredths behind Reece. The GTX felt good today, but the Montreal track was wet. He was on hard tires—so was everyone—but he'd switch to soft halfway for more speed.

"Adam, that was perfect," Bruce said.

Adam tailed Reece like a love-struck groupie. This was a replay of Monaco two years ago, catching Reece's splashes—a horrible way to spend a race. But Reece tended to get fatigued around lap forty when tailed relentlessly like this. Adam had to hang on and focus through the difficult visibility and play the tactics right. Chad and Bruce were better tacticians than Reece's guys.

Fifteen laps later, Adam was still staring at the same sight, dizzy from the effort—a migraine was threatening. The sun had come out with unexpected force, and the track had dried up.

"You're coming in," Bruce said. "It's safe for the soft tires now."

"Roger that." Adam swerved into the pits. If he did it just one lap before Reece, he'd gain the advantage.

"Good going," Bruce said. "He hasn't stopped yet."

Adam was too keyed up to answer. He drummed his thumbs on the steering wheel in agitation as the engineers changed the tires. "Come on, come on," he urged them. Was it his imagination or were they slower than usual?

"Shit," he heard.

"What?"

"We got the left and right rear tires mixed up here," Bruce shouted. "Hang on, Adam."

Oh for the love of Christ!

"Go, go, go," Bruce yelled, making the signal for task completion. Adam slammed down and rejoined the field. That was one disaster of a pit stop. It could cost him the race.

"Where am I?" he asked anxiously.

"You're in fourth. But no one else has changed yet, mate. You'll make up the time. Revs 7 now, mate. Revs 7."

On his faster tires, he overtook Hänninen and Voutilainen, who always seemed to drive in tandem, then Anderson. He breezed past Reece, who hadn't changed his wets yet. He was in the lead now, and he'd be there to stay.

"You've got a lead of four seconds, mate, that's perfect."

Take that, Reece! Another twenty-five points would give him a nice margin. And a psychological advantage.

But then something seemed wrong. Terribly wrong. Before any monitors could signal, he felt it in the fuel transmission; the acceleration wasn't powerful enough. Why it didn't show up before he couldn't tell, but this was a disaster. Could he risk going on? Pushing a little harder? Hoping it'd hold? Christ, no …

He did another lap in the agony of indecision, ignoring the hullaballoo in his headphones—his team in disarray as the impossible had happened. It was all meaningless now; he'd have to stop. Bates was behind him, a five-second gap or so, with Reece behind him. Gaining rapidly. Jesus. Ten laps to go.

"Will she hold?" Bruce asked.

"No."

Fuel injection. The readings on the instruments told him nothing, but he was sure. The engine lost responsiveness, and his driving would be inaccurate, unpredictable, dangerous to others. Impossible, but it was happening. Coming up to the fifteenth corner, Adam knew it was over.

"I'm coming in."

In the pits he flung up his visor. "Fuel injection. Get me out of here."

The engineers swarmed around the vehicle with concerned faces. Bruce waved them back and came up to Adam. "You sure?"

"Yes, I'm sure." The steering wheel was lifted and Adam leapt out.

He let rip on the team. "Who checked it last? Who's responsible? This is not a wear and tear issue. This was faulty at the start. And how the hell could you get the rear tires mixed up on the pit stop? How is that even possible?"

His face was bathed in sweat, and he wiped it off with his forearm. Journalists and cameramen were sprinting over. Adam turned away and retreated into a crowd of engineers. Bruce came up to him and grabbed his elbow. "Mate. Just go, before they're all over us. We'll talk later."

Adam stormed off, torn by frustration and anger. He wanted to get into the safety of the VIP area, away from the vultures.

Sorry, Eddie. I can't believe it either.

• • •

Viv couldn't believe it as she watched the replay of the green figure storming off the circuit. She felt awful for Adam but even worse for herself. Once a driver had a no finish, he was a volatile animal, out of bounds.

And that meant no interview.

"And he's gone, folks. Fontaine is out. Fontaine is *out* of the race," Rick yelled with unconcealed relish. "This will be his first did-not-finish this season. Oh, what a bitter disappointment for Fontaine, who would no doubt have held onto that first position had this not happened. Depending on how the rest of the race plays out, he may find himself slipping down a notch or two in the overall rankings. Viv, what do you think?"

"He's certainly not going to be happy," she said, trying to shake her somber mood. A driver with a DNF was like a footballer with a red card, a bear with a sore head.

"It must be a serious problem for him to give up like this. Let's hope to find out the reason as soon as we can. Meanwhile, Bates has charged ahead of Marlowe, and if nothing else happens, that will be the final placing."

Adam would be raging. He'd clam up. The way Ronan and Maddux used to stew and burn and shut the door when a race hadn't gone their way, especially when they'd been leading and something had happened to kick them out of the race. Those were the worst times. She'd known enough to make herself scarce, to do her own girly thing on those nights—stay in her room and have a nice scented bath, read a book, forget that she was dating a Formula One driver. She didn't have that option this time.

The race was over. "And after three races, it's 72 points to Marlowe, 68 to Fontaine, and 63 to Bates," Rick yodeled. "Fontaine has slipped off his top position. This is such a close championship so far, folks. It truly is neck and neck as we head over to Hungary in two weeks."

Viv waited for the signal from the director and sighed with relief. Rick poured some mineral water into her paper cup. "It'll be nice to start the Euro tour next week, won't it? Hungary, Austria,

Germany, Belgium, Spain. Three whole months in the same time zone. We won't know ourselves."

She managed a tight smile. Under normal circumstances, she'd share his enthusiasm, but as things stood now, she probably wouldn't even see the Hungaroring. She packed up and headed down to the VIP tent to get some interviews.

•••

To her surprise, Adam sat hunched at the bar, eyes glued to the screen replaying the race. She moved along the edge of the crowd so she could observe him from a safe distance. There, she ordered a double gin and studied him from her high barstool. People came up, clapped him on the back or the shoulder, exchanged a few words, nodded and then melted back into the crowd. No one stuck around. He may as well be covered in people-repellent.

She gulped down the gin only to realize it was a stupid idea on an empty stomach. She texted Liam the race result because he'd said he wouldn't have Internet access in his boring meeting, and he always wanted to be the first to know. She smiled, picturing her younger brother reading her message under the boardroom table.

MAR, BAT, AND, NJU.
FON had a DNF!

"Hello," a crisp male voice resonated in her ear. A voice she now recognized immediately.

"Stop sneaking up on me, Adam." Seeing his exhausted expression, the tightened line of his mouth, she told herself to be cautious with her words, not flippant. To tread very, very softly.

The barman handed them both a paper cup of ice water. She sunk hers in one unladylike gulp.

He finished his at the same time. The cut on his forehead was bruising yellow around his bandage. He looked even paler than usual, and there were purple shadows under his eyes.

She exhaled. "I'm sorry about the race."

"Not exactly a stellar moment."

"I'm not going to hound you about it now, if that's what you were wondering. I realize you need some space just now."

"You don't want to interview me because I lost the race?" He crumpled the paper cup in his hand. "Why not?"

She wadded her own cup for good measure. He still refused to make eye contact. "Well—do you actually want it now?"

"I promised you an interview." He made a move to go.

"Okay … okay." She tried to keep panic out of her voice. This was her one shot, and she wasn't going to let his exhausted, bitter expression shake her. "I mean, if you're sure …"

"Take it or leave it, Vivienne." He inched his body toward her, and she felt another wave of alarm. On her high stool, she was at direct eye level with him.

"Yes, of course. Will you come to our studio for it?"

"No. I need privacy."

"Well, where would you suggest?"

"I'd suggest my room, but"—his mouth twitched—"inappropriate."

A warm sensation enveloped her—just like every time he was this close to her—and he seemed to be making a habit of it lately.

"Very inappropriate," she agreed. "What about my room then?"

He shifted backward in surprise. She counted one blink in the silence and waited for the next. She hadn't a clue why she'd said that.

"Your room?"

"Yes, I can set the cameras and mics up myself. It would still be a televised interview."

He remained impassive. "What number?

"Um, 3089. Shall I write it down for you?"

"No need. I'll be there once I get cleaned up. An hour from now." He turned quickly and made his way toward the back exit.

Had she just agreed to interview him in her bedroom? One hour from now? Oh boy, she'd need all the help she could get to set up a makeshift studio in that time. She pulled out her phone again and started calling.

Chapter 15

After Sarah and Joe the cameraman left her bedroom fifty frantic minutes of equipment mounting later, Viv rifled through the clothes in the narrow hotel wardrobe. She held up a blue silk blouse to the light to check for stains and grabbed some safe black trousers. Much better than the confining skirt she had on now. She changed quickly and opened the window for some fresh air.

Oh God, her nerves were all out of kilter. She wanted something personal, a whole set of revelations about the man. But after a no-finish was abysmal timing to ask Adam such things.

She switched on the TV to find repeat coverage on the race and to discover the reason for the car's failure. Fuel ignition they were saying. Something that shouldn't happen. From her experience, this kind of preventable error made the drivers even more irritated.

A knock sounded on her door, a stronger rap than the typical room service one. She slapped down the lid of her laptop and jumped up.

From her stocking feet sans high heels, Adam towered over her. She felt vulnerable but hid it by ushering him into the room. "Would you like a drink? I have a delectable selection from the mini bar, with which you are no doubt well acquainted."

"Thanks, brought my own." He produced a whiskey bottle from behind his back, and strode over to the chairs by the balcony where she'd set up an impromptu interview studio.

She peered at the bottle. "Ardmore. Not bad."

"Want some?"

"No thanks."

He inspected the microphone setup with a critical expression. He then backed off to look out the window.

"Your view's better than mine," he said. "Christ." Adam swung around. "What's that?"

Her phone was ringing, the squawking ducks ring tone, in crescendo. She flapped her hands looking for it. He located the phone on the bedside table and handed it to her, wincing at the noise.

"Sorry. It's Sarah; I have to answer this or she'll be calling me all night."

"Go for it," he said.

Viv turned away from him and walked with the phone toward the bathroom door.

"Coming to the bar after?" Sarah asked.

"Not tonight."

"Everything okay?"

"Yes, yes," Viv said, with all the naturalness of an Al-Qaeda hostage with a gun pointing to her head.

Sarah's voice reduced to a hush. "Is he talking?"

"Give us a chance."

Adam was examining his fingernails in a show of not listening.

"I'll leave you to it then," Sarah said. "Want me to call back again in an hour just in case?"

"No! I mean … it's fine."

"I'll go then. But I'll call you first thing." Viv knew she would, too, so she turned the phone off and lobbed it onto the nightstand.

He perched against the armrest of one of the typical hotel room chairs. "Nice ring tone."

She chuckled. "Every time I see my brother, Liam hijacks my phone and puts something ridiculous on it because he knows I'm too lazy to change it."

"Do you see him often?"

"Well, not since I started this job, but I'll see him at Silverstone when we get there. He's based in London. Programmer for a private bank. Seven years younger than me. I love him to bits."

"Of course you do," he said, looking down. He ran his fingers through his hair. The call had distracted him. "Does Liam like Formula One?" he asked in a stilted tone.

"Yes, yes, he does. Very much so."

"Good." He looked over again. She was beginning to feel like a science experiment the way he kept sneaking glances at her as if to make sure she hadn't tiptoed away. "Do you like Formula One?"

"Yes, of course."

"But is this what you want to do with your life?"

She opened her mouth to give the formulaic answer and then stopped. His lonely, somewhat feral quality enticed her to drop the perfect, poised journalist act and be honest with him. "No, it's not. I just ended up here. In Formula One I mean. I do want to be a journalist though, yes."

"It's a strange place to start."

She shrugged. "I know. But it is what it is."

He waited for more.

"Journalism is a tough nut to crack, and I take my opportunities as they're dished out to me. I got this one handed to me on a silver plate. I would be stupid not to make the most of it, regardless of my past."

"Yes, I understand."

She pressed the camera on, focusing it on the two armchairs by the balcony door, her makeshift studio. With the backdrop of glittering hotel lights, tall palms, and smoggy Montreal skyline, it didn't look too far off a professional studio setup, and it was real.

Satisfied, she beckoned for him to take one chair, and she sat in the opposite, sliding an empty mug toward him. She poured a measure of gin into her own and settled back on her chair.

"We're pretending it's coffee, okay?" She waggled her eyes toward the camera. Crossing her legs, her bare foot accidentally grazed his lower leg. Even through denim, she felt the hardness of his calf muscle. She caught his eye for a quick moment, and that's when she saw it—the flash of understanding, the unspoken man-to-woman communication. *Oh, sweet Jesus.*

She bit her bottom lip and focused on pouring the tonic into her gin and keeping her feet to herself.

"So," she said, brightly. "Let's start. You don't mind if I take written notes as well, do you?"

"Do what you need to." Adam, whose attention had been wandering around the room, came back to focus on her. He looked at the camera and seemed to be calculating something. Pushing his armchair back, he splashed a good measure of the single malt into his mug. He dragged the chair forward again and held up his mug in toast. "Nice coffee."

"That's a wide-zoom lens in the camera," she teased.

"No, it's not."

She grinned. He was right.

"Let's begin with your recovery, Adam," she said. "The ankle and leg injury."

"It's fine now," he said, tapping out Morse code with his long ring finger on the table. "Doesn't affect my driving in any way."

She'd interviewed *children* who were more comfortable. His eyes wandered. He kept rubbing his jaw, shifting his position. He didn't smile. His whole demeanor screamed *I don't want to be doing this.*

"And the head injury?"

"That's fine too. I can still do everything I could do before."

"You were in hospital for seven months in Belgium, right?"

"That's correct."

"Why there?"

"Why not?"

"Well, why not a US hospital, as you were resident in the States at the time of the accident?"

"I preferred Belgian."

"French-speaking staff?"

"There was that. Plus the fact that Wallonians are a discreet lot."

Viv chuckled. "I'll take your word for it. I don't know many, apart from yourself, and I think we can agree that you play your cards close to your chest."

He nodded. Then shrugged.

"Yet you agreed to this interview," she prompted.

"I prefer it come from you, if it must come from somebody, and you keep assuring me it does."

She'd cut this bit out in her edits. This was a tad too personal. "Why me?"

"You talked to Villiers."

She put down her pen. "So?"

"You didn't make up some bullshit story around it."

"Well, I didn't have all the facts, and I work for the BBC, which kind of likes stories to be based on fact."

"You protected Al-Saeed."

Cut, cut, cut. She wouldn't be able to use any of this. Maybe it made more sense to forget the interview and try to understand the man. No wait, her job. Mack! She needed camera footage no matter what.

"You also didn't mention the oversteer ... to Reece."

"Of course not. Why on earth would I do that?"

"I don't know." He averted his gaze.

Viv sank back in the chair, appalled by what she suspected was going through his mind about her and Reece. She stood up and turned off the recorder and the camera. "Look, I promised you I wouldn't mention it, didn't I?"

"If you're involved with him, you're compromised." He tapped out more Morse code.

Her hackles rose. "I told you there's nothing going on. Even if I have—in the past—slept with a driver—it doesn't mean that I'm going to sleep with every driver I happen to meet, now does it?"

"Why did you split up? Maddux, I can understand, but Hawes? Did he not treat you right?"

She fought to control her temper. "Look, we are so not talking about this. Could we please switch back to *me* asking *you* the questions now?"

"And yet you want me to talk about my history. For all I know, you leaked a story, and that's why Hawes dumped you—"

She stepped away from the camera. "Where is this coming from, Adam? Read my lips, I dumped Ronan ... although I do prefer to think of it in other terms, and it was nothing to do with what you're saying. I wanted ... more." She put a hand to her pumping temples and sat back down on the chair opposite him. Adjusting her body into regal pose, she fixed him with what she hoped was the coolest of gazes but suspected wasn't. "More in the sense of commitment, you understand?"

Adam frowned and raised the whiskey to his lips, wetting them with the amber liquid. He looked at her solemnly and took a longer drink.

Why oh why had she let him know all this before she'd wrung a drop of information out of him? Yes, according to him, this was the most interesting thing about her still. How could she have dumped one of their golden boys? Who did she think she was, in other words? It was the same old resentment and hawkish curiosity that had followed her since day one of this job.

She crossed her arms and eased back in her seat. He mirrored her actions. Their elongated shadows flitted across the walls, interacting, colliding with every gesture in the glow of the lamp. A long silence followed.

"We're not here to talk about my love life," she said and rose to switch on the camera again "Now, let's talk about your race today. You must be very disappointed with your did-not-finish." God, he was bringing out a snarky streak in her that she didn't even know she possessed.

"That was unfortunate. We need to fix the problem and make sure it doesn't happen again. And it won't."

"How can you be so sure?"

"Preparation. Losing happens. It concentrates the mind. It reveals weaknesses in the engine, the team, the system, the driver."

"You seem very calm for someone who didn't finish, and who's fallen down a place overall to second."

"You expect me to sulk about it?"

"Well, for instance."

"That's not my style."

"Hmm." She licked the sticky tonic off her lips, scribbling down "sulking not my style" on her pad with a frowning smiley beside it. Bluffing probably, but maybe she could make something of his stoicism. She looked up and caught him staring at her with his dark eyes.

"Did I say something interesting?" he asked.

"No, you've been terribly boring so far. This is my to-do list for tomorrow."

In one smooth, panther-like move, he reached across the glass table and swiped the pad from her lap.

"Hey," she yelled, leaping up, grasping thin air. "Give me that."

"Nope."

"Honestly—behave yourself, Fontaine."

He slid back into his chair and scanned her notepad at his leisure. A slow smile formed, instantly brightening his features. She stared at him, at the sheer novelty of his amused face. He looked like a different person.

"I'm on your to do list?" He chuckled—a sound she'd never heard before. It made her scalp prickle, in a good way.

"For tomorrow?" he asked. Here, bathed in the soft glow of her bedroom lamp, it was nothing short of a miracle how alluring he'd become. His gaze roamed her face with a new tenderness. An entrenched journalistic instinct flared up and made her rise slowly from her chair. She fiddled with the camera viewfinder, getting him into focus against the muted light.

Click. Adam Fontaine with bedroom eyes and a sensual glow. Click.

She'd nailed it. Photo of the year. Cover of *Time* magazine.

Triumphant, she looked up again. For once it was she who had to break off the eye contact. This interview wasn't going the way she'd planned. It wasn't going at all. The only thing going was a bedroom ambiance so thick you could cut it with a plastic baby knife. Major mistake. *Earth calling Viv. Come in, Reporter Viv for the Beeb* …

"Do you mind if we continue the interview?" she asked, clearing her throat.

"If you must."

"I must." She saved the photo and changed the camera setting back to video mode.

"Did you always want to be a Formula One driver?"

"Since I was sixteen, yes." A small, pained smile crossed his face. His eyes turned downward and flickered in a manner that suggested he was searching memories, painful ones.

"And before that?"

"I've always liked machinery. When I was four, I wanted to be a mechanic. And I became one. But I guess being a driver is a more aspirational choice."

"It depends on what you're aspiring to," she said. "Fame, fortune, women … I mean, if you like those things, they go hand in hand with being an F1 driver."

He remained silent, his intent gaze doing all the talking.

"I'm not sure you *do* like those things though," she pressed.

"I like you."

"Okay, that's it." She leapt up to switch off the camera.

She felt a presence behind her. Spinning around, she was unprepared for how his hard chest a mere inch from her touch would affect her senses She nearly knocked the 3,000-quid camera from its tripod. "W—what are you doing?"

He cocked his head shyly as if to say, "Your move." His gaze wandered from her eyes to her lips and neck … and then back to her lips. This was the hungry look of a starving man, and she had an urge to feed him.

He eased her fingers from the camera, and she let her hand go limp. "You don't need to put me on your to-do list," he said in a low tone with the undercurrent of male animal. He squeezed her fingers in his tough, leathery hands. "I'm right here."

"I … can see that." She allowed her gaze to rest on his mouth. It was a sensitive mouth, one she'd studied many times, with a tiny tilt upward left of the bow of his top lip, through which a hint of white teeth flashed. Until now, she hadn't noticed the delicate laughter lines etched into those sculpted cheeks. How did he get those?

He leaned closer, and her chin tilted up to him of its own accord. His gaze searched hers, as if testing her resistance one last time, then grew heavy lidded. His lips brushed against hers, easing her into the kiss. His teeth explored her bottom lip and then sucked gently. Something told her this wasn't just for fun. This man would never be just for fun. He would always be intense. About everything. Her body thrummed with excitement.

His mouth pressed into her, and he slid his tongue inside, rubbing slowly against hers. Single-malt flavored, smoky and smooth. She reached up to cradle his neck, feeling short hairs at the back of his skull brush against her fingertips. It felt dizzying, intoxicating, drugging. Like she was in free fall—like something she'd been planning on doing for ages.

He continued kissing her until she couldn't think anymore. She lost all sense of time or place. Her whole body had woken up to his touch, to the power and the need that emanated from him.

His hand slipped to her neck, and he kept kissing. "Vivienne," he whispered. He pulled back and set his forehead against hers.

Her mind went blank, lost in a burning need that set her body throbbing. Those hands, she wanted them all over her. It had to be him. And it had to be now. That was all her brain could currently manage.

"Do you want this?" His breath tickled her ear, sending a delicious quiver down her spine. "I know you have a job to do."

She nodded and pulled him by his belt nearer to the bed. She searched his dark eyes for a sign. Her mouth burned with the sensation of him, and her thoughts thickened with sheer animal lust. They stood in silence.

He pulled her in and brushed his lips across her cheek. It felt glorious. Shivers rippled across her skin.

"I like you, too," she whispered.

She saw an innocent, almost childlike satisfaction spread across his features. He angled his head and kissed her, his lips warm, insistent. She lost herself in the taste of him, the whiskey and the commanding feel of his mouth. He advanced forward until her back pressed against the wall. He cupped her head in his hands, and his torso pressed into her. She felt his hard musculature and the hollow of his abdomen. The warm, clean scent of his skin gave her a huge rush. And that was with his T-shirt on.

She ached for him, and the burn of desire coursed through her body. They didn't break the kiss. Viv's fingers moved down from his neck and curved around his shoulders, pulling him in, trying to get closer, but with clothes on she couldn't get close enough.

His mouth moved over her jaw and trailed down her neck. Her spine quivered as he licked her sensitive skin along her collarbone.

"Do you trust me?" he asked.

"Yes."

He moved his hands down her back and smoothed his palms over her butt, pushing his fingers into the waistband of her jeans, beneath her cotton thong. She leaned her head into his chest and felt his heartbeat and breath speeding up.

"Kiss me then," he said.

She fitted her mouth back to his, back where it belonged. Her hands scrambled now, pushing up under his T-shirt, running along warm, taut skin. After a mini-eternity of bliss, he held on to her forearms and broke off the kiss.

"Take this off."

She unbuttoned the fiddly buttons on her blouse. His glittering eyes followed her every move. When she stood half naked in front of him, he stroked below her breasts with his thumbs, outlining the rib cage, as if committing her shape to memory. He ripped off his own shirt and pulled her in close so she could breathe in the heat of his skin. He smelled of hotel soap. She needed more now. That sensation of him pressing between her legs suddenly became the sole thing in her universe.

He trailed a finger down her torso, slowly between her breasts, stopping at the top of her jeans. "I've wanted to touch you since the first moment I met you."

"Why didn't you?"

"I didn't know you. I don't get involved with women I don't know." He trailed his fingertips over her breasts, and she gasped as he narrowly missed each nipple. For the lucky women that he did get involved with, he knew what he was doing. She closed her eyes and felt a growing dampness in her underwear.

"Why's that?" she murmured. Talking was becoming an extreme effort, but she'd kick herself later if she didn't find out these things.

"They're either locals that I'll never see again or touring groupies that I will."

Her eyes popped open. "But journalists are okay, huh?"

"Sometimes I have to make exceptions," he said with a glint of mischief in his eye. He tugged her hips into him and held her tightly. Bending with his mouth to her ear, he asked, "Let's lie down."

"Mmm." She planted a kiss at the base of his neck, wriggled free, and slid down on her back onto the cool sheets of the bed. She looked up at him. He looked sinfully good half naked in his black jeans. She held an arm up to him. He clasped her fingers in his, kissed them and then mounted the bed, knees on either side of her legs. Gently, he took her shoulder and pushed her back onto the pillows. His gaze rose to meet hers. "I don't have protection."

"Oh, it's okay. I do. Bathroom."

"Would I find——?"

"No, no, I'll go."

From the bathroom she could hear the crunch of his zipper and the whip of cloth as he undid his jeans. She fished out the box of condoms from her toiletry bag. When she looked out the door, she saw him wriggle out of the jeans, the hard lines of his torso drawn in all the right places, and some jagged scar lines running across his abdomen in parallel with his ribs. She forgot to breathe.

She strode back to the bed, more than ready for him. She didn't want foreplay. Not anymore. She gave him a pleading look, hoping he'd understand, and he did. He zipped down her trousers and pulled them off in two decisive tugs, throwing them over his shoulder. They landed on the miniature coffee machine on the side table. She laughed, lightheaded with anticipation.

Next came the panties, which he looped around his fingers at the seams. He kissed where skin met cloth along the top rim. He pulled them down an inch and kissed again … and again until the cloth was stretched across her hips, then further down, until he'd exposed her most secret parts to his mouth. His tongue explored the soft folds in probing caresses and then slid inside, caressing her clit. She clenched up and gradually relaxed into the exquisite pleasure. Her breath came erratically. He sat up and cupped his hand where his mouth had been, and his gaze flickered to her face. She gave up any semblance of control at that point. "Adam, please—"

He planted his hands on either side of her shoulders and leaned his body over her. He held the plank pose with one arm as he opened the box of condoms with his other, fishing one out, and putting it between his teeth.

She wrapped a leg around his. "Just … do it, would you?"

"Look, you try doing this balancing on one arm," he said out of the side of his mouth.

She giggled. "Oh here, let me." She whipped the condom from his teeth and ripped it open, smoothing his underwear down impossibly hard thighs to his knees. She took a moment to run her fingers along his long shaft, pleased at how his face tightened with pleasure. She watched, fascinated—his jaw clenched, skin taut, more like a man in pain than pleasure.

"I'm close," he said, muscles bunching in his neck and shoulders. "Too close." She rolled on the condom quickly and slid back under him. He placed his hands on her thighs and parted her legs so he could kneel between them. His face was serious now, his eyes blazing.

Words stopped. So did thought. Only skin on skin mattered, pleasure and movement, smell and touch. Adam eased himself into where she waited for him, and her inner muscles clenched around the unfamiliar, glorious length of him … further and even further. Every muscle in her being tightened into a frantic rhythm. And she was already near. So near.

All they could hear was their breathing and the hum of air-conditioning. Everything within her gathered and shattered. He came seconds after, with an anguished groan. Through her haze of euphoria, she saw the ecstasy in the way his eyes tensed, before his face relaxed by a micro-degree back to its normal, shuttered state. He eased his full weight down on her for the first time, a comforting heaviness. She wrapped her arms around his shoulders and dug her hands into the damp hair at the back of his skull.

All she could think was *wow*.

Chapter 16

Viv opened her eyes and peeped over the edge of the duvet. She squirmed, thinking of the wonderful passion of last night, and marveled at how soundly she'd slept afterward. They'd done it three times. And she'd done it again—slept with a Formula One driver.

The space beside her was empty. She shot up. Had he gone?

Then she saw him through a wide slit in the curtain, in T-shirt and boxers, sitting on her balcony, chin propped on hand, peering into space. Heart-stoppingly gorgeous, but tense around the forehead. She could read his face better now. Something told her he'd been up a long time.

She climbed out of bed, took a dressing gown from the hook, and switched on the coffee machine. It hummed, breaking the silence. Out of the corner of her eye, she saw him stand up and occupy the doorway.

"Coffee?" she asked.

"Yes, please." He made no attempt to come closer, to touch her like she wanted to be touched. To kiss her senseless. No, he just stood there, blocking the morning sun.

She didn't know what to say. Words had a way of dividing people. The minute she opened her mouth it would either strengthen or weaken what they'd shared—mind-blowing sex and a deeper connection than she could ever have thought possible. All she wanted to do was hold onto this warm buzz and shut out the reality of the world they were in, the reality of who he was.

Whatever happened, she wouldn't cling. That's what they hated most of all.

"I guess I'm holding up your schedule?" she said, leaving the opportunity wide open for him to bolt out the door. After all, it was seven thirty already, and that was late in Formula One driver terms.

"Guess again." He came over and trailed his lips down her neck, awaking the delicious feelings all over again. Her body fired up, and her doubts smashed to smithereens.

She shivered. "Thanks for last night."

"Don't thank me," he said, eyes glowing. "You've no idea what you've done to me. I feel … alive."

She had no answer to that. None at all. Except to say she'd felt so in the moment, not worrying about anything or anyone. She'd been in a place where time stood still. But none of that sounded particularly sane. And it sounded clingy. She handed him his coffee.

"So—" they both said.

"You first," she said, unable to lift her gaze to meet his. She longed for him to clasp her into his taut body, and he could probably read that in her eyes.

"What are you doing tonight?" he asked after a gulp of the coffee.

"Tonight? I—I hadn't planned anything." Even if she had, which she couldn't recall right now, she'd cancel everything, absolutely everything. "Sleeping?"

"Why don't you come to my room for a change?"

She nodded.

"Come meet me at the circuit after the practice runs."

She took a step back. "Um, is that a good idea?"

"Don't you want to see me?"

"Oh, Adam, of course I do, but—" She pressed her fingers to her forehead, trying to think. "At the circuit? So publicly? That's a bit … complicated."

"It's not complicated." He put his cup down and rubbed a hand over the stubble of his jaw.

"What I mean is, we have to keep this one under the radar of the press and, well, just about everyone else, too."

"You mean sneak around?" Adam's voice cooled to the temperature of permafrost.

"Well, yes, if you want to put it like that. We don't even know what *this* is ..." She reached for his arm and trailed her finger along a vein from his elbow to his wrist. "I want to see you. We'll still see each other. I can't have my boss and everyone else thinking that I'm sleeping around with the drivers."

"Are you?"

She slapped his arm. "Just you."

He didn't answer.

"Adam, I'm a journalist now. This would be the end of my career. I have to report on you guys. I can't be seen to have favorites."

He rubbed his forehead, looking confused, then took a seat on the bed. Viv sighed inwardly. This was what happened once people opened their mouths—hateful reality invaded the cocoon of loveliness they'd wrapped themselves in for that night of fantastic sex.

On the other hand, his idea of being seen in public with her was from Cloud Cuckooland and even she in her sex-numbed state of mind could see that.

"I'm afraid it has to be on these terms—secret—or not at all."

"Secret?"

"Yes."

"That's nice. You get to choose," he said.

"What?"

"You choose which parts of your life you get to hide and which parts get opened to the public. Convenient."

"Adam, it's to protect you as well."

He winced. "Yeah, I know. Sorry. I'm not a fan of sneaking around."

"You don't have to. I'll do all that. You do your thing. I'll come to your hotel wherever you are. I'm a pro at dodging the press. Anyway, I'm sure you don't want our private lives plastered up as headlines."

"No."

"Well then. That's settled."

Adam stroked her cheek with his forefinger and let it linger on her chin, vestiges of a smile lingering at the side of his mouth. "Do you always settle things your way?"

"Hey, we came to a mutual agreement here." She lifted her chin higher. "Speaking of which—we need to finish an interview."

"You are joking."

"Not at all. I think I have about five usable seconds in total where you're actually saying something and behaving yourself. We need a new date, Adam. Strictly professional, of course."

"On one condition."

"Name it."

"You come to the ballet tomorrow night with me."

"You strike a hard bargain."

God, ballet. She'd not seen a performance since she'd watched her best friend Emma Daley graduate to the London School of Ballet at the age of seventeen. Aside from the cost of tickets, she'd never wanted to be reminded of what might've been. "Are you saying you just happened to buy one ticket too many and are at a loss as to what to do with it?"

"Something like that, yes."

"A proper, live, TV, BBC-exclusive interview?"

"Yes."

"Okay then, you've got a ballet partner."

He grinned boyishly, and it was worth it just to see that. He bent his head and kissed her, and it made her quiver with the memories of their night together.

"I do have to go now though," he said, breaking off the kiss.

"Go, go, go." She shooed him towards the door, handing him his wallet he'd left on the side table, overcompensating for the way she'd started to melt inside. Another kiss like that and she'd be a puddle of goo on the plush carpet.

When the door closed behind him, it had the effect of a bucket of ice-cold water. Who was in Cloud Cuckooland now? One night of sex and she'd forgotten how to *think*. The Montreal ballet house wasn't a private bedroom. Okay, it was a formal setting, not as bad as a nightclub, but still, it was public.

One lucky camera shot, and the press would be on fire with the news of their "affair." And all this before she'd got a decent interview with him. Either he was more devious than she was giving him credit for, or he had lost his head as much as she had.

Thank goodness it was tomorrow night and not tonight. She'd need at least a day to recover.

•••

Vivienne wanted them to meet in the café across from the ballet house, like she'd researched the location beforehand and figured this was the best way of not being seen in public. Fine by him.

When he saw her standing in the light of the streetlamp in a pale yellow, chiffon dress, white jacket, looking angelic, he wondered why the whole world hadn't stopped to stare at her and take photos. He wanted to pull her into his taxi and drive off somewhere more private entirely.

He paid the driver and stepped out, adjusting the lapels of his tux. Normally he felt okay in a shirt and suit, but today everything felt too tight. One night's absence from this woman had almost driven him to despair, thinking their night together had been an illusion, worrying that she'd somehow slipped away from him. But the fact that she was here now gave him hope.

"You came," he said.

She turned quickly, eyes wide. "Of course."

"Thanks."

"Just holding up my end of the bargain."

"Wearing this dress?" He took her cold fingers and placed them on his forearm.

"What's wrong with it?"

"Nothing. You look … " he fought for words "… ethereal—far too good for this world."

"Not so bad yourself." She laughed, a rich, soft laugh that made him long to tug her to him and devour her with kisses. Her eyes wandered to his face, his neck. He felt ridiculous for not kissing her, but her body language was ambiguous, confusing the hell out of him.

"Let's get inside," she said. "I'm uncomfortable standing here in public, even if the demographic is all middle-aged and predominantly female. Not your average racing aficionado."

"Indeed," he agreed. "One of the reasons I enjoy ballet."

"How did you get into it in the first place?"

"My mother brought me to a show—*The Nutcracker*—one Christmas a few years ago. She lives in New York now. She's lived there since … well, since I was sixteen. I went to humor her and so I wouldn't have to talk to her new boyfriend. I didn't expect to like it—but I loved it. The precision of the dancers' movements, the defiance of nature, the danger."

"The complete control?"

"Yes. In some ways it's like driving. All the preparation, the mental and physical perfection expected, the inherent risk, the total reliance on a two-hour performance on the day."

She nodded. "The insane competition, the horrible politics, and the ugliness under it all?"

"Yes, and yet, when you see a perfect performance, it transcends the bad stuff."

"So true," she said, thoughtfully. "What about your mother? Was she a ballerina?"

"God, no. She's a diplomat, and I think her hobby as a girl was negotiating pocket money raises from her parents. She was more bookish, I suppose. Has a way with people. Can convince them to do anything. Can't think why she married a farmer like my father. What did or do your parents do?"

"Dad was a teacher—geography. Mum's a nurse, part-time now. Very middle class. Lower end of middle class, actually."

The bell sounded for entering the theater. They settled into their seats in the middle of the darkened auditorium, with a perfect view and acoustics.

Despite the much-hyped, debut performance of the lead ballerina, despite the flawless choreography, his eyes were drawn constantly from the stage to Vivienne sitting beside him, where a performance far more intriguing and private was playing out. She wasn't watching as a normal observer—but as someone who had lived through the rigors of the dance. Her spine tightened on the difficult leaps … he could sense the ripple of tension coursing through her when the prima donna stretched into a high-extension arabesque.

Her chest swelled when a line of ballerinas took the fore of the stage in a line of mathematic perfection. Her fingers twitched on the armrest. He smoothed his hand down her wrist and covered her fingers. She tensed for a second, her sharp knuckles pressing up against his palm, but then she flattened out her hand under his, letting it go limp. He kept his hand there, moving it back and forth, communicating his opinion of the performance mixed in with his own thoughts of pure lust.

He let the music swirl over him, moving his forefinger in slow three-four time along the V of her middle and ring fingers. Her hand clenched, and she turned to look at him, glassy-eyed. He continued caressing the tiny valley between her knuckles and was gratified to notice her chest heaving, her neck relaxing its regal pose against the plush chair. If she were half as turned on as he was, they wouldn't make it past the first intermission.

When the intermission lights pinged on, it was like a rude intrusion into their privacy. He pulled her hand to his mouth and kissed the knuckles he'd been caressing. He glanced up to let people pass them on their way to the aisle.

"This is … taking a lot out of me," she said when they sat alone in their row. Her cheeks flamed pink, and her pupils were dark, swallowing up the hazel of her iris. She fanned herself with her free hand that clutched the program. "I'd forgotten how … charged … ballet can be. How utterly absorbing. I felt pains I've not felt in fifteen years."

"Mental or physical?" He leaned his head closer, grazed his lips against the irresistible curve of her cheek and then sought her lips with his. She opened slowly, beautifully, and he pressed deep. He was feeling pain, too, and she was the only one who could relieve him. He wanted her to understand this. This was torture. Mental *and* physical.

"Mmm," she replied. Her fingers trailed along the top of his stiff collar and up along his jaw. He could rip off this blazer, this shirt if she just said the word to get them out of here. He watched her face as he moved his hand to where her dress hem cut across the middle of her thighs, as he slid fingers into the hot space between her legs. He slid his tongue into her mouth again. Her body arched forward. A small moan came from deep in her throat as he inched his fingers ever closer to her core.

"Adam." She pressed out the word with her lips against his. "Don't make me come in a goddamn theater."

"Why not? Nobody's watching."

"Let's get out of here. Look, I know you forked out over $300 for these tickets, but I swear I'll pay you back and—"

He covered her mouth again with his. Ridiculous talk. He'd pay a hundred times as much to be teleported into a bed right this very moment.

"Come on," he said, rising. The semi-darkness might just about cover the obvious effect she had on him. He strode through the crowds milling around the tables in front of the bar, through the sonorous buzz of middle-aged chatter, the heady scents of expensive colognes.

Only seconds away from the large gilded doors that marked their freedom, his phone buzzed in his trousers pocket, agitating his erection further.

"Christ," he muttered and looked at caller ID.

Saskia.

She could wait.

He opened the doors and clenched his jaw as an elderly couple shuffled through first, before Vivienne, with a speed that would make a tortoise look nifty. The phone buzzed again in his pocket. Vivienne gave him a curious glance.

"Aren't you going to answer that?" she asked. "I'll get us a taxi." She turned away and stood arm raised at the edge of the sidewalk, her shapely back leg tilted up in a half-arabesque.

Saskia rang a third time. She never did that.

He pressed answer. "*Oui?*" He didn't bother concealing his irritation.

"Adam, Dad found out you were here, and he threw a complete tantrum. Not that he'd have wanted to see you, but just the principle that you'd come here behind his back and—"

"Saskia, this is not the time. I'm—"

"That's not it, Adam. He had a heart attack!"

"What?" He gripped the phone tighter. His heart clenched.

"You heard me. He got morose, storming around, banging pots and pans, everything and everyone getting on his nerves. I wouldn't mind, but then he had to sit down. I mean he was mixing fertilizer one moment, and the next he had to sit on the bench in the garage. Jeff told me. Short of breath, he said, but I think it was a heart attack. A minor one, but still."

"What? What did you do?"

"Jeff was with him. He rang 911. The ambulance came, and the medics took him in after a bit of an argument from Dad. We're here now in the hospital, waiting for the result. A nurse came by to say he's okay, but we're waiting for the full diagnosis. I blame myself. He should be doing regular checkups at his age. But he refuses to go."

"He's too scared they'll find something wrong with him, and now look what happens," Adam said, bitterly. He had to undergo routine medicals, and he hated it, too. That much he'd inherited from his estranged parent. But he wasn't as stubborn as his father. "I'm guessing the last time he saw doctor was when Mum was still in the house."

"Yes."

"Were there any signs?"

"Well, in hindsight, yes. He'd been complaining about shortness of breath going up stairs, but we'd put it down to lack of physical conditioning. He claims a good Cab will make him immune to heart attacks. Adam, I'm scared. If he goes—"

"Don't say that."

"—I don't know what I'll do. The winery can't run without him."

"Sure it can. You and Jeff have been doing most of the work for two years."

"But it's he the customers come to see, not me. The big ones."

A shiver rippled through Adam at the truth of this. Why did this have to happen now, when he'd so little control over what he could do? He had to calm her down. "He's had a scare, Sask. But people do at his age."

Vivienne was motioning to him. She'd got a taxi.

"Look, call you back. I'm outside. I have to go. Soon as I'm back in my hotel, okay? Wait for my call. Don't talk to a soul about this."

He shoved the phone back in his pocket. How could Dad have worked himself into such a frenzy as to cause an actual physical heart attack? Was that even possible? Whatever—it was up to him to manage the consequences now—to get Saskia calm enough to think sensibly again and deal with the paperwork and insurance. But more important, they'd have to plan for whatever press interest this might have stirred up in the hospital. He had to walk Saskia through exactly what to say—Jeff too—in case a journalist came knocking, which could happen any minute.

• • •

When Viv turned around to tell Adam to get in the taxi, she was looking at a different man from three minutes ago. His body was rigid. He nodded curtly and slid inside the car as if in a daze. No smile. No playful tugging on her hand. A strange metamorphosis caused by a short phone call. He sat leaning onto his knees until the momentum of the taxi taking off seemed to wake him up.

"God, sorry, Vivienne." He took her hand in his. It felt big and warm and comforting, but the guarded look on his face reminded her so much of their earliest encounters that she felt her desire cooling down. Rapidly. The dampness that had spread in her panties seemed to mock her now as she grew ever more uncomfortable sitting in her tight cocktail dress in the stuffy taxi.

"Who was that? Do you have to go somewhere?" She was used to these last-minute urgent meetings spoiling everything.

"Um." He rubbed his jawline. "That was my sister."

"Your sister in Santa Ynez? Saskia?"

"Yes."

"So—is she alright?"

"She's fine."

His tone and body language screamed otherwise. Should she intrude? Give him time to say it? She bit her lip, racked with indecision. Why was he looking out the window? God, surely he could tell her if there was something wrong? It wasn't like she'd broadcast it to the world.

"Adam? You can tell me. Whatever you say to me in private stays that way—by default—unless you want me to say something. Do you understand?"

"Yes." He reached for her hand, but his eyes showed strain.

"Do you trust me?"

"Yes." His fingers clasped around hers, just short of the point of pain. He sought her gaze. The guy was being honest at least, if not completely open. But his business was his own until he chose to share. Number one rule in dating drivers—give them space. Let them decide, or else you never knew where you stood with them.

"Good," she whispered. "Look, we don't have to be together tonight. If you need time to … I don't know—"

"Maybe it's better," he said. "I feel too … I don't know … aggressive right now."

A jolt of reluctant interest shot through her, firing up her system. Her nipples hardened at the illicit thought of him releasing that pent-up aggression in some high-energy sex.

"Not in a good way." He squeezed his eyes tightly and massaged his temples for a few seconds, then straightened. He pulled her into a soft kiss and muttered, "I'll make it up to you, I promise, but I need figure out some stuff alone tonight."

"That's fine," she said, hating her body for responding to him while her brain was yelling at her to leave well alone. "My hotel's before yours, so I'll pop out, and you drive on. You call me when you're … you know—"

"I'll call you."

She wobbled getting out of the taxi, and her vision blurred with sentimental tears as she clacked through the lobby in her stilettos. *Get a grip, McCloud.* She still had to pack for the long-haul flight to Heathrow tomorrow. She didn't need another night of passion, what with all the risk and everything. Too many people milling about—not only was the BBC staying in this budget hotel, but half the American press as well. It was for the best. Really. It was too soon anyway to expect him to treat her like a girlfriend or anything.

She also had a piece to create on the subject of all this soul searching—Adam himself. For God's sake, they both had jobs to do—this wasn't a holiday camp. If she couldn't separate the emotions from the job she was put here to do, then she was already in big trouble.

Chapter 17

Budapest, Hungary

The BBC troops landed in Budapest airport the next day after a long and grueling flight from Montreal with a stopover in Heathrow.

Viv didn't go to bed like everyone else after checking into the hotel. She'd been awake for thirty-five hours on the go, and the temptation to flop into bed was enormous, but she buried herself in her laptop—editing the "interview" video and preparing a script from her notes. Despite having spent so much time with Adam in Montreal, he'd given her precious little camera time that she could use.

She typed up her narrative feverishly; it had to be raw, fresh, real. Emotive language, emotive backstory. Piecing all the snippets of information from Mack's files and from Adam's brief answers together, she could just about pull off this documentary. She'd use her own voice to save time. A brief mention of the Fontaine Fans website wouldn't go amiss either. The fans were starting to amass. Still a small bunch, but enthusiastic. Her eyelids fluttered as she remembered the intensity of their lovemaking, twisting and turning on the satiny bed sheets. Then the evening with him at the ballet. She'd never wanted anyone so much and then been so thwarted. She turned back to her keyboard, gritting her teeth, forcing her eyelids to stay up.

When she finished, she rooted out a photo of him for the title screen. It was from after the race in Bahrain, where he was talking to an engineer with the desert sunset in the background. Nothing compared to the ones she'd taken in her bedroom—but she wasn't ready to unleash those on the public. They were *hers*.

The result was a ten-minute piece, "Adam Fontaine—The Man Behind the Helmet." The final touches like music and graphics rendering would have to be done with an expert like Sarah, but this was the beef, as her boss would say. She closed the laptop and collapsed into a dreamless sleep at 6:00 a.m. local time.

• • •

After breakfast at noon, she headed to the lounge beside the hotel reception to call Sarah to ask for help with the music and editing for her video. "I'm in my room, be down in ten," her colleague replied cheerfully, sounding like she'd gotten a full night's sleep.

"Great." Viv lay back and closed her eyes, enjoying the perfect proportions of the plush armchair, a heavy, elegant 1920s relic that epitomized this hotel. How easy it would be to nod off. She was so, so tired …

Someone touched her cheek. Someone was still touching her cheek, trailing a finger down from her eyebrow to the edge of her mouth and lingering there. It was pleasant … very pleasant. She opened her eyes dreamily.

Reece stood there, immaculate in a tux with a first-class, smarmy smile to match.

Yuck. She lurched forward, fully awake now, rubbing her cheek. Had she drooled?

"God, what time is it?"

"Five past one, Sleeping Beauty."

She'd been asleep for ten minutes. Her eyes trailed up his dark suit. "Why are you all dressed up?"

"Sponsor meeting." Reece flumped down in the armchair opposite her. "But, hey, my schedule tonight's opened up real wide."

"Has it indeed?"

Reece peered at her face. "You look tired, babe."

"That's because I am."

"Let me carry you off to bed. I promise I won't touch."

She shuddered mentally. Was it her imagination, or was there something behind his words, some emotion lurking deep under the perma-tan? "I couldn't, even if I wanted to. Important stuff to do. Sorry."

Sarah breezed into the lounge at that moment. When Reece turned, the young technician stumbled backward, almost knocking over a brass lamp. She reddened to the roots of her red hair and mumbled something incomprehensible. Her knees wobbled under her black lacy skirt as she approached.

Oh, God. Struck dumb, the poor woman. Viv sometimes forgot that other BBC employees didn't have the same exposure to the drivers as she did. "This is Sarah Deegan, program technician," she explained, coolly. "Sarah, you know who this is."

Sarah nodded, still mute. Reece scanned her thin, reedy body, and judging by his expression, categorized her into the "maybe" group. The young woman squirmed under the scrutiny. He nodded, and stood. Sarah backed off a step like a frightened deer. He brushed past her on his way out saying, "Bye, darlings—see you around."

It took Sarah several moments to recover, standing like a schoolgirl staring into space.

"Bad idea, whatever you're thinking." Viv prodded the chair Reece had vacated with her foot.

Sarah flopped down on the same chair and gripped her arm. "He spoke to me! He's so sexy in real life, too."

"He's eye candy, nothing more." *Not even eye candy for that matter.*

"I know, I know. Lord, he's so … young."

"Older than you, Sarah."

"Yeah, well, I know, but …"

That love-struck grin lasted the whole three hours they spent on their laptops, selecting music and editing clips. Viv wrestled with her own thoughts as she replayed the clips of Adam, careful not to play any of the more-intimate moments in front of Sarah. Where was he? What was he doing? Why hadn't he called since he landed? It would be nice to show him this piece before she sent it to Mack.

When she was satisfied that her documentary was final enough, she sent it off to Mack. Sarah was busy on her phone, so Viv waited.

"Thanks so much for your help, Sarah."

Sarah widened her eyes as she called off. "That was Catherine. She said Adam Fontaine called the studio."

Viv's heart jumped. "What?"

"Twice. He asked for you, but obviously you are here. Guess what, he said he'd do a live interview."

"Oh." *He didn't have to announce it, did he?*

"Yeah. So Catherine gave him a studio slot."

"Catherine?" The morning show anchor would tear him to pieces given the chance.

"Yeah. Mack's all excited, Viv. What's wrong?"

She cleared her throat and looked out the window. "Nothing. I suppose I'd better call him and thank him." She had to get away from Sarah pronto she could talk to him.

"I'm going to check out the office facilities," she lied as they passed reception.

"Sure, see you up there later." Sarah headed to the elevators to their rooms.

Walking past the open doors of the restaurant, she noticed Mack at a table with a bunch of gray, senior executives who were joining the crew on the European leg of the Grand Prix. Groaning, she slid out of view.

Joe the cameraman came up alongside her and asked about setup times in the afternoon. Viv answered tersely, but it was too late. Mack had spotted her. He beckoned her over to his table. She cringed and trudged across the dining room.

"Afternoon." She smiled at the round of four pasty-faced, middle-aged men.

"This is Vivienne," her boss said, "We've just been looking at that piece you sent me." He motioned to his iPad and beamed like she'd been awarded the Pulitzer. She held her tight smile in place, wishing she could walk on. "We've made it public."

"I enjoyed it. It was gutsy. Gave Mr. Spock some character, some … color," the man to her left said, folding his napkin in his lap.

"Sit down, Viv," Mack said. "We appreciate your efforts on securing a date for the live interview with him, too. I'm presuming that was your doing. Better late than never, eh?"

Approving nods all around.

"Yes, Viv's full time," Mack announced. "Probation period ends next week, and she's here for the long haul."

Viv let the news seep into her system. God, the relief was almost unreasonable, but she didn't want to give her horrible boss the satisfaction of knowing she'd actually been worried or anything.

"Thank you," she said. "And will you allow me to conduct the Fontaine interview, too?"

Mack pulled a doubtful face and shook his iPad. "Well, you went a little too gentle on the guy here. Besides a fresh attack will get different results. Anyway, Catherine's our interview girl—we all know what a tiger she is."

The round of men laughed. The way he'd said it, his comment was not without sexual innuendo. Not that Catherine would touch any of these porkers with a barge pole.

"She's got first dibs, but you can always ask her if you like."

Oh, bloody fantastic. There was no way in hell Catherine would give up her prize.

As they yapped on among themselves, she picked at her nail polish under the table. It was unbearable sitting here listening to their shoptalk on the antics of the upper echelons of their organization. She excused herself to escape to her room. Eating was impossible.

She'd gained the respect of BBC senior officials. So it was safe to say her job was secure. More than that—she'd gained respect. But where was the wave of relief she'd been expecting? Now all she felt was an itchy kind of agitation, resentment almost. Was that normal?

It was her hormones talking. She couldn't let her private life get in the way again. Adam was … lovely, but the way he shut her out suggested she was just a nice-to-have on his list of priorities. Although dissimilar in temperament to Ronan and Maddux, they all had that in common. She didn't want to give him up … not completely … but she'd have to be extra careful from now on. No more ballets. No more anythings in public.

Chapter 18

"What's the latest?" Adam asked Saskia.

"He's out. He's home. He's grumpier than ever."

"Okay, that's good then. Is he taking any precautions?"

"They gave him some pills he's supposed to take every morning. I don't know, Adam. I can't monitor him all the time. He keeps saying he's fine; it was nothing."

"Well, make sure he takes it easy. No heavy outside work."

"Would you like to come here and tell him that yourself maybe?"

"Considering what set him off—the news that I'd been home unannounced—I don't think that's a good idea."

"Yeah, well. I just want him fit and healthy so he can walk me down the aisle come December. Of course, he's claiming he'll be dead before that day ever comes."

Adam frowned. "And blaming me for his own death as well as Eddie's. Typical."

Saskia's laugh was harsh. "Listen to yourself. I've a good mind to elope to Vegas and leave the two of you to fight it out of your systems."

After that call, he wanted to talk to Vivienne so he'd feel better. Dad was just being his belligerent old self. He'd live on another forty years, tormenting everyone around him with his impending next attack. But there was no answer on her mobile.

Adam bit into his knuckle. Where the hell was she? Not at her work. Nowhere in the hotel or around the circuit. No one at the BBC could tell him. This was his only morning off. He'd wanted to show her a bit of Budapest, or if he got lucky, entice her to his bedroom—his or hers, didn't matter. Nothing mattered. He wanted more. He needed more.

Why hadn't she called him back yet? She wasn't the play-hard-to-get type. He said he'd call, and he'd called ten times this morning. Had she even made it over to Europe or been re-assigned somewhere? Or was it personal—pissed off about their evening in Montreal being cut short? But how could he explain that whole mess with Dad without explaining the colossal mess that was his life?

Vivienne should get to know his positive side before he subjected her to all the ugliness he hid inside. She'd think less of him; how could she not? Any sane person would. Reece had brushed it off, but he could hardly be classified as sane. The trick was to be more like the charismatic guys she'd dated or hung out with. Keep the focus on her. Keep it light. Wasn't that the first rule of dating women? Make them laugh?

He was pretty sure Ronan didn't fill her ears with his problems with his own father—a felon. And God knew, Maddux could hold a marathon talk on his troubles with sponsors and money and the rest of it. Only they didn't fall into that trap, did they?

He had to see her. Why wouldn't she switch on her goddamn phone? He couldn't function. He flopped on his bed in frustration and pulled up his laptop to check the weather forecast.

Hungaroring, with its sixteen turns, was almost as treacherous as Monaco, and he didn't like it one bit, even in the best of conditions. Flicking through websites, he landed on the BBC and the first thing glaring out at him was "Fontaine—The Man behind the Helmet." Then he saw her name under it. His blood ran cold. What was this? God, she better not have said anything …

He watched the video with growing unease. He'd agreed to an interview to prevent this very thing from happening. When the hell had she done all this? This morning?

She was presenting him as the goddamn elephant man—a recluse that needed pity. His frown deepened on the part about his family. She mentioned "family tensions" when he was sixteen, the loss of his brother, and suggesting in the same breath that he felt somehow responsible for the winery. He threw the laptop aside and got up again. They had to talk about this.

• • •

Viv needed three goes before she let her call to Adam ring long enough for him to answer. Her nerves were shot. What was she? Sixteen?

He answered immediately. "Where were you?"

"Um, out and about with Sarah, our technician."

"When can I see you?"

"Now?"

"Good," he said. "I know your room number."

"Yes … okay."

Within minutes, there came two sharp raps on her door. She sat up and swung her feet onto the carpet.

She opened the door a crack. Adam stood in the corridor.

"Can I come in?" Despite the tension, she broke into a grin. God, he looked good.

He strode in, shutting the door behind him with his fist. He took two steps to her, his chest heaving under the dark blue T-shirt, his dark eyes focused on her, watchful.

She forgot everything she'd been thinking about.

He slammed his lips onto her open mouth and pushed her up against the wardrobe. She caved. Her body pressed into him, coming alive again. Her nipples hardened against his chest. He lashed her with his tongue and crushed his body tightly against her breasts. Heaven had just opened its pearly gates again—

He drew back. "See?"

"See what?" she panted, irritated that he'd broken off.

"How much I needed that? This—separation—it's not good."

"Hey, you'll survive if I can."

"And what's this?" He tore out his smartphone from his pocket and held up the display of the BBC website and her video. "What the hell, Vivienne? I thought we'd just agreed to a new date. You didn't have to make stuff up."

She looked away. So he didn't like the piece. Question answered loud and clear. "Is that why you called the station and gave the interview to someone else?"

"I promised you an interview. You weren't there in the office when I called. But I had to schedule a time."

"Okay, but you may have handed over your life to a different interviewer now who's quite the bitch. Catherine Price."

"How could I have known that? I think—I think it's for the best anyway. If we're on TV together ... well, maybe *you* can be professional in front of a camera, Vivienne, but I can't. I'll only want to—" He stepped closer, eyes glowing, "you know."

"Yes, yes, okay," she said, splaying her palms on his chest.

"And if I choose to say nothing to this Catherine, then at least you won't get the blame for being a bad interviewer, *but* you'll get credit for having secured the interview."

She held her fingers to her forehead. "That's ... twisted, but yeah, okay. Look, the whole point of this was to make you approachable, likeable, *nice*, remember?"

He paced around, saying nothing. She was definitely getting through on some level, so she continued. "What's your problem with the piece?"

His expression darkened. "All this Fontaine Fans stuff. Why do you encourage them? Give them publicity? They mill around my family home, tormenting my family, and you give them cred? I thought I told you I didn't like it. It's—it's disappointing."

She sighed. "Adam, your family—"

"What about them?"

"My question exactly. I've told you about my brother, my family. My past love life even. You've given me nothing. Nothing at all."

"Because I know where it would end up." He shook the phone in his hand. "It's funny how you want to dissect my life in public, even to interview me in public, and yet you won't be seen dead with me."

He looked at her, then ran a hand through his hair. "Sorry. That's unfair. I know. You're just doing your job."

She sat down on the bed, tugging the duvet to cover her knees. The irony stuck her, and not for the first time. But was he using that as a shield? So she couldn't get too close? Too intimate?

"Adam, I've respected your privacy within reason. But I had to say *something*. Yes, about your family, too—you didn't just drop to Earth from a different planet, despite what some reports are saying. People need to know the basics so they can connect to you and see you as the good guy you are. I nearly died when I saw what happened in Bahrain—you know, after the race. That bottle could have slashed your eye out."

"You think you can prevent that?"

"No, but it brought home to me what you *needed*." She held her face up to him.

"Let me be the judge of what I *need*." His voice was gentler. He sat down beside her on the bed. He stroked a thumb across her cheek, then the other. He kissed her lips gently, then urgently. His mouth trailed down her neck. "But promise me this: Get off my case."

She nodded. Right now, she'd agree to anything. As long as he kept going.

"I just need you," he said.

•••

They'd done it again. Adam shook off the blanket and the lingering feelings of lust and something more tender. He wished he could be locked up in this room with her until Sunday's race, but he had a strategy meeting to get to in ten minutes. He couldn't afford to get mushy-brained now.

And it would always be like this—until the end race in Monaco in four months. Snippets of time together and lots of sneaking around. Hardly the level of attention she was used to from the likes of Ronan and Maddux, but it was her express wish to keep it secret. Anyway, once it was over, he'd have all the time in the world to make it up to her.

As he dressed, he watched her sleeping. Vivienne looked beautiful naked, snuggled into fetal position on the satiny sheet with a serene look on her face. She managed to be fit and yet natural looking, beautiful and yet real. Everything about her was like honey—her voice, the looks she gave him, how she maneuvered him from one topic to another, how easy on the nerves she was, playful, confident and harmony-seeking. Five days and two continents into this relationship, he was one lucky bastard, and well he knew it.

"Wake up," he said.

"Oooh what?" Viv raised her head and grinned at him. If her hair were long, it would be tousled. As it was, her spikes were just a tiny bit wayward, and it was incredibly cute.

"I have to go."

After a lingering kiss, he traipsed reluctantly down to the garages. Bruce was inspecting the rear axle of Albany's car. Albany waved when he saw Adam.

"What's the verdict on the GTX?" Adam asked.

Bruce nodded. "Injection. You were right."

Albany shot him a look. "Bad luck, mate."

"Who was responsible for checking it?"

"Marc. He's real sorry; won't happen again."

"Cut him some slack, Adam," Albany said. "Marc's done overtime to get the car shipped, and it's arrived quicker than anyone else's—he knew someone in customs. So you can at least give him credit for that."

Adam nodded.

"The engineers all have girlfriends now," Albany continued. "Happy as pigs in muck."

"Yes, I know," Adam said. And they weren't the only ones. An image of Viv naked on the bed flashed in his mind, and he couldn't be as angry as he wanted to be. Not by half. No, he was unfortunately rather like a pig in muck himself.

Bruce looked guilty. "Like you said, mate, there may have been an excess of partying in Bahrain. I had a word with them, though. Reece will not be welcome in that garage again, you may be sure. We've set up a night watch and all."

"Good," Adam said, unclenching his teeth. "Hey Marc, good move with the customs."

Bruce and Marc both stared at him like he'd spurted a second head.

"What?"

"Nothing, um—" Bruce began. "Marc, go check that suspension one more time, would you?" He turned away, but not fast enough to conceal a wide grin.

and Voutilainen. They've brought half of Finland here to Budapest, just like every year."

Her commentary went on and on. When Adam stuck behind the stupid safety car that lost him precious seconds over Reece, she fought to keep all frustration from her voice. At one point she very nearly swore at Reece.

"Well, that was fun," Rick remarked when they were off-air. "Viv, you got very animated. If you're not careful, you'll make me look like the levelheaded one."

"Impossible," she retorted. "I just wanted the best man to win."

She pretended to be engrossed in her phone to prevent any more home truths slipping out.

With Ronan, she'd been new to the F1 scene, and she'd overlooked a lot as she'd adjusted to the thrilling life on the road, speeding around the globe—a different city every two weeks, staying in posh hotels and attending splendiferous parties.

She'd weathered the driver's different moods depending on how the races went, and grinned and borne the constant publicity. She'd adapted to the madness, and it had worked out fine. By the end of her time with Ronan, it was clear that his career obliterated everything else. He'd given her the option of keeping the affair going—surface only—without even realizing that was what he was doing. She'd declined. It was an occupational hazard with these guys. And that was fine.

But then not long after, Ronan had met Cassidy and discovered he *did* want a serious relationship after all, that he *was* capable of commitment. This was Ronan Version 2.0.

She'd anaesthetized the blow by hanging out with Maddux, who made her laugh—Maddux, the bad-boy Texan who wanted fun. There was no ambiguity regarding commitment between them, as there was none, and no sex either. It was a move that benefitted both of them in terms of keeping the press happy and the stalkers away. And yet, to everyone's surprise, Maddux got serious with

Brynn not long afterward. They were suddenly marriage material. Enter Maddux Version 2.0.

She knew she was being immature, but it hurt that both men had found who they did want after her, even though such a turn of fate had seemed next to impossible while she had been with them. Strange that.

Then there was Adam. He didn't ride the rough times; he dove right in. He seemed to take perverse pleasure out of making things more difficult than they needed to be. It was impossible to tell when he was in a good mood and when not because his manner hardly differed in either case, and that was somewhat disconcerting. But also reassuring. Something told her there wasn't an Adam Version 2.0 waiting in the wings, ready to burst out the minute he encountered Ms. Future Bride. If there were such a woman that could so transform him, she couldn't imagine what she'd be like.

Chapter 20

Hockenheim, Germany

The F1 season was in full swing. After Hungary they moved through Austria into Germany, like World War II occupation in reverse. Adam had clinched Austria in retaliation for Reece getting Hungary, leaving the gap between them the same, with Reece a mere four points ahead.

The races started to become a blur to Viv. The gaps in the points table widened between the elites—Adam, Reece, Maddux, Ronan, David Anderson—and the less fortunate.

Adam went over all the team tactics with her in the evenings after each race, explaining why they'd decided to do what they'd done, what had worked out well and what hadn't. On air, her new insights into the sport surprised even her. She was hitting her stride, finally incorporating all she knew from following F1 as a fan with her dad and Liam, then on the circuit with Ronan, and now polished off with the added knowledge from Adam's analyses. She judged situations correctly, sometimes even better than veteran commentator Rick.

And people noticed. When the other drivers talked to her, they looked her in the eye instead of roaming all over her body. Well, most of them anyway. At press events, sponsorship types asked her what she thought the chances were for specific drivers.

In private, the past three weeks with Adam had been wonderful. Sure, they didn't have much time together, but what they had was intense bliss. Their schedules were unforgiving, particularly his, but they managed to meet up when he didn't have any late strategy meetings and she didn't have a press event or have to help with packing and moving. They'd seen another ballet together in

Cologne, Germany, and spent whole nights away in secret hotels away from F1. But she always made sure to return to the BBC's cheaper hotels at night.

It was different with Adam. She never felt relegated to the back seat despite his schedule. But having to keep it so secret was an additional hardship that cut their time together even shorter. They had scarce time to talk, and when they did, it was about the race or the preparations for the race.

The most difficult times were the VIP tents after the races and the press events where drivers mingled with the journalists. That was when Viv discovered just how good Adam was with stealth. He was a genius at hiding his feelings—his expressions rarely giving anything away unless his guard was down, usually on sheets as soft as butter at the hotels they escaped to whenever possible, and he had a reputation for sobriety and abstinence that he didn't actually deserve. She had enough journalistic experience to be able to remain stonefaced whenever she came in contact with him in public, stealing a glance now and then, but never pushing her luck. So nobody suspected anything. In Germany at the Hockenheimring press conference, Adam shared the stage with Albany, his second driver, and Reece and Maddux with their second drivers. He had said his short bit about Gatari's chances in the championship, and now he was off camera, looking down, jaw held in his fingers, playing with his phone.

She got a text a few seconds later.

Schönes Fräulein, let's get out of here.

Good idea, she texted back.

She raised her head, and their eyes met. He looked away quickly, pretending to be engrossed in what Reece was saying. Viv suppressed a giggle.

Where? she typed. She enjoyed watching his eyes flicker as the text came buzzing in.

Holiday in Wallonia he wrote back.

This time her giggle came out as a snort. Luckily the moderator had just said something funny, and everyone else was laughing, too.

Cleopatra Ballroom 5 min.

* * *

Adam was serious about a mini-holiday in Wallonia. He had a few days off the schedule because the gap between races this time was two weeks instead of one, and Germany to Belgium was a mere bunny hop in comparison to the stretches they'd traveled between the Middle East and the States, and the stretches they would soon be covering between Europe and Asia.

"We can do a tour, visit the estate where I grew up. It's a guesthouse now, but it used to be a farm."

She couldn't hide her surprise. Mini-break? Where he grew up? Their relationship was leaping forward in light years. What did this mean? Ronan had never suggested a mini-break.

"Sounds wonderful," she said, snuggling into him. And it did.

They took a train from Frankfurt am Main to Brussels Nord, as he had a sponsor meeting in Brussels. Ronan and Maddux wouldn't have been seen dead in a train; they had to fly everywhere, first class or private jet.

"That's because they're not European," he explained.

"Ronan's British."

"My point exactly."

"*I'm* British."

"Well, I'm working on Europeanizing you." He gave her an ambiguous look over the rim of his café crème in the Speisewagen of the Deustche Bahn ICE train.

"Which entails what exactly?"

His eyebrows quirked. "A certain element of *je ne sais quoi* mixed in with *je ne regrette rien*."

"Well, for your information, *ma chérie*, I got all that. Some *I don't know* mixed in with *I regret nothing*. Why does it sound better in French? And don't forget *voulez vous couchez avec moi*. Look, I know you're taking the piss at my ballet-terms-only French."

"I'm excited," he said. "*Qu'est-ce que je ferais sans toi?*"

"What will I…?" she deciphered slowly. "No, what *would* I … do without you?" She smiled as it hit her. "That's very romantic, Adam."

"Not at all. It's the truth."

She warmed inside and reached for his fingers on the table. The remaining passengers in the café wagon left.

He slid out from his seat and came around the table to sit beside her. Without a word, his mouth slanted over hers, and his tongue darted into her mouth. She slid her hands up under the hem of his shirt and ran them along the hard planes of his back. His kiss was full of want, of greed, and something more. His fingers roamed under her blouse, touching all the parts he could reach, telling her she was as irresistible to him as he was to her.

His hand slid slowly under the hem of her dress, kneading the soft skin of her thigh with his fingers. Probing, teasing, while he watched her reaction.

Before she could think, he pulled back and held her hand to his lips, kissing it. She released a frustrated sigh. The ache he'd started deep inside of her was never going to be soothed with a kiss. But they were on a train so …

He looked speculatively toward the back door of the carriage. "You reckon there's an empty compartment down there somewhere?"

"Maybe." She shrugged. "What do you have in mind?"

"Let's go." He grabbed her hand, leading her out.

The first two compartments were totally free. Few people traveled in first class at this time of night. He opened the glass door and pulled her in, pushing her up against the window. Standing against him like this, her body molded into his, they started to move together to the rhythm of the train. Her skin prickled with awareness, and her insides sprang to life. Every nerve in her body welcomed him back in a way she couldn't control. His hands mapped the lines of her breasts, her torso and her hips, and his erection prodded into her softness with every thump of the train.

His tongue continued in her mouth, and his hands sought her bare flesh until she squirmed with need. He reached down and pulled her leg up to his hip, sliding his hands under the hem of her dress. His hand was so close to where she needed it, she let out a whimper.

He grinned and licked along her bottom lip, teasing. She grasped his head tighter to tell him she wanted it, yes, even here in this train carriage. She didn't care.

His chest rose and fell, and his eyes bored into her. "Try doing this on an airplane."

"No," She laughed. "I haven't, and I wouldn't."

He cupped her ass and yanked her into his body, into his hard erection. "Not even with me?"

"Unless someday I fly first class with you."

"How far are you willing to go on a high-speed train?"

"As far as you're taking me, hotshot." She sucked in her breath as he moved his hands up her midriff and stopped beside her breasts. Her body was perched on the edge of need; it responded the moment it got the touch it craved. His thumbs made contact with her nipples, which hardened instantly.

"Come, talk to me," he said.

She leaned back and grasped a vertical rail, closing her eyes to allow the sensation to overwhelm her other senses with each gentle up and down stroke of his thumb. The rail was the only thing stopping her crumpling in a heap. Her head clouded, all witty comebacks obliterated in her brain.

He leaned in to suck her bottom lip and then pulled back to meet her gaze. "Come." He sat down on a seat and patted his lap. "Sit down."

With an uncertain glance out the compartment's glass door, she hiked up her dress and placed her knees on either side of him, lowering her center over his lap.

A secretive expression flitted across his face, making her want to cradle his desire and to own it, control it, to devour him. With his dark eyes fixed on her, he inched the hem further up her thighs. Her lips parted in anticipation, and her eyes darted to the door.

"Stop watching the door," he said. "We'll hear if it opens. I'll hear." He squeezed her thigh. "You just relax and tell me what you want, because I want to feel you inside. His fingers brushed over her, sending a jolt of electricity to her sex.

"I—I—"

"I want to be inside of you, to feel you all around me, to hear that sound when you give it all up to me."

She nodded wordlessly, and then he gave her what she needed, capturing her mouth with his, parting her lips and taking control over her every shiver of reaction. He pulled aside her damp underwear with his thumb and touched her clit. A wave of pleasure coursed through her, and her moan was smothered when he covered her mouth with hers. She panted out her desire in quick spurts.

While his mouth captured hers, his fingers parted her cleft and teased the skin there so that every part of her hummed with pent up need. Still caressing her, he slipped two fingers in, waited for her gasp of acceptance and pushed in deeper.

She groaned at the exquisite sensation, desperate for more. She flexed her hips, opening herself to him as far as possible. Her head lolled back.

"You're so ready. I want you like this when I enter you."

His words edged her closer to that cliff. His fingers thrilling her flesh made her forget they were on a train, speeding through Belgium's flatlands. The risk of being caught like this only heightened her arousal. They wouldn't be able to stop if the pope himself walked in.

His fingers worked up the stimulation her clit needed to send her soaring to the highest point, then the intense, deep wave of heat enveloped her, as her body disintegrated into a sparkling cloud dust of ecstasy.

He withdrew his fingers and pulled out a condom from his back pocket, pulled down his zipper and positioned himself at her entrance. She took the condom from him. If there was one thing he couldn't do, it was open a damn condom quickly enough. He flashed a tense, grateful smile. She smoothed the rubber onto his erect cock, and he then guided her hips so he had access to her entrance.

When the tip of his cock entered into her, her body threatened complete meltdown, of connectedness, of wanting him. It obliterated thinking; only sensations mattered.

She sank slowly onto him, feeling every solid inch of him as she maneuvered herself fully onto him. His voiceless growl and his fingers digging into her hips were all the response she needed. She leaned forward and covered his mouth with hers, grinding against him in time with the train.

His whole body tensed and she tightened around him in response, sliding up and down. With her tongue she coaxed his mouth open and demanded for him to take what he wanted, what he needed, because she sure as hell needed all of him.

Soon his body demanded to move in his own rhythm, a faster rhythm, faster than the rocking train. She watched his face, fascinated by how the cheek muscle tightened and the veins on his temples pulsed, a sure sign of imminent climax. He thickened inside of her, and her body exploded in warm pleasure again and she rocked against him. Gripping her hips , he held her in place as his orgasm let rip though his body. He slammed his head back against the wall of the carriage. He let out a moan that was swallowed up by the noise of the train.

She kept watching his face, the sweet release, the slackening of his chiseled jaw for just that brief moment, and the warmth and vagueness filling his eyes. He sat like that for some time, staring back. Then he gathered her to his chest for a sweet moment and kissed her lips softly.

"Qu'est-ce que je ferais sans toi?"

• • •

As they left the flatlands, driving south in a rental car from Brussels, the terrain started to change, becoming greener and hillier with every passing kilometer. The clouds broke up and allowed some of the high-June sunshine through. Instead of turning east at Liège for Spa-F they headed west toward Namur and their final destination, Rochefort.

He was letting her drive. This was definitely a first. Her F1 exes would rather have been buried alive than to allow that. At first, she worried that Adam would be a terrible passenger, but he seemed at ease and didn't once comment on her driving. That was because she was an excellent driver. It was nice to be able to prove it for once.

The car was quiet for stretches of the journey. She didn't know about him, but she was still reeling from that amazing sex on the train. She'd never be able to travel by rail again without thinking of that. She was still all fired up. At least the task of driving kept her attention off his body.

This mini-break was going to be heaven if it continued like it'd started. And she was flattered that he wanted to show her his old family home. Especially as he never talked of family. She knew no more now than she did before about his childhood in Belgium or of his youth and coming of age in Santa Ynez. Maybe this trip was his way of telling her something, without having to tell her?

His sister Saskia called frequently, but from his monosyllabic responses afterward, she knew not to go there. Given the chance, he tended to take those calls in another room or skip answering altogether. She had to give him time on that one. Why bring up contentious issues when they had so little time to talk at all?

"Where has this been all my life?" she asked, slowing the BMW down on the empty road to gaze at the hills with their dense green covering, villages huddling on meandering rivers with bridges. "I mean, I thought Spa-Francorchamps was picturesque enough, but this is … amazing."

He reached out and rubbed the back of her neck with his strong fingers. He didn't comment on her little swerve, but kept kneading those muscles so they were humming for joy.

"Where have *you* been all my life," she moaned.

"Drive on, you haven't seen the best part."

The way the dull-colored houses hugged the roads so tightly, packed together in each narrow valley, lent the place a sense of community and an age long forgotten. With its low clouds, Belgium did bleakness in a way no other country managed, elevating it to a grim kind of beauty.

They arrived after an hour at Rochefort and Adam's instructions came faster and faster as they departed the main road and trundled down country lanes.

They finally stopped at a large estate of rolling lawns and thickets of trees The gray stone house perched at the top of the low hill commanded a view over the surrounding countryside, which consisted of more and more of those forested hills. The more-distant trees appeared a shimmering gray-blue.

"That's it, isn't it?" she said in an awed voice. "That is where you were born and grew up?"

"Yes."

"What is it now?"

"A guesthouse."

"Will we stay there?"

"Nah. That would be weird, although the Bertrands who run it now are very pleasant."

Didn't he want to stroll memory lane on his mini-break?

They got out, and he took her hand in hand to walk the grounds.

"Was it a vineyard back then?"

"No." Adam pulled her in and kissed her on the lips. "My mother … she was a diplomat in the EU Commission who transferred from the US State Department and specialized in American-European trade agreements. This place is almost equidistant from Brussels and Strasbourg, so it was perfect for her. The little fruit farm that my father maintained behind the house was just a hobby really. His job was to maintain the house and look after us kids. That's where I learned to get up early—fruit picking."

"So why did you all move to the States?"

"Well, even the Commission downsized. She lost her job. My father had always had a dream of running a winery. My mum's from near Santa Ynez, and she had parental pressure to come back and I think she missed home. So, they upped and left when I was fourteen and bought a small vineyard with the money they got by selling off this place."

"That must have been quite an adventure for you kids." Viv stroked his hands with her thumb as they walked. She couldn't help feeling she was in interview mode, but she desperately wanted to know. "I mean, you were in the middle of secondary school at that stage."

"I hated it. I had to leave my car here. My karting club."

"And your friends …?"

"There weren't many.

She squeezed his hand. He didn't look at her. What kind of fourteen-year-old missed a car more than his friends? Come to think of it, what kind of fourteen-year-old even *had* a car, not to mention one that he'd built himself?

"I spent all my free time with … my brother." His expression hardened.

"Eddie," she said in a low tone.

"Yes." He was crushing her hand and no doubt didn't realize he was doing it.

"Come on," he said. "We should get to our guesthouse so we can relax in peace and quiet for once."

"I like the sound of that."

• • •

It didn't take them long to find themselves lying together on the white-linen-covered bed, from where they had a view of a country garden in early summer bloom.

"It's nice to have some privacy." Viv was hungry for him. Before he could make a move, she slid her hand up inside his T-shirt and trailed her palm down his hard chest, relishing the sensation of hard muscle and hair across the taut pectorals. Her insides melted; he was an addiction, and she was getting her fix.

Adam's hand curled around the back of her neck and brought her mouth to meet his. All her pent up frustration, which had built up since the train, exploded within her. He slid his tongue into her mouth, stroking her own and then teasing her teeth and lips. Of all things French, the kissing was the best part.

His fingers moved to her breast, and she gasped as more parts of her body stared to fire up. She inched forward to get more of him, and his other hand held her in place, cradling her shoulder blades in his long, tough fingers. She pressed into him, rocking against him to get closer.

Now his kisses were fierce and hungry, his mouth moving over her jaw and neck. He gently pushed her back.

She lay back on the cool linen, and he undid her jeans and cast them away. He undressed and slid back onto the bed beside her, leaning on his elbow. He let his gaze drift over her body, naked from the waist down. His hand traced her stomach, teasing her in a slow circle around her navel. Then he moved down.

"Every part of you is exquisite," he said softly, moving down to stroke her sex in languorous sweeps, leaving a trail of fire in their wake. "I don't know where to go next." She had no answer for him. Her brain had frozen up, and the only message coming out was … *don't stop.*

But his fingers knew where they were going. She panted as they entered her, driving her mad. He studied her face as she gave in to pleasurable moaning. Her desire for him was unceasing, primal.

A groan escaped from deep in his throat. He seemed to get as much pleasure from giving as receiving, especially when he'd found some new way to make her lose her head. As he was doing now, kneading some spot inside.

"I want you … now," she managed to press out.

His fingers eased out, and he grasped her by the hips and turned them both around so he was on the bottom, holding her crushed into the length of his entire body.

"Then take me," he said, smoothing his hands over her buttocks.

Her hands slid down his biceps, enjoying how her weight could restrain him, or at least pretend to.

"With your T-shirt still on, I can't see anything," he complained when she sat up to roll on a condom. "Come on, off with it, we're not on a train."

"You just have to imagine it," she said, gritting her teeth as she eased herself down onto his rigid cock. His head jerked to the side against the pillow, eyes shut in pleasure.

"Oh God," he breathed.

She sat up and tugged off her T-shirt, but something moved outside the window in her peripheral vision.

"Oh God!" She pulled herself off him and scrambled off the bed.

His eyes flew open. "What?"

"Out there. People."

Was this it? Had the paparazzi caught up with her again?

Chapter 21

Adam groaned. His system was still thrumming with pre-climax pleasure. He was still hard as hell. He'd been that close to—

"People outside," Vivienne hissed again. She clutched up her T-shirt from the bed to cover her breasts.

Adam sat up. Then he, too, stood.

"Stay away from the window," she urged, pulling his arm. She yanked the floral curtains closed just as he got a glimpse of a group of about seven kids loitering in the lane at the back of the garden.

"Vivienne?" he laughed, pulling the T-shirt away from her chest. "They're tiny kids."

"God, sorry." She smiled and looked sheepish. "Knee-jerk reaction. I'm so used to being followed by paparazzi." She peered out through the slit in the curtain again. "Yup, these little guys look to be about six years old; they wouldn't even understand what we were doing even if they saw."

"Did this happen a lot with you and—?"

"No, just now and again," she said quickly, her face flaming red. Whether because of embarrassment or lying he couldn't tell.

"Are there any compromising pictures or videos of you out there?"

"No. Nothing like that." She came to sit on the bed beside him. "In fact, the thing with Maddux? It wasn't even a … thing."

"What do you mean?"

"We didn't have sexual relations."

"No?" This astonishing news blasted through any remnants of politeness he still maintained.

"And Ronan?"

"Well, er, that was a normal relationship, or as normal as could be under the media spotlight."

Damn. "I see." So at least Maddux had been platonic. And she'd weathered all this gossip and slander about them? Why?

"So ... what about you, Adam?" She looked at him earnestly. "What's your past when it comes to relationships?"

"Since I came to F1 two years ago, there's been nobody. I had a tough first season and then the hospital."

"No nice Wallonian nurses to look after you?"

"Some were very nice, but I was stuck to a bed."

"That never stopped anyone," she teased.

"Maybe I'm a little fussy." His eyes trailed over her curves as she lay beside him. More than a little fussy in fact. Why sleep with someone you didn't want to spend the morning after with, the whole day after with, your whole life after with? At least in theory. There had to be that theoretical possibility there, or else he couldn't do it. With Vivienne, it was there.

Other women he met around the F1 arena tended to project their own ideas onto him as to what he should be—a playboy, a superstar, or at the other extreme, a strange robotic savant—and they were disappointed when they discovered he was just what it said on the label: a Formula One driver first and foremost. As a result they never got near. Vivienne never deluded herself in that way. She got him. She also seemed to understand there was more underneath.

She seemed to be happy with his answer because she was smiling again and snuggling into his side. Not for the first time he wondered how in the hell Ronan could have wasted his opportunity with her.

"What about before that? When you lived in LA?"

"Yeah." He looked down at his hands. "My double shift at the garage didn't leave much time for that. And I drove at night. But now and again I'd meet a girl, yeah. There was a sister of another racer, and a sponsor executive. Didn't last though. I was somewhat ... intense ... about my racing career back then, and I had all sorts of money problems, too. If I'm to be honest, Vivienne, I wasn't great company."

He raised his eyes to hers. "This is my time off. My *only* time off, and this is how I want to spend it … with you. Let's not talk about the past. It's not a good place."

Just the now mattered. And the theoretical future.

• • •

The minute they got to the Spa-Francorchamps circuit three days later, Viv's Zen bubble of contentment burst. Bruce called Adam, telling him there were complications with the rear wheels' suspension, and he got stuck into testing that on the circuit. She didn't see or hear from him for the rest of the day. What a bucket of cold water after the luxury of a mini-break. But such was a driver's life. And a driver's girlfriend's life, for that's what she was now, public or not. No matter how close she thought she was getting to him at times, the third person in the relationship—the car—always fought back for his attention.

The following day, Adam had to stay overnight in Brussels, and she had no way to go with him and still keep her working commitments. At least it gave her the perfect opportunity to join in the social events with her colleagues.

"Come on," Sarah said. "You never do anything with us these days."

"Sure. Where's the party again?"

"Nautilus Oil's in the Marriott ballroom. Everyone will be there, from the top-of-the-food-chain car owners to the lowliest media support staff, like me. Our photographers are on full alert."

"Why?"

Sarah smiled. "The parties at Spa are always the raunchiest for some unknown reason. It's the one place the drivers will party before the race."

Viv texted Adam, who said he'd meet her there directly from free practice at the circuit. She'd not seen him since he got back from Brussels this morning and had been hoping to sneak off with him. But she had to keep up appearances.

"Come on, I love this song," Sarah pleaded, tugging her arm in the direction of the dance floor after about half an hour of people watching. "Let's dance."

Viv looked around warily. "I'll pass."

"Oh come *on*."

Then again, when had she ever refused to dance to this before, and why was she doing so now? Of course Sarah couldn't dance on her own, not with all those drivers there. Viv simply had to go with her. It was becoming clear why Sarah was still single and would remain so; she was as timid as a mouse where men were concerned and secretly pining away for Reece. Viv scanned the room for a better alternative for her young colleague.

"Okay, okay, I'm coming."

Bodies jostled to the rhythm on the dance floor set up in front of the two DJs' mixing desks. The effects of an almost two-week gap without much travel between races were evident in the drivers' elevated energy levels. The DJ had chosen the perfect music to get them inspired. Either way, the room came alive with gyrating bodies.

Out of the corner of her eye, she spotted Adam come in the main door with his manager, Chad. Her primal instinct told her to go over and throw her arms around Adam. Her brain said *don't you dare*.

Everyone was here; her two exes, Reece, and all the drivers and the engineers. Although her exes were engrossed in their partners, sharing the same dance floor made them all too tangible as living, breathing men—Ronan's way of flicking back his floppy fringe impatiently, Maddux's smooth way of prowling around. She did her best to avoid eye contact with any of them.

"Oh my God, I'm going to faint," Sarah said in her ear. "He's looking at us."

"Keep your cool."

Reece stepped into their little circle. He eyed Sarah up and down and sidled up to Viv. "The gang's all here tonight."

"Indeed."

"Rich pickings."

"Oh really?"

"For you I meant. I'm only browsing tonight."

"How perfectly sedate of you, Reece."

"Even the wicked have to rest sometimes."

"I suppose they do."

"Of course," his hand slid onto her waist and down her ass where he left it resting. "I'd make an exception for you, in this teensy little scrap of silk you're calling a dress." He cupped a buttock firmly.

Viv gave a yelp and glared at him. "Hands off, Reece."

He didn't budge, but kept staring into her eyes.

Her gaze darted around the dance floor. "Reece—"

Should she cause a scene by battling him off? *Oh God* … the ballroom was swarming with reporters. She squirmed, but Reece's hand was going nowhere. Yuck. Over his shoulder she saw Adam, fighting his way through the swaying crowd, watching them intently. *Thank God.*

"Just relax, babe. Let me hold onto my fantasy a few seconds more, hmm?"

She clenched her teeth. Then she felt an arm tugging her away and separating her from Reece. She whirled around.

Not Adam. Ronan. He'd been standing a lot nearer. His fair eyebrows shot up as hazel eyes assessed the situation in an instant. "Steady on there, Reece. Viv's not into the old dirty dancing lark." Ronan winked at her. "Well, not that I know of anyway."

She smoothed down her dress and fought back sheer mortification. "Yes, thanks, Ronan." She searched around for Adam, but he'd disappeared into the crowd.

Ronan's gaze bounced from Reece to her and back again. He shrugged. "I'll just bugger off and mind my own business then."

"You do that, Hawes," Reece replied. "We got it all under control here."

"Glad to hear it, Reece," she said pointedly. "Thanks, Ronan. We'll take him at his word then."

The last thing she wanted was a scene with her ex and goddamn Reece. The two golden boys of F1 battling it out. Another quick scan of the area told her Adam had definitely left.

She grabbed Sarah's elbow. "Ladies' room. Come on."

Sarah pounced on her when they'd entered the relative quiet of the bathroom. "Why didn't you dance with Reece? He likes you."

"He likes everyone, Sarah."

"I don't understand you sometimes," Sarah said, pouting her freshly made-up lips into the mirror.

"No? He's not a nice person, Sarah. Don't try anything."

Viv felt her phone vibrate. She took a cubicle to read it in private.

Come to me now. My hotel.

She flushed the toilet and came out. "I've a headache, Sarah."

Her friend's eyes narrowed. "You'd leave me to face Reece— this not nice person—out there alone?"

"You're a big girl now."

"You're up to something. Come on, where are you going?"

"Sarah, I'm going to bed." Which was true, in a way. "And you're not alone, our whole team is here. Joe the cameraman seems very nice."

Sarah twisted her freckled nose in scorn. Then she waggled her eyebrows. "Well if Reece comes on to me, *I'm* not going to say no."

• • •

She hailed a taxi and reached Adam's hotel within ten minutes. When he opened the door of his bedroom, Viv felt agitation rippling off him in waves. His gaze burned with an intensity that looked almost painful.

He grabbed her into his chest. "Are you okay? How dare he touch you? I wanted to flatten him, Vivienne, I—"

"Shhh," she said, holding her finger to his mouth and then replacing it with her lips. His anger, his possessiveness was turning her on. He pulled her in tightly and kissed her, but then broke off equally as sudden. In three long strides, he reached the window and glared, but she doubted he noticed a single detail of the moonlit courtyard.

"Reece wants to destabilize me so he'll win. He thinks this is his way to get to me. He's got us all figured out. But I will not let that bastard derail me. I cannot."

"Oh, I hate him, too. You think he knows about us?"

"Maybe. Who knows? I'd guess he suspects." Adam spun around. "Vivienne, it's time."

"Time?"

"To come clean. If we'd been there as a couple, this would never have happened."

"It's just Reece being a prick, Adam, really. We can ignore him. Let's … hang on until the season's over."

He turned back to the window and addressed her reflection in the dark glass. "How can I stand there and watch him put his hands all over you and not do anything about it? I know you had to keep a brave face out there, but how far would you have let him go if your goddamn ex hadn't shown up?" His hands curled into fists against the windowpane.

She approached him from behind and slipped her hands around his waist. His rigid posture relaxed by a fraction. "Reece wasn't going anywhere. Trust me, Adam. I'd have kneed him in the balls if I'd had to."

"Hmph. Wish you had."

She pressed her chest tightly into his back and slid her hands down his abdomen to his groin. He inhaled sharply and flattened his palms against the glass for support. Zipping open his jeans, she slipped her hand inside, feeling the length of him as he hardened. He offered no resistance. "It's just us," she said.

"Yes." His fingers splayed wide as she tightened her fingers around his cock. She had a feeling he'd agree to anything she said as long as she kept going, and this intoxicated her. His breathing accelerated and his fingers trailed ten parallel lines of heat down the condensation on the glass.

He stiffened, swung around to face her, grabbed her wrists, walked her backward to the bed and tossed her flat on her back. Before she could even kick off her shoes, his arms flew under the tiny skirt of her dress and whipped off her underwear with a speed that left a breeze against her most vulnerable parts.

He straightened and held up her lacy underwear. "You're not getting these back until the morning."

"Adam—"

"No." He stuffed the garment into his jeans pocket. His expression was a mixture of triumph and lust.

Damn. Her cocktail dress was teeny, Reece had been right about that. Adam was forcing her to stay there.

"You win," she breathed. "I'll stay. Dirty tactics though."

"Plenty more where that came from." His hands slid slowly under the dress, this time covering her where her underwear used to be. Rotating his palm against her sex, he filled her with sudden, wanton greed for more.

"Yes ..." She couldn't think when he was doing that with his hands.

"Vivienne, you know," he said, rubbing faster, "reporters have been known to date sportspeople. It wouldn't be the end of the world if they found out."

"Mmm-hmm … I'd rather wait until … um—"

"Until when?" His eyes were watchful.

She shut her eyes. Until she was sure? She couldn't say that.

"Until when?" he repeated. He was manipulating her, and she wasn't falling for it.

"I don't know, Adam. Until the season's over and we know what we're doing?"

"I know what I'm doing."

"Good, well keep going."

She didn't want to think or talk or anything … just to feel her insides succumb to the sense of him mastering her pleasure. Nothing else mattered … nothing else.

• • •

Adam won in his old home country, to the joy of the Gatari team and the Wallonian press. He was now 151 points to Reece's 158. There was nothing between them except a snowballing rivalry.

The BBC team had to go back to London HQ on the Eurostar train instead of wasting money in hotels. Viv was determined to exercise some control over the live interview with Adam. All Mack would say was that it was going ahead in two weeks in their London headquarters when they got back from Japan, and that Catherine was definitely doing it. The least the anchor could do was be forthcoming about what she had in mind for it.

"I just want to get an idea of how you're going to steer the interview, that's all," Viv said in her most reasonable tone in the staff kitchen.

"Trust me, Viv, I'm a veteran interviewer."

"But what'll you ask him? I mean, you've only got fifteen minutes. What'll you be concentrating on?"

"Why do you care?"

"It's my interview. I secured it."

"Well, I think you'll find that Mack wants me to do it, so I have complete creative control."

"Yes, I know. Fine." She had never liked Catherine Price much. Now she officially hated her.

Their voices were raised, and Viv was fully aware the whole canteen was listening in, from the boom operators to the cameramen. "Catherine," she pleaded, "Don't grill him on the family too much, or the past. He's … sensitive about it."

"He's … sensitive about it," Catherine mimicked Viv's concerned tone. It got a giggle from a nearby table of nature documentary engineers.

Viv shook her head and gave up.

"And why would you care about that? I think I'm entitled to know how you secured this interview if I'm going to be conducting it. Otherwise he might completely surprise me on air."

"Oh, I doubt that very much." She marched off.

"How interesting," Catherine called after her. "Maybe that'll be my first question to him."

...

She rendezvoused with Adam in Spain on his precious week off before the race in Barcelona and warned him about the interview. They lounged on a beach near Malaga in the July heat, on the opposite side of the country from everyone, Adam disguising his face with a ridiculous, wide sunhat. Viv remembered this area from holidaying with her parents as a kid—half of Britain came to Costa del Sol in the summer—and she knew a secluded, rocky beach to escape to. As she watched her lover's taut torso flexing in the white sunshine while he caressed her arm, life had never been so good.

"That's okay," he said, shaking the sunscreen bottle. "If you're fine with it?"

"Yeah." She let the dark brown sand flow through her fingers and land on his toes. "I've made peace with the situation. It's kinda hard to let anything get to me sitting here next to you."

"I'm doing it for you," he said, rolling over and smearing the cream on her back, making her shiver. "And only once for that matter."

"Okay," she squirmed under his attentive touch. "And it's already helped me keep my job. Oh I wish we didn't have to go to London and Japan and Brazil and China."

"Don't forget Russia," he said trailing his tongue across her shoulder.

"God," she giggled, "that, too."

She knew with such a grueling schedule, these romantic interludes would be chopped to a minimum. They'd be jetlagged, dealing with logistics, dodgy infrastructure, transfers, customs officials and setting up studios in places where the languages made everything take ten times longer. As an F1 girlfriend, she'd skipped some of the more challenging destinations, especially when packed together in succession. Now she had to take it in her stride and still look perky on TV.

But as long as she did see him, that was all that mattered.

Chapter 22

Suzuka, Japan

Of all the stupid situations to be in, this was the worst. It was enough to make Adam want to take a seat in economy class. Only an hour into the eight-hour flight from Madrid to Nagoya, his nerves were raw from dealing with Reece's mind games. Whose idea had it been to book them beside each other? This would be a bumpy ride.

Reece had a no-finish in Barcelona, and this was probably the reason for all this asshole behavior. He'd come in third, and Maddux had clinched his first win.

"Watch a film, Fontaine," Reece said straight after the pilot announcement, slotting his headphones into the armrest. "It'll help you relax."

"You're the one who needs to relax."

"Or you can talk to me. How's your lovely sister these days?"

"Getting married," he retorted. Two years ago, Reece had met Saskia when she'd come to Adam's second race, in Texas, risking the wrath of Dad in doing so. Reece had, of course, singled her out and lavished his attention on her. Adam had been friends with him then and actually encouraged it. God forbid. She'd had a lucky escape because Reece had had a sponsor meeting that night. He'd hate to think what might have happened.

"Who's the lucky guy?"

"A Californian. You don't know him."

"Do you?" Reece scoffed. "Considering how much time you spend at Emily's Hill."

"I'm going to watch a film." Adam yanked out the remote control and pressed the first film that came up in the menu.

"Who're you bringing?" Reece asked before he could put on the headphones.

"None of your business."

"Hmm. Look, Adam, this life"—the Englishman motioned around the tastefully lit, first-class cabin—"is good, I'll grant you, but it's a touch unreal, wouldn't you say? A sister's wedding is real. You need someone real to hold on to."

Adam dropped the headphones in his lap and looked out the window. This advice was so ironic, he'd just let Reece hang himself with his words.

"We drivers ... we're a strange breed and we need real people in our lives."

"The people in your life are 100 percent real are they, Reece?" Adam pictured the anatomically enhanced grid girls that perpetually surrounded the bastard off the circuit.

"Well, I'm going through a phase, but I did have Alice."

Okay, he did have Alice, the nice, normal Italian girl, last year for about four months. Adam had heard about it but not seen it. Four months would be a record for Reece. Had it actually meant something? Hard to believe, but he wasn't about to get sucked into this pointless conversation. Reece was obviously after something. "That's nice, Reece, maybe you should get her back if she meant that much."

"Yeah." Reece fiddled with his own remote control now, tapping the buttons in agitation.

Adam sank back to watch the film, not quite sure who'd won that round.

• • •

He bolted awake when the announcement came for Nagoya Airfield. Amazingly, he'd slept most of the trip. Things were looking up already. As countries went, Japan was soothing—the quiet, gentle, unassuming people left you alone, and the foreignness of the writing system prevented one's brain from going into overdrive assimilating the information all around.

He tossed the travel bag over his shoulder and exited from arrivals alongside Chad. He'd succeeded in separating from Reece at immigration control. Judging by the shrill acoustics of the crowd on the other side, there were a lot of young women—Reece fans, no doubt. He checked his phone for a signal—always touch and go with these carriers. He couldn't wait to hear Vivienne's voice back in London. She wouldn't be here for another four days.

"Would you look at that," Chad said when they passed through to arrivals. He pointed at a bevy of what looked to be schoolgirls waving and cheering.

"What? Japanese people in Japan?"

"No, you idiot. Look at who they're shouting for."

Adam turned his attention to the placard one was carrying. The girl carrying it bounced up and down in the excitement of being noticed. The placard was a huge black and white shot of him in sunglasses, in dire need of a shave, taken God knows where.

They started clamoring—there must have been fifty at least— and they squeezed past each other and past other normal people to get closer to him. He shrank back. "Let's get out of here."

"Smile, for crying out loud." Chad beamed at the girls and waved his chubby arm, eliciting a cheer. "See? They're mad for you. Even I'm getting adoration by association."

Adam grimaced. Their squeals amplified the closer they got to the railings. Now they were near enough to reach out and grab him, which some of them did. The sea of thin, milky arms, clutching smartphones, clambering for his attention, dark heads bobbing in enthusiastic greeting, overwhelmed him. A flutter of homemade banners featured more shots of him he'd never seen before, with assorted hearts and other symbols he couldn't understand. Incredible.

Cameras flashed—professional ones, too, not iPhones. The Japanese press was here. Adam made an honest effort to smile, but it seemed so at odds with how he was actually feeling. All he wanted was a dark, quiet bedroom and the company of one woman who wasn't due to arrive for another four long days.

In the serenity of his white hotel room at the Suzuka circuit, he rang Saskia to get the latest on Dad, more for her sake than his. She'd be devastated if Dad couldn't walk her down the aisle in December.

He'd had another "episode." Saskia hadn't been there herself, but one of their new hires had known to ring 911 immediately.

Adam clutched the edge of the duvet. He'd not expected a repeat incident. But it looked like Dad wasn't bluffing. This was serious.

"New hires?" he asked, trying to deflect attention from his alarm.

"We've, like, a steady stream of visitors now with your Fontaine Fans website. It was one of them who stayed with Dad the most in the hospital—this old dame whose husband follows your team. She was even wearing your green shirt. It was the first thing Dad remarked on when he came around."

"What? Why would she—? T-shirt?"

"Yeah, we're getting, like, about six groups a day now because of your site. We've hired extra staff, Adam. Don't tell me you don't know this?"

"I had no idea. But Dad hates them."

Saskia's loud sigh came over the line, a hiss of static. "We're doing great financially because of them, and they're nice, even if they don't know the first thing about wine. So much nicer than the wine snobs. Dad's happy; he can pawn off the bad stuff on them. He's more worried about his health, Adam. As am I."

...

When Vivienne arrived at his door four days later during qualifiers, Adam lifted her up in a huge embrace, devouring her face with kisses. "Thank God you're here."

"Hey, it's only been a few days," she said, chuckling.

"Far too long. It's been terrible—rear wing problems, and the track's deteriorated since two years ago. But never mind. How've you been? How was your trip?"

"Fine, yours?"

"Great. I got attacked by a squad of Japanese girls at the airport, and every time I leave the room, I worry they'll follow me and smother me. I don't think I'd cope."

She nudged him. "Oh, I think you rather like the attention."

"Yeah, right."

"Hmm. I can see I may have some competition now." Her eyes shone, teasing him, but there was an edge to her voice. Could she—possibly—be jealous? Even slightly? He laughed aloud.

"What's so funny?" She frowned, digging her toe into the carpet.

"Vivienne? You cannot be serious."

She turned to him, eyes widening as if belatedly understanding his meaning. "No, of course not, dummy. It was me who encouraged this to happen, remember? I engineered this."

"Precisely. You engineered it."

"So, of course I don't mind if you get mobbed by a bunch of perfect, porcelain-faced Japanese girls and it gets broadcasted on prime time news in downtown Nagoya. Not in the slightest. Okay, I'm mildly peeved."

"Well," he said, smiling and pulling her into him. "Let's see what they're up against, shall we?"

She responded immediately, as her body latched on to his. Her nails dug into his shoulders as his tongue prized her lips apart.

Her eyes widened, her hips pressed against him and she moaned. Just watching her surrender so quickly to his touch made him determined to make her climax loudly. His hard cock twitched in recognition of her naked lust.

"Now," she said cupping his groin in her hand. "Inside me."

He scrambled for the condom in his back pocket.

She swiped it off him, rolling it onto him. "No thinking, Adam, just do it. Now," she ordered. Her face was hard, her nostrils flaring.

He pushed her back across the duvet, parted her thighs, and entered her with such force that her head banged against the headboard. She gasped.

"Oh God, sorry," he said.

"No, Adam, it's good." Her body was slick and so ready for him. He lost all control, thrusting into her. Just when he felt he might be too rough, she hooked on to him with her legs, drawing him in with a viciousness that urged him to pump even harder, faster.

He liked her when she was jealous.

She strained against him as she climaxed again, arching with a force that pushed his hips upward. At his moment of release seconds later, he opened his eyes and found her staring at him, pupils so huge they swallowed her irises. He lost himself in that shared communication. He heard his own voice groaning out, and he collapsed on her.

• • •

"It *is* quite a nice change from being booed off the circuit," he said, propping himself up on his elbow hours later at 3:00 a.m. when Viv stirred and opened her eyes. It was difficult to sleep with her smooth curves molding into him. He kept wanting to wake her up and repeat their lovemaking.

What was it about her he couldn't get enough of? Yes, she was beautiful and smart and independent and yet passionate about people—passionate about him. He'd always kept his relationships far from work, but with her, the thought hadn't crossed his mind. And no relationship had ever turned so serious so quickly.

He tickled her nose with a stray feather that had escaped from the duvet.

"You see?" she murmured, still half asleep. "I bet you feel a lot more relaxed now going into the race on Sunday, even with Suzuka's high-speed corners."

"I do." He trailed his hand down her cheek. "But that's not because of any manga girls."

She smiled, and her eyelids fluttered and closed.

He watched her breath come and go in her chest, and tenderness squeezed his heart. "When this is over in four months, I'll give you all the time you deserve—if you want it."

No reply. She was asleep. But her mouth curled up to one side as if she was dreaming something pleasant.

• • •

Viv traipsed groggily down to the hotel lounge to have a call with Mack. The time difference meant she had to get up at five, but with all the globetrotting of recent months, her inner clock had no clue what time it was supposed to be anyway.

"Having fun out there?" Mack wanted to know.

"Well," she coughed, "I've just got here. But I'm all set up and ready to go."

"Good." He yawned audibly. It was bedtime for him. "Now, you know how we're playing this. Japan is neutral territory, so ramp up the rivalry aspect in your commentary. We want a nice little three-minute piece on the Marlowe-Fontaine bickering before the main commentary on Sunday. That'll set the stage nicely for Catherine's interview back in London next week."

"Sure, no problem."

"Fontaine's got some freak following over there. He's big in Japan. Play it up. Give it some sparkle for once. Girls screaming. All at Fontaine. Then some screaming at Reece, that kind of thing. If you can get the fans to mud wrestle, all the better. That's what we want, isn't it?"

"Um, yes, it's how we've played it all along."

Mack wheezed with laughter. "Do I detect a note of possessiveness? That's what we want—emotion. Go on with you." He broke off the call.

Viv sat, twisting the phone around in her lap. What did Mack mean by that? Possessiveness as in Adam being her pet psychology project, or something closer to the truth entirely? She headed to reception to inquire about the possibility of getting coffee this early. There was no way she could sleep now.

Why had this project seemed so important to her anyway? Now that Adam *had* become popular, all it did was make the press about him even more ridiculous, vindicating all his reservations.

The lone receptionist, a twenty-something model of perky perfection, straightened to attention when she approached.

"Well, I'm wondering if I could get some coffee this early?"

"Yes, they have set up the restaurant for breakfast. Please go this way, and they will help you, Mrs. Ah ..."

"McCloud. Ms."

Viv sank down onto a seat near the window in the dark restaurant. A kitchen maid had telepathically received the message that she needed caffeine and brought her a huge silver pot of coffee. As she sipped the piping hot coffee, she watched the sky grow pink and then orange as the sun rose slowly. The setting, gently fragranced by fresh orchids, was so conducive to quiet contemplation.

Mrs. McCloud. The receptionist's innocent words mocked the complexity of her relationship. Her relationships, plural. She would be thirty in January, and she looked old enough to be a Mrs., but she felt light years away from matrimony.

What was she doing, risking not only her job, but also her heart by following Adam this far in the game—the sixth-to-last race. This was so different from her relationship with Ronan. Yes, they were both tenacious F1 drivers, but her connection with Ronan had been all surface and mirrors. Attraction, camaraderie, but nothing even approaching the depth she had with Adam.

She loved so many things about Adam. His innate honesty—he had no idea how to sugarcoat anything and was all the more trustworthy for that. His intensity, while not uncommon in F1 drivers, sent a charge through her. He cared so passionately about cars and races, it should've been a blot against him after her experience with single-minded F1 drivers, but it wasn't. She admired it in him.

She'd felt this way about ballet in her youth, but she'd given the dancing life up. Her personality didn't lend itself to being so single-minded for all of her life. People and real life distracted her in the best way possible. Journalism had a draw on her for these very reasons, but it didn't consume her. The only thing consuming her thoughts right now was Adam.

And yet Adam seemed incapable of holding a conversation in either the future or the past tense. The past to him was dead. His future lasted until the next race and then drew a blank. This guy took living in the present to a whole other level.

He had no plan for failure, and failure was defined by anything less than first place. And that was the hell of it. He'd been right when he'd said it was all about winning. They had blinders on, the lot of them—and she was a big-picture person. One who liked to know where she was headed—career, family, location. Back in Montreal, he'd said he'd get out when he won, but that was before they were together, before he had to be careful about what he said. Could she trust him on that?

And what if he didn't win? She wasn't about to play second string to a car for the next decade. He'd move on to the next season with even harder determination than he had coming into this one. And if he won? Same thing, except he'd be jealously defending his title, just like Reece was doing this year. Why was she drawn to men like this? Men whose profession made them so unavailable?

What about her own profession? If she came out in one piece at the other end of this BBC stint, she'd still need a job. And what would they give her? What did she want? She couldn't imagine covering footballers and that whole scene. Olympic coverage perhaps? Or local UK reporting—but as a newcomer who looked good in front of the camera, they'd give her the fluff between the news. No matter how serious she tried to look with short hair and glasses, producers always wanted to put her in the fluff.

Maybe she could do serious reporting in the United States. Maybe then she and Adam could let themselves go, allow the truth to be known. She wouldn't ever have to go back to F1.

But until then, she had to play the game right. The worst thing she could do now was to appear unprofessional and let her emotions impair her reporting ability. If anyone found out about her relationship with Adam, at least they wouldn't be able to replay footage of her reporting and laugh in hindsight at how biased she'd been. No, she'd always erred on the side of cold where Adam was concerned. And, regardless of what Mack said, she'd continue to do so.

She felt a presence behind her and swung around.

"Adam!"

"May I join you?"

"This is dangerous," she hissed, glancing around. "If they catch us here together, it'll be the story of the month—"

"Don't worry. It would be normal for a driver to take his seat opposite the most beautiful woman in the room."

"No, no. Not good."

"Okay, whatever you say. I'm not staying long. I've to check the car before we go into parc fermé. A shipment came in last night. I want to get a test run in before anyone else. We need to adjust the rear wing—"

"Fine, fine, I understand," she said. He was miles away, in motor-racing land, calculating the points, strategizing the turns, worrying about the engine. Unreachable. His mind was flicking through the engine's bill of materials, all the permutations, searching for the reasons he was bound to win this one. This was not the time for existential angst about their relationship.

Not that there ever was a good time for that.

Chapter 23

She returned to the hotel after a brisk morning walk on the streets of Suzuka. The hotel was running an exhibition of Japanese art in the lobby. The watercolors looked delicate, ephemeral, and the polite gathering offered an oasis of calm in the hustle and bustle of the F1 hullabaloo.

Stepping away from the fourth impression of Mount Fuji in a row, she spied Reece two paintings down. On his arm he had a beautiful Japanese girl, with ultra-gloss hair and expensive accessories. He looked bored. His face brightened when he saw her, and he sauntered over, leaving his date staring intently into a painting.

"Hey babe," he said, "getting sick of Mount Fuji yet?"

"Don't babe me."

"Yeah. Just wanted to apologize for the incident in Spa. I was a little … inebriated. It shouldn't have happened, and I swear, it won't happen again."

"It's okay, Reece. Apology accepted." Viv made a move to get away.

"Cool. I wouldn't like it standing between us, you know." Reece blocked her way.

"No, no worries on that score. So, are you looking forward to racing on home turf next week?"

"You bet. It's time to get back on top of the table. Fontaine will never beat me here. "

She nodded noncommittally.

He lowered his voice. "Look I know you two have a … thing."

"What?"

"I've been watching you. I know Fontaine. He's different now. He can't hide it, and neither can you."

She bit her lip. As long as there was no proof, this was just noise. Besides, he could be bluffing. What could he possibly know? What evidence did he have? "So what're you going to do about it? Tell everyone?"

"It's none of my business." Reece shrugged. "As the man himself would say."

He had nothing then. "So what was all that in Spa? Some kind of test of my fidelity?"

Reece grinned. "Yeah, I mean, if I were going out with someone like you, I sure as hell wouldn't be hiding it."

"Unless I asked you to?"

"Ah." Reece's eyes narrowed with understanding. "I see. Professional distance and all that. All well and good, I suppose. Once the season's over there'll be a big announcement?"

"I don't know," she said, trying to sound nonchalant. "Maybe."

"But he's taking you to the wedding, right?"

Viv's cool shattered. "The … wedding?"

He grimaced as if in pain. "Oh man, this is seriously fucked up."

"Reece, what wedding?"

"Uh … " He scratched his neck, and looked around as if hoping for salvation from somebody, anybody.

"Reece—?"

"His sister, yeah? Saskia? Heard of?"

"Oh."

"You—want a drink?"

"No thanks, Reece. I'm fine. I'm just … going." She walked off. *Going nowhere.*

She sank down on the nearest chair in the empty hotel dining room, feeling sick and woozy, a heaviness pulling her heart down. So Saskia was getting married, and Adam hadn't seen fit to tell her. Which could only mean one thing—he didn't want her to go. He didn't want her there with his family. Maybe there was a simple explanation, but that one seemed to be the simplest and the only one.

The question was, what should she do about it? Kick up a fuss, whine and demand to be invited? That way he couldn't refuse her, but if he didn't want to invite her, then she didn't want to be there. She had no place there. She could even live with that if he'd only *told* her.

Quashing the impulse to ring him and demand what was going on, she drummed the phone against her palm, thinking furiously. Would it open a can of worms? Would it upset him? Was this another Reece trick? Reece was desperate to win, just as Adam was. He'd try anything. Even lying about that. But it was an odd thing to lie about, a sister's wedding. No, it must be true. But she wouldn't upset Adam before this race, which was going to be difficult enough for him.

She could cope with the winning obsession. Drivers had to be like that to a certain extent. But Adam was sharing less and less these days. After four months, was it too much to ask to let her in? Given how he treated his family, maybe she couldn't expect him to treat her any better.

Hang on. She had to talk to him. ASAP.

• • •

Adam came to her room on short notice. She skipped the BBC dinner and knew he was skipping his team's traditional pre-race dinner to make the time to see her.

"I've only got five minutes," he said, then stopped suddenly. "Hey—what's wrong?"

She shook her head briskly. "Nothing. How's the car—all set for tomorrow?"

"Yeah, I'm just hoping it doesn't rain. I'm starting on softs. Sixty-five percent chance, though, at the latest forecast, so we may revise that decision." He bent to kiss her, and she responded, although the voice in her head was screaming to address the issue first.

"I met Reece this afternoon," she said.

"Yeah? I hope he kept his paws off you."

"He was impeccably behaved, with some Japanese woman. We were at the same art exhibition together."

"Hmm." Adam cast a glance at his phone. "Anyway I've to get to the race strategy meeting now. I'm already late. Let's talk about this later."

"But this is important!"

He frowned. "Reece is important?"

"No. Talking is important."

"So is preparation," he said. "After the race—"

"After the race? After the race? I can't believe this. After the race … is before the race!"

He ran his fingers across his brow. She could almost see his synapses burning with pre-race calculations. This wasn't entirely fair of her.

"It's fine. Just … go."

He regarded her for a silent moment. Then he moved in. "Kiss me before I go."

She hesitated. He saw it. He flinched, but his expression grew determined. "I won't force you."

"Oh, Adam." She lunged into him. "What's going to happen to us?"

He kissed her, rougher than usual, turned, and strode out of the room. She blinked back tears while watching him shut the door behind him. Was she being a complete bitch, attacking him with this before his race? She'd never have done this with her exes. But wasn't she allowed to care about what they might lose, even if he only had one thing on his mind—winning?

• • •

She cleaned herself up. She applied an extra layer of foundation, and two of mascara. She had to rise above it. Life would go on as long as she held up her end. She left it until the very latest moment to enter the studio, when everybody was in a pre-transmission frenzy. This meant ignoring Mack's and Sarah's calls and invoking their anxiety, but tough. The rules had changed.

The makeup artist was the first to accost her when she showed up.

"It's okay, I've done my own," she began.

He dabbed her eyelid with highlighter. "Why you people can't leave it to the professionals, I don't know. You DIYers all think you're Kate Middleton on her wedding day."

Viv felt so far removed from a royal princess that she burst out laughing in the kind of breathless way that left her dangerously close to sobs, but she pulled herself back from the brink.

Sarah came rushing up. "You're here! Don't need to tell you that Mack's having a conniption."

"You're right, Sarah, you don't need to tell me that."

Studio lights burned into her retinas. Her smile was breaking cracks in her makeup. Her soul had been hollowed out with a spoon. She'd managed an hour of this, but how much longer could she keep going? She knew her voice sounded dead, vacant.

"It looks like the championship is boiling down to an epic duel of Hunt-Laudian or Hamilton-Rosbergian proportions," Rick intoned, nodding at Viv to follow up.

"Yes," she said, cocking her head to give the impression of a comfortable discussion in front of the TV, "this type of rivalry is always exciting to watch, especially when each race is so crucial. Fontaine and Marlowe are too close in points now to be able to ignore each other, though that's what they would most like to do.

We have black and white personalities here, and they're clashing on several levels."

Rick nodded. "Given that they were once teammates, it looks as though that camaraderie of two seasons ago has all but died out."

"It happens a lot," she added. "The drivers have to become hardened during the years of competition, to focus on the goal, nothing else. They often turn into quite nice guys after they retire, and they've even been known to become friends again."

Rick laughed, and she forced herself to join in. It took effort to say these words, because they were true. All she wanted to do was go to the garage, grab Adam and ask him where they stood.

"Well, well, well, the Japanese public is sure laying it for Fontaine. Listen to that cheering out there in the stands."

Viv kept a smile plastered on her face. "Yes, he's popular here."

Rick, bless him, had noticed her slow reaction, her inability to keep up a steady stream of commentary on the duel between Adam and Reece, and he came to her rescue by blabbering enough for two.

"Fontaine has always considered Reece Marlowe his benchmark," he said. "But after Marlowe's no-finish in Barcelona, it could be that Fontaine is now going to surpass him." His gaze darted to her, and she nodded automatically but didn't agree.

She cleared her throat. "Yes, Marlowe is a fantastic driver, but his lifestyle may hold him back at times. Fontaine is ready for the challenge for the title, as this race and many others have shown." *Don't worry. His lifestyle will never hold him back*, she could have added.

She watched the race dispassionately. In the grand scheme of things, who cared who won?

And there he was, standing on the podium, once again his body rigid with anger for having come second to Reece. Ridiculous, really. She looked away from the monitor and focused on the cables of the cameras.

Maybe it was time to wake up and smell the petrol.

"And next up is Silverstone back in Old Blighty, and it looks as though Marlowe has a fight ahead to hold on to his championship. Now they're neck and neck, with Fontaine on 184 points to Marlowe's 183, and Bates trailing behind on 153 points. It's all still to play for, folks. After the break we'll have extended coverage of the race and an interview with Marlowe's team chief, Charles."

Time was up, and everyone started dismantling the studio and removing their personal effects for the trip back. Viv went through the motions like a robot. Next stop, London. She couldn't wait. She needed a dose of real life again, away from this madness.

Chapter 24

Silverstone, England

First item on the agenda was to do this TV interview with Catherine Price from the BBC. Adam groaned inwardly. Yes, he'd promised it, and Vivienne had claimed it had done her career good. So at least there was that. But now he had to follow through. And this was live.

Since Vivienne was in his life, he'd become more confident about doing something like this—but only in theory. Actually doing it was another matter. She'd landed last night and headed straight to London. He had to come direct to Silverstone for team meetings. She'd been unreachable all morning but texted to say she'd make it in time to watch the interview behind the scenes. A good luck kiss would have made all the difference.

The BBC studio by the circuit was larger and more disorganized than he'd expected it to be—at least as a naïve observer. Apart from the area in front of the camera, chaos reigned—men and women with rolled-up shirt sleeves and headpieces dashing to and fro, shouting out directives. Cables twisted around furniture, coffee cups balanced on any flat surface available. This was Vivienne's natural environment. How could she stand it?

He leaned forward on the leather couch in the brightly lit studio, not quite sure where to look—into one of the cameras, at the interviewer, or at the audience who were taking their seats slowly and staring at him. Maybe he shouldn't have refused to do the full rehearsal, because then he'd have a clue what to do.

The makeup artist tiptoed up to him.

"No thanks," he said.

The makeup artist glowered at him, his powder box suspended inches from Adam's nose. "There's shine—right … here."

He flinched.

"We're good, Danny," Catherine piped up. "He's fine as he is." She motioned impatiently to the cameramen and sound technicians. "We'll just do a little sound check and then we're ready to go live."

Countdown sounded, and he twisted his fingers in his lap.

"We're honored to have you here today. Adam, I don't believe you've done many live interviews before?

"No." He shrugged.

"Well don't worry, this audience is very well behaved." Right on cue, they cheered and clapped. They were clapping for themselves, not him; they clearly wanted him thrashed by their golden boy, Reece. Some even had the audacity to wear the signature red Reece fan shirts. He couldn't see any neon green out there.

"Why did you avoid interviews in the past, Adam?"

"I'm not great on TV," he said honestly.

The audience laughed.

"I think you're just fine," Catherine said, a flirtatious note fluttering up her pristine, BBC-English accent. "I think you can go out in public without being ashamed."

It elicited a few catcalls from the audience. He fought the urge to shake his head. Vivienne had told him to keep his head still.

"Seriously though, how do you feel going against Reece at the Sepang circuit in Malaysia after the way you crashed season before last?"

Adam frowned. Of course, she couldn't say what really happened, could she? For all he knew, she probably believed Reece's version. What would Vivienne tell him to say here?

"Well, Reece and I have had our differences … especially after that race, but at this stage of the game, I can't afford to dwell on that. There's so much else to think about—the car, the circuit, the weather, the team tactics, the points table, and my own ability to give it all I've got."

"And you do publicity, too, don't you?"

"Not much. I did in the beginning when I joined F1. I was sponsored by Alstrum Turbines. But I'm not deep in endorsements at the moment, er, Catherine." He looked into her rather plastic looking face. The texture of her skin seemed … wrong.

"Not yet," she grinning. "Maybe after today?"

The audience chuckled. At what he wasn't really sure.

"Why not do more publicity, Adam? Maybe on French media?"

He fiddled with the bottom of his T-shirt. "Living in the public eye has always been difficult for me."

"Indeed it's not for everyone. I think a lot of people would sympathize with you there. But in your own case, why would you say that is, Adam? All drivers have a private life, but we never hear you talk about how you turned from a seventeen-year-old schoolboy running away from home to the superstar driver you've become. Is it true that your younger brother's death still affects you to the extent that you're considering undergoing psychiatric treatment?"

His heart hammered. What? "No, I'm not … but as anyone who has lost a family member—especially a younger brother who looked up to you—will know, it leaves a void that is never filled. That remains raw. Having the public, reporters, poke at it in the name of entertainment just seems wrong to me. I don't want sympathy. I want it to be left alone."

There was a collective gasp. Catherine was frowning as much as her botoxed face allowed.

"Your brother—" She had to consult her notes, and he wanted to kill her for not caring enough to remember "—*Eddie* died at age fourteen in a quad bike accident. So tragic for you. For your poor parents! I believe they divorced that same year. Do you think it was due to grief?"

"Possible," he said, through gritted teeth after a long pause. Her phony smile wavered.

"Yes, quite, I understand," she said. "That's a family tragedy and a half. Now, let's talk about the race and the championship. Let's watch the footage of your last win in Spa-Francorchamps ..."

• • •

Viv sat watching the interview on the screen in her office upstairs. She grasped the arms of the office chair. He'd come out with *that*. On live TV. To Catherine? Catherine Price who'd stolen her interview from her?

Of course, Catherine had used her arsenal of interviewer tricks and gotten lucky, but why, oh why couldn't Adam have confided in her before about how much he was suffering because of Eddie? She could have helped him ... talked him through it. Catherine had dug to his core in one blundering move and exposed him, whereas she'd only scratched the surface after months of skirting around his sensibilities.

She let the interview run on, hardly taking in what was being said except that they'd retreated back to safe territory—the race, the points table, the rivalry with Reece—the stuff the audience wanted to know, Reece fans the lot of them.

How could Adam do this? It made a mockery of everything she'd tried to do, of everything she'd tried to be ... in her career, and for him.

God, she'd really had enough of this shit.

She texted his phone.

Meet you outside men's toilets after interview. Ask where they are.

She reckoned it was the only place she could talk to him in private without his press agent, Catherine's minions or anyone else hovering around. The only men allowed used those toilets were the guests.

Adam's regular footsteps soon sounded on the tiled corridor. She peeped out from the doorway. He was alone.

"There you are," he said, reaching out to her. "Thank God that's over."

She stepped aside, avoiding him. "No. Not here." She scanned the corridor both ways. "Let's go in."

"Here?"

"Yeah."

Adam slid in without a fuss.

She leaned her back against a washbasin for strength. "Adam, I can't do this." The words echoed in the tiled room, sounding weird, forced, rehearsed. But it was out there now.

"What's wrong?"

"It's everything."

"Everything?" His dark gaze bore into her. "Explain."

"I need to know where we stand now. Where I stand. I can't just wait for the next race and the next championship."

"There won't *be* a next championship."

"Why not?"

"Because I'm going to win this one."

She clutched the sides of her head. "And if you don't? Are you still getting out then?"

His mouth flattened into a grim line.

"See? You can't answer. That's exactly what I'm talking about."

"Vivienne, how can I answer? I've six races left. *Six.* This is my chance—don't you see? It'll never come again. If I admit—even to myself—any doubt in my ability to win this, then I've already lost."

"So what? So what if you do lose?"

"No." He paced around the washroom. "If you can't bear to be around me until the end of season, that's fine. But let me do my thing for the next six races—here, Sepang, Shanghai, Sochi, Sao Paolo, Monte Carlo Nine weeks. Then it's over."

"It's not just nine weeks, Adam. You've defined your *life* around winning a race. You're addicted to it. You'll only get *worse*."

"Worse?" he echoed.

"Worse than you are now. You're addicted to the idea of beating Reece. So much so that you ignore everything else that's going on in your life."

"That's not true."

"I hear Saskia's getting married. Married!"

"Vivienne, I—"

"When were you planning on telling me? Or is December too far ahead on your calendar to plan me in?"

"What has Saskia's wedding got to do with anything?"

"*Everything*. Do I really have to spell this out?"

Adam rubbed his forehead. "But it's … after the championship." He looked and sounded so genuine that she believed it wasn't a conscious choice after all. Just the F1 blinkers. But that was just as bad.

"Don't look at me like that," he muttered. "I don't even know if I'm going myself."

"How could you *not* go to your own sister's wedding?"

"It's complicated."

"Try me."

His expression hardened. "Vivienne—no. Let's not go there. Another time, okay? Please."

Her indignation soared. "Winning a motor race won't change a thing, you know."

He looked down.

"And your family will still be as broken as it was before."

"Leave my family out of this discussion." When he looked up again, his eyes were as cold as his tone.

"Fine." She held fingers to the sides of her head, turned, and strode toward the door. "This discussion is over anyway. And as far as I'm concerned, this relationship, too."

And because it was spring-loaded, she couldn't even slam the door.

Chapter 25

Malaysia

Adam had a sleepless flight, and when the plane began its descent into the Kuala Lumpur airport, he felt his spirits sink even lower. Should he have let Vivienne storm off? If he'd grabbed her and begged her to stay, he'd have to explain from the beginning. From Eddie. This wasn't something he could do on the spur of the moment—in a men's toilet. And not because some talk show bimbo had somehow forced the words out of him either.

Dragging Vivienne into the mess that was his family would take time, patience, and a lot of explaining, and he wanted to do it in his time, properly. She'd think differently about him, not in a good way, and he needed to mitigate that damage.

Her flight was due here in KL at five—an hour ago, or at least the flight she'd told him about last week, and she hadn't texted or called since then. Now there was no sign of her around. This was his last hope. If he wanted to see her, he'd have to loiter around the BBC studio. Catch her off-guard somehow.

At least good old Bruce was there to meet him in the arrivals hall. He'd been on the same flight.

"You checked the forecast?" Bruce asked. "Any word on thunderstorms?"

"Not yet. But it won't be accurate until Saturday."

"You're looking worse for wear. They give you some dodgy food up in first class?"

"No. I don't know." Adam hadn't been able to eat at all. Two beers hadn't helped him sleep.

Bruce gave him a sympathetic glance. "You're thinking about that accident, aren't you? Look, mate, it's normal when you come back to a crash site for the first time. Best thing is to do a round of the circuit first thing. You worried about that hairpin?"

"No," he said, truthfully, but now that Bruce mentioned it, his leg ached with psychosomatic pain up from his right ankle to the knee, in memory of the crash two years ago.

"Well, if there's one place you need to qualify ahead of Reece, it's here. Look, forget about Silverstone—home territory—he was bound to win, okay? You got Spa after all."

Reece had pipped him at the post in Silverstone, and the crowd had gone mad with joy and schadenfreude for Adam It would be easy to blame the argument with Vivienne for his inability to shake Reece off on lap fifty-eight, but that way of moping would cost him the championship.

He checked into the hotel with Bruce, but declined to meet up with the crew for dinner. He went to his room instead and ordered room service, hoping he'd be able to fall asleep afterward. He sat in bed with his laptop, browsing his mail for something to do that didn't involve thinking about Vivienne. But of course he was looking for an email from her, just in case. There wasn't one.

He was about to close the email window when a subject title caught his eye. "My brother." He scrolled to that message halfway down the list. Reading it, his breath caught. It was from a forty-year-old man who had heard his interview with Catherine and identified with his situation. He'd lost his own brother in a car accident twenty years ago. An accident in which he'd been driving. He lived with the guilt every day …

Adam clicked the mail shut and shifted uncomfortably on the bed. No, he didn't want to get involved in other people's grief. Wasn't his own enough? Why lump their feelings on him? Who did they think he was? Gandhi? Ann Landers? A shrink? He just drove cars.

The skin crawled on his neck when the subject headers started to leap out at him: *I miss my brother, too. Sharing your pain. Alone now.* He forced himself to read those, from not just siblings, but also people who'd lost partners, children, parents.

The messages about lost brothers and sisters were the ones that affected him the most, and he couldn't resist peeking at more. These surviving siblings often were overlooked in the face of child-loss and parent-loss, which were deemed more profound by outside sympathizers in general. And most of these mourning brothers and sisters felt guilt. Whether they were even present at the time of death didn't matter. They felt the guilt for being alive. Yes, he knew that one.

"Christ," he said aloud when he'd read about thirty of them. He'd never thought about others out there who might be suffering the same way. Some of these stories were worse than his own. His eyes were burning, and it wasn't just from the glare of the screen.

Then he read the message from a local Malaysian boy of sixteen whose fourteen-year-old brother had just died in a road accident. The older boy, Aqil, had been driving a motorbike, and the brother, Ahmed, had sat on the back. They had been on their way to play soccer. He had swerved to avoid an oncoming truck and Ahmed had fallen off. He'd watched his brother die, bouncing and rolling in the road. Had held his hand.

Exactly like he and Eddie.

The accident had happened just three months ago. The boy was in agony—the letter made that apparent, and the decisions he made now would affect him forever. Adam wanted to reach out through the electronic ether and tell this boy, "No. Stop it now. Let go of it—the blaming, the guilt and the self-hate." Once it took hold of Aqil's psyche, he'd carry it around, like an illness he would never shake. And it would get worse with time, not better.

He'd lived to race because normal living after the accident had been too painful. They'd all reacted in their own ways—Saskia as the martyr who'd tried to save the family. Mother, who'd run away seeking a new, more intellectual life. Father, who'd lumped the blame on him and become fanatical about obscure wines. And as for himself ... only F1 driving—the thing Eddie had loved and aspired to—had made any sense. He funneled everything into his driving, his cars. And fixing things. Because the one thing he needed to fix, he couldn't.

It may not change anything, and it may just be a random drop in the ocean, but Adam had to write back.

•••

Viv entered Mack's office in the London BBC HQ at noon, bracing herself for his reaction to seeing her still here and not in Kuala Lumpur where she was due to land—right about now. She couldn't work in the F1 arena anymore. This was screwing with her mind. It was totally unprofessional of her to let it get to her, but it would be even more unprofessional to do a shoddy job. Her performance in the Japan studio was testament to that.

"Mack, do you have a minute? I'd like to talk."

Her boss waved her in, all smiles. "Sit down, Viv."

"I ... wanted to talk to you about my job direction. As you've probably noticed, I'm not on the plane to Kuala Lumpur, and, well, that's because I feel I'd like to steer away from F1 commentary the way—"

He stood. "And I suggest we play this the smart way."

She stared at him. Of all the reactions she'd expected, this wasn't it. "What do you mean?"

"Okay, so this—affair—"

"What?" She sprang forward in her chair.

"Changes things somewhat, I'll grant you that. But," he paused and flicked fingers upward in the air as if conjuring up suitable words, "let's handle this the smart way."

He knew?

Mack sank down again. "You do an exclusive, of course. How I fell in love with a Formula One driver. That sort of thing. This is the ultimate humanization. From robot to man. Romancing the Spock."

"But how do you know?"

"Viv, don't be naïve; you can't hide something like that." He smirked. "Everybody knows. Hotels have staff; the walls have eyes—come on, who are we kidding?"

He rubbed his hands in glee, ignoring her open-mouthed horror. "We'll have fun with this one. The public will love it. There's a dearth of scandal about the royal family this autumn, and this'll plug the gap nicely. But we have to keep it exclusive to us, so you and Fontaine will have to sign agreements not to spill to anyone else, all right?"

She pushed back her chair with a noisy screech. "Plug the gap? Exclusive? What are you talking about? Are you even listening to me? We're not together. We've split up. And where am I supposed to go from here?"

"Look, be pragmatic. The world will have forgotten everything by next season, and you'll be able to report on the races same as this year. I can get a replacement for you for the next five races if I must. But you have to play it my way now that this has happened."

"What if I don't agree to this exclusive—this invasion of the public into my—into our—private lives?"

Mack's eyes narrowed. "Oh, you'll agree."

"I won't. I don't."

"Don't forget that this little romantic interlude happened on BBC expenses."

"I did my job," she retorted. "You paid me a salary."

"We can pay you extra for this exclusive, too. A lot extra."

"Stuff it."

Mack's expression grew cold. "Then don't come here looking for work. And by here I mean the entire corporation."

"If my career here depends on selling my private life off like this, why would I? I thought you hired me for my journalistic capabilities."

"In a certain context, yes. I thought that your … way with the men would help add a bit of sparkle to a subject that is—let's face it—dry. And you did that. You should be happy. Now that your personal situation's changed—and may I stress because of your own choices and your own actions—and you feel you can't do unbiased commentary, let's deal with it in a way that is mutually beneficial. The offer, as I understand it, stands at 30,000 pounds. Tax exclusive."

Laughable. If her heart weren't breaking, she probably would be laughing at this. She might even find it genuinely funny. But he'd picked the wrong time to come with this kiss-and-tell bullshit and the wrong woman.

"You can sod your job and your exclusive. I won't do it. I quit. I quit the entire corporation."

His eyes widened. She turned on her heel and marched out the door.

"Trust me, this is your best option," Mack called after her.

All eyes followed her as she walked red-faced back to her desk. Her fingers trembled as she turned on her laptop, preparing to erase any personal files before they blocked it.

This was the right decision—every bone in her body vibrated with the conviction of that—but now she was careerless and back at square one. Square minus one if you considered that she was a laughingstock for the whole industry now. Square minus a million without Adam.

She forced back tears of frustration by sheer willpower. She'd been prepared to put up with so much that wasn't right about this world only to discover it was all wrong, all rotten at its core. She'd been a fool to think Mack could help her get on the career ladder. She was fodder to him. Fodder for the news machine. For his little empire he had going. When it came to deception, the story was every bit as fake behind the camera as it was in the world they were reporting on.

Was *nothing* real anymore?

The blinds on Mack's office were pulled down. Sarah came out of nowhere to appear at her elbow, timid and pale. "What's wrong?"

"I'm quitting."

"Oh my God, no. Why? No, you can't do that. Viv, think about it, please—"

Viv grasped her arm to stem the outburst, sensing the terror in Sarah's eyes. "It's time. I can't take this anymore. It's all fake. It goes against everything I believe in."

"But what will you do?"

"I'll find something. Anything. I'll go back to the pharmaceutical industry and report on drugs trials. I don't care—"

"But Mack's your only way up the ranks here. You won't make it anywhere in the BBC if you don't go via him."

She snorted. "Mack is precisely the person I need to get away from. It's okay Sarah, we'll stay in touch."

She trailed back to Liam's apartment in misery. The worst thing was, Adam was already en route to Malaysia, and she missed him horribly. But she wasn't going to follow him. She was going to stay in London with Liam, with family.

Adam had been right on one thing, though. Her job and "humanizing" him was not as important as his right to privacy. He was already human before he met her, albeit a reticent, suffering one who only wanted privacy, and she'd been so arrogant as to decide that he needed more exposure. It was no wonder he'd blocked her off.

Chapter 26

London

"Come on, sis. You know you want to." Liam took Viv's bishop and rolled the ivory piece between his fingers with a smug grin.

"Damn you." She pushed a reluctant pawn forward, not really concentrating. "No, Liam, I don't want to. I'm serious." Three days it had been now, three days with her little brother as her only company. She appreciated being able to stay in his London apartment, which boasted a spare box room of a bedroom where she'd been holed up mulling over everything that had passed, but she did *not* appreciate his attempts to cheer her up.

"Come on, when was the last time you missed one?"

"An actual race, not qualifiers? Well … three years ago, I suppose."

"Then you don't want to start missing one now, do you?" Liam caught her eye, and then his gaze flickered down to where he was about to checkmate her king.

"That's *why* I want to miss it. It's taken up too much of my life already. Besides, it's on at 8:00 a.m. our time. I'm going to have a lie-in this Sunday."

"You don't do lie-ins."

"I do now. You can bring me breakfast in bed and tell me the final ranking."

Liam drummed his fingers on the side of the chessboard. In a horribly piquant way, it reminded her of someone. "Please don't do that."

"Holy mackerel, someone's touchy."

"When was the last time you broke up with someone?" she asked. "Touchy doesn't even begin to cover it. I shouldn't even be here with you. I should be in a bedsit getting drunk with my girlfriends, except they're all off being successful across the globe." She slumped back into the sofa. Liam had won anyway. Just like the last two games.

"Giving up?"

"Yeah."

Liam gathered pieces off the board and put them into a velvet bag. "Count yourself lucky you got in deep enough to mourn him. Mine never last more than two or three dates. Story of my life. Maybe I should look for a sportswoman. What do you think? A Russian tennis player? A triathlete? Or one of those synchronized swimmers? They're seriously kinky."

She threw a cushion at him. "Stay away from athletic people. A nice, safe, banking employee is what you need."

"And you need your head examined. I didn't even get to meet him! That would've made my year."

"I'm sorry about that," she said sadly. "You'd have got on. If it's any consolation, I didn't get to meet any of his family either. In fact, you could say he really went out of his way to avoid that happening."

"Well, I have a load of bankers who want to meet you, my famous, TV-presenter sister. You won't be single for long."

"Load of wankers, you mean." Viv pictured Kieran, the last one she'd dated. "I'll pass."

They sat in silence, Liam slowly filling his bag of chess pieces clink, clink, clink, Viv watching him vacantly as she ran through the series of incompatible men she'd dated in her life.

"You know what?" she said. "Maybe I will watch a little bit. The start. You know, to see if there are any crashes."

Liam grinned. "Knew you'd cave. I'll set the alarm to seven fifty, just in case."

• • •

Adam found the street using his phone's GPS. It was off a squalid market, rife with people, chickens, spices, foodstuffs. All he could see was a typical open-front restaurant with sacks of rice lining the crooked pavement out front. He located the serving woman and asked for Aqil.

"Ah, Aqil …" She nodded vigorously and pointed upward with a soupspoon. One floor up.

He climbed the dark, narrow stairway that stank of cabbage and unidentifiable pungent vegetables. The house door was painted a bright blue. He knocked. A wizened old woman in a shawl answered, toothless, but with a mesh of kind wrinkles around her eyes.

"Aqil?" he asked, pretty sure that she wouldn't understand a word of English.

"Aqil! Aqil!" she croaked. She turned her beady eyes back to him, searching him with a mixture of curiosity and suspicion. Was it her other grandson, Ahmed, who had died, or how did she fit into this tragic picture?

A tall, thin boy came through with a slow, sulky gait, typical of any sixteen year old. The old woman gestured to where Adam was standing at the door.

Aqil turned and stared. His arm shot to the woman's to prevent her from walking any nearer the door. His mouth opened, but no words came out. The woman made a questioning sound.

The boy held his hands to his head. He started jabbering in Malay, or what Adam thought was Malay until he got used to the sounds and discovered it was English, or something like English, with many consonants glossed over.

The boy slowed down after a minute and started speaking a more intelligible version. "You got my email?" he asked. "You came to see me?"

"I did. That's why I'm here. I wanted to check that you were doing okay. I'm sorry about what happened. About Ahmed."

At the mention of Ahmed, the old woman's hand clamped to her mouth, and she nagged the boy again so that he'd translate. He calmed her down with a few words, and then in another torrent of words he pointed to Adam, then to a small TV at the back of the room, then back to Adam again. She stared at Adam, backed off, through the same narrow doorway from where Aqil had appeared.

"She get tea, yeah? Come in, sit here. I can't believe this. I can't believe this. Why did you come all the way here?"

"Aqil, where is your family? The rest of them?"

"Oh no, they're not here. They sent me here."

It was as Adam suspected. "Because of what happened?"

"Yeah, they think I will feel better away from there."

"Aqil, listen to me. You have to go back. Talk to them. Share your pain with them. Explain that you're hurting as much as they are. If you don't, you'll carry this forever, and you may never see them in the same way again."

The boy shook his head. "No, no, I can't do that. They say I killed him."

"And did you?"

"No, of course not. He's my brother. I told you; I told you. It was an accident. He fell off the bike."

"I know that. You know that. They know it, too. They just want to blame someone. But you have to fight for your right to be accepted in your family no matter what, and you have to do it now, Aqil. Or it'll be too late."

Aqil looked up in anguish. "You help me? You go there?"

And so Adam found himself driving out to a rich suburb of KL with a boy who had turned from sullen and timid to someone he knew was bright and inherently hopeful under all the recent bereavement. Aqil wanted to be a civil engineer. Or an architect. He had set ideas. And he knew more than Adam did about F1 history. The guy was a walking encyclopedia. Adam tried to catch him out as they navigated the crazy streets of KL:

"Okay, who finished sixth in the Australian Grand Prix of 2007, after starting last on the grid?"

Aqil thought for a moment. "Felipe Massa."

"Who made his debut in the 2007 US Grand Prix, when he was nineteen?"

"Sebastian Vettel."

"How many races did Michael Schumacher win in 2000?"

"Eight—no, nine!"

"Damn," Adam said. "I give up." They both laughed. Aqil stopped laughing abruptly in a way that reminded him so much of how raw he'd felt after Eddie. How it had felt wrong to laugh or smile at anything. He looked at the grim set to the boy's mouth.

"It's hell, isn't it? He'll never go away. He'll always be there. And that's a good thing. Your job is to live the life you have so that one day when you talk to him, you'll be happy because of the things you've done."

Aqil nodded.

He left the boy at the automatic gates with some local currency to get back to his granny when he was ready. Adam knew his gesture could only have symbolic value at best. The rest was up to Aqil. He promised to get him two seats in the grandstand. Did he have any other brothers?

"No, a sister. She'll come."

"Even better,"

"You win for me?"

"Don't worry about that. You go get your family back."

"Like you got yours?" Aqil asked.

He shrugged. "I'm working on it."

Driving alone back to the hotel, Adam felt a tight bolt of anger being twisted counter-clockwise, letting the pressure eke its way out. It wasn't a comfortable feeling. It opened up the way for too much to get in, and it was emotionally exhausting. The raw vulnerability in Aqil's eyes brought home to him how far he'd come since he was sixteen—how far down the wrong road. With any luck, Aqil would take the right turn when it came to deciding how to carry on with his life.

Chapter 27

Sepang, Malaysia

Adam ran into Reece in the lobby and couldn't help overhearing his ridiculous conversation with the poor receptionist. Reece was trying to get a room change so he could have a view of the pool area, like last year. No doubt he wanted to inspect the female guests in their beachwear so he could choose which one to attack next. Mid-negotiation, he held up his forefinger and turned around.

"Fontaine, sorry to hear about … you know."

"Save it." He looked about for another receptionist. Reece apologizing for anything was just about as disingenuous as things could get.

"Look, I had nothing to do with it." Reece held up his palms. "Just so that's on the record."

Adam looked past him. Another receptionist had come to the desk. He marched over to the young Malaysian man.

"Adam," Reece said, sharply.

"What?"

"For old time's sake, man, I had nothing to do with it."

"What are you talking about?"

"The thing with Viv. Someone tipped them off, but it wasn't me."

"Tipped who off?"

"The press." Reece held up his phone.

Damn. So the gossip had started, had it?

"Wasn't me," he repeated.

"Forget it." Adam wanted him to shut up so he could think about what this meant. Vivienne would hate it. Especially now. Didn't matter who had leaked the story.

"And I've nothing to do with her quitting either, got it?"

"Quitting?"

Reece frowned. "You don't know? She quit, right? The Beeb? I just heard. It's official."

Adam spun and walked blindly away from reception, forgetting what he'd come down for.

Why would she quit? But she'd have said something, surely? And she wanted that job. It was her best way into journalism. Other journalism. She'd always mentioned how being a serial F1 driver girlfriend made her queasy, but queasy enough to give up on a career choice?

God. Quit? Where was she now?

He'd assumed she'd be here reporting. In Malaysia. That they'd still have a chance. Or at least that he'd still see her and gauge her reaction to being apart—to see if it was wrecking her mind just as much as it was wrecking his. He'd assumed she was all right, that she'd hang on until the end. And then things would be easier.

But this meant she wouldn't be here at all.

Or ever again.

• • •

"No," Chad said for the third time. "Don't be a moron. Even with a direct flight, you'd get there Wednesday afternoon, local time, earliest. You'd have to leave that same evening to get back here by Thursday evening. You'd miss the practice runs. I forbid it. End of."

Adam stared straight ahead, determined to wait it out.

"Not to mention you'd be sleepwalking for the qualifiers. You never sleep on those international flights," Bruce added, quite unhelpfully.

"Fine." He raised his hands in a gesture of surrender.

"Sorry, mate," Bruce said with a nod of sympathy.

Chad gave him a look of disgust.

"We'll see you at dinner?" Chad asked. "In the Red Room? They're doing French cuisine tonight. I'll need your help in selecting my wine."

"Yeah."

Adam traipsed back to his room and slumped on the bed beside his packed holdall. He flipped his well-worn passport in his hand for a moment, deliberating, looking at the eight-year-old photo of the very serious young man on the first page.

Then he stood up.

Fuck them all. He was going to London. He'd find her, and he'd beg her to think again. Ask her to come with him to Saskia's wedding. Having Vivienne sharing his life was more important than his grievances with his ailing father. More important than anything. If he could ever forgive the old codger remained to be seen, but until that point, he needed to get his priorities straight in his own life. Otherwise he was still living for Eddie, wallowing in old wounds.

That was not what Eddie would have wanted.

Chapter 28

London

Adam arrived at the shiny black door of Dreyfuss Lane 304, dog-tired, hoping the stale air of the airplane didn't cling to him. Even first-class plane travel made him feel filthy. She wasn't answering her phone. If the house was empty, he'd just spent a lot of time sitting in an airplane for nothing.

An auburn-haired, earnest-looking young man with blotches of freckles on his nose opened up. His eyes blinking in the sunlight were so exactly the shape and color of Vivienne's that Adam knew who he was in an instant.

"You're Liam."

Liam, whose expression had changed in a millisecond from polite to awestruck, was gasping. "Adam Fontaine! I—I've set the alarm to see you at 8:00 a.m. on Sunday. But now you're here on my doorstep. Um, I'm not quite sure I'm not seeing things. Shit, Viv's not here. I mean, she is *here*, but not right now. She's out. Sorry—I'm blabbing, aren't I? I—I tend to do this when I'm shocked … I mean, pleasantly surprised—"

"It's a family trait," Adam said, smiling. "Do you know when—?"

"—she's back? I don't know for sure. But please come in. Forgive me. Come right this way. There you go. God, you're tall. Yeah, I'm working from home today. Hence the mess. But wait. Aren't you meant to be in Malaysia? Free practice and all that?"

"I'll pass on that question."

"I don't know what time she'll be back." Liam held a hand to his jaw. "She's out talking to a prospective client."

"Prospective client?"

"Yeah, she's got this new job. Well, she's sort of creating this new job. She's starting her own agency. PR agency."

"PR agency? Really?"

"Yes. Sit there, Adam, please. There you go. See when you've had TV exposure as she's had, it generates interest within the right circles. You can hit the ground running because people want a piece of your expertise and automatically think you know what you're doing."

"Well she does know what she's doing."

"Yeah, actually," Liam agreed.

"Any idea when she might back?" Adam glanced at his phone for the millionth time that afternoon.

Liam rubbed the back of his neck, looking pained. "I couldn't say. She's at the mercy of London traffic. God, she'll kill me. I know I'm supposed to be doing something polite here like offering you tea or something." He wrung his bony hands in a show of anxiety. He was more highly strung than Vivienne. "Do you want tea?"

"No thanks."

"Coffee? I do have real coffee with beans and shit."

"It's okay, Liam, I'm just here to see your sister."

"Yeah, I get that. Right. Right. I'll call." He walked around in a circle as he punched the phone.

"I've tried," Adam said. "But maybe she'll answer to you."

Liam tried. "No luck," he said after a few tries. He shot Adam a woebegone look.

They sat down on the couch together. Adam's gaze landed on the old-fashioned clock on the mantelpiece, ticking away. Five o'clock. He had to leave back for the airport at seven, latest. "And you've no idea who these clients are? Even whereabouts they are in London?"

"No. South End, she said, but that doesn't narrow it down much."

"Christ," he said. "I can only wait until seven."

"She may be back by then. If the traffic is good, which"—he looked at the clock, crestfallen—"it never is at this time."

Adam rose. "I won't take up your time."

"What?" Liam laughed in a strangled manner. "You're just going to leave?"

"Yes."

The younger man jumped up. "Well, write a note or something. Otherwise she'll say it's a hoax. She won't believe me."

"No. I'm not sure she wanted to see me anyway … we've … I've … it's complicated."

"If you saw the way she was moping around here, you'd have thought twice about coming back here, too."

"Moping is she?" Hope ignited in his chest again.

"Seriously. It's unbearable. Can you—please—take her off my hands?"

Adam laughed.

Liam smiled, too. A very Vivienne-like smile.

"Look," Liam said. "If you're going to be in London for the next two hours, it may as well be here rather than in an airport lounge, right? And well—*Top Gear*'s on, if you wanted to see that?"

Adam hesitated.

"I have beer."

"No, really I—"

"It's Belgian."

"Yes, but—"

"Trappist."

"Which one?"

"Westvletern 12."

"Don't do this to me."

Liam marched off triumphantly to the kitchen.

He sank back in the black leather couch. The room was small, neat, typical twenty-something male with obscure dark posters, assorted gadgetry, plugs and adapters strewn over the simple wooden coffee table, and a huge TV with a workstation taking up one wall of the room. The only evidence of Vivienne being there was a soft cardigan hanging off a chair and a faint whiff of her Daisy perfume in the air.

His gaze landed on the printer because there were printouts beside it with pink and green colors that looked familiar—

He wandered over.

"Oh, yeah, that. FontaineFans.com," Liam said, coming into the room with two bottles of Westvletern. "You can blame me. She liked the colors, but after a while I didn't think they were the best for you. Hope you don't mind."

"I gave her a hard time over it," Adam said ruefully. "I never considered how much time she must have put into it. And for the life of me I still can't understand why."

"Well, it is a bit … *girly*. Maybe that's why she told me to shut it down." Liam shrugged and picked up the TV remote. "It was probably as well because the traffic was reaching the limit my provider could handle. Some Japanese kid took it on. Bought the whole shebang off me for 5,000 quid."

The strains of the *Top Gear* theme tune filled the living room. They watched in fascinated silence for forty-five minutes, broken only by their laughter.

It was long enough to learn there were few things better in the world than watching *Top Gear* with Vivienne's brother in this cozy living room. The warming caramel finish of the Trappist beer almost mellowed the bitter taste of the absurdity of taking a flight from Malaysia to London without seeing Vivienne herself.

As the ending tune rang out, Liam shook his head. "God, I'm so sorry. That's a long old way to come for a couple of beers."

"Not just any beer," Adam reminded him. "Good company, too."

"There was that," Liam said. "Now will you please leave me some proof for Viv that you were here?"

"Tell her I said the beer's better this year."

Liam exhaled. "You're not making this easy for me, are you?"

He grinned. He shook Liam's hand, and a bolt of sadness shot through Adam at the thought of never seeing him again. In a short space of time, he'd met someone he could be really comfortable with. And that didn't happen too often. "Bye, Liam."

"Good luck Sunday. We'll be watching."

• • •

"Liam, don't be such a wanker. It's not funny," Viv said three hours later. She slumped on the sofa and kicked off her pumps.

"See where you're sitting?" her brother insisted, "He was right there."

She ignored him and rummaged in her handbag for her phone. "Battery ran out. Look, I'm loading it up now, and if there isn't a message from Adam Fontaine telling me he's in London—or as you say, was in London—then *you* are making the coffee tonight." It was typical of Liam to joke around but really unlike him to be so goddamn *cruel.*

Liam shrugged.

She settled back with a copy of his last week's *The Economist* with no intention of checking the phone. "It's your turn anyway, so I think you might as well start making it now."

"Viv, check the frigging phone."

She gave him a withering smile and pressed the phone on. Her heart jumped. No joke—Adam had called at 17:05, three hours ago, and at 17:07 and 17:15 and ... there was no message.

"But ... but he's in Malaysia, preparing for the race," she said, dumbfounded. "Isn't he?"

"Well, he's on his way back there now, I'd imagine. He said to tell you the beer tastes better this year."

Viv frowned and searched her brother's freckled face. When had she told him that?

"Four empties of Westvletern in the kitchen. I'd never drink that much on my own."

Liam was either getting much better at lying, or he was telling the truth. And the evidence was piling up.

"All circumstantial," she muttered, stomach lurching. *Good God. It is true. He'll mess up his qualifiers, the stupid man!*

• • •

In the middle of the race, Adam groaned aloud; the thunderstorm had hit the Sepang circuit on lap twenty-four, a fierce wind blowing in from the east. Having started in seventh position and fallen to eighth on lap two, things were going from bad to worse.

"Gotta hold on 'til the pit on lap twenty-eight," Bruce said. "We'll tell you when. Watch out for debris at the end of the straight."

Adam heard the strain in his engineer's voice. Bruce had been so disappointed with him only qualifying seventh that he'd refused to talk to him all morning. But during a race, feelings had to be pushed aside, along with any self-doubt, or regrets, or fatigue.

The only consolation was that Vivienne wouldn't have to comment on this drastic performance on live TV. With any luck she wouldn't even be watching the race. He hadn't heard a thing from her, even though Liam must've told her he'd been there. So her feelings were clear.

He was using the aerodynamic tow from Anderson in front, which helped on the straights but not in the corners. And Ronan Hawes right behind was dying to overtake, so he had to fend him off by reducing the available angles going into the corners. All the time.

"Stick to one line," Bruce warned. "Keep it legal."

"Yeah, I know."

Give it up, Hawes.

But then in the second corner on lap twenty-nine, just before the pit stop, Hawes found his angle and overtook.

"Damn," Bruce and Chad yelled simultaneously.

"You're coming in," Bruce said, all the frustration audible now.

• • •

"Noooooo!" Viv and Liam leapt up from the sofa in unison.

"Why did he let him overtake?" Liam moaned. "Boyfriend one overtakes boyfriend two."

"Information overload," Viv said, ignoring the comment. "He's got drag from Dave Anderson in front to think about, and Ronan's been up his ass the whole race. He can only change his angle once in a corner to ward him off—any more than that, and he'd be accused of deliberately blocking him—but he went a bit too narrow there."

"You saw all that?" Liam asked.

She shrugged. "This is my job, you know? Uh, was."

Her brother picked up the sheet of paper they'd used to work out the points. "So if he's in ninth now … he'll pick up two points and he needs more than that."

"Anything can still happen," she said hopefully.

"No, Reece's got it in the can. Look at him, smug bastard."

Reece's red car was a few seconds in front. Catherine was doing the commentary, and it grated to hear her blunder her way through. The way she eulogized Reece's driving, you'd think she'd had a fling with him. The minute the thought formed, Viv felt thoroughly ashamed. Wasn't this the very prejudice she'd fought against for so many months?

"Ronan's in, too," announced Liam.

She glanced up from her calculations. "Please don't let him overtake Adam in the pit."

"Remember the time Adam's crew got the tires mixed up?" Liam said.

"I'll never forget. But that was before we … got together."

"What's he like? After a race? Before a race? Is he like Ronan?"

She sighed. Liam knew Ronan a little from having met him after two races. They'd got on well as fellow British men with friendly dispositions, but she'd felt it was surface only. She'd have paid good money to have seen Adam interacting with Liam. "No, he's not like Ronan," she said. "Before a race, he's intense but calm. After a race, he's … intense but calm." She frowned. "Not much difference really.

"And he's not afraid to be critical in either case," she continued, "but also very open to suggestions and willing to treat me as an equal when he talks about it …" Her voice trailed off as she got stuck on remembering Adam after his first no-finish in Hungary, how he'd mastered his emotions and good naturedly sat through the torture of an interview with her, which had turned into … their first scorching hot kiss and lovemaking.

"That was the impression I got all right," Liam said, and stood up to pull over the curtain as the late August sunshine was zapping in at eye level. Viv sensed he was fishing for information, but she was in no position to tell him how she felt. She hardly knew what to think herself.

"Viv, look, he's fallen to tenth."

She buried her face in her hands.

"Viv?"

She raised her head.

"How on earth did you manage to do live commentary on this? Look at you; you're a sniveling wreck."

"Shut up."

The remainder laps went by in silence, Viv unable to speak, and Liam scribbling down calculations—the permutations that would still allow Adam to win the championship. It was a close finish, with Maddux coming in first to surprise everyone. Reece came in second. Good old Maddux snuck past him on the penultimate lap. Adam followed ten seconds later in ninth. Despite his lowly position, the camera sought him out after the race because the only two men who could still win outright were he and Reece. No other drivers mattered anymore.

"And there's Adam Fontaine, the man in green," chirped Catherine, "the man they call Mr. Spock. He's had a disappointing finish here in Sepang, and he may have just handed Reece Marlowe the championship on a silver plate today. We'll just have to hold our collective breaths until we see the final finish in November."

• • •

After Malaysia came China, Russia, Brazil. Every Sunday or second Sunday brought a new continent for the F1 squad, and Viv had to admit she was glad she wasn't traveling with them. To schedule the final races in this way was an act of cruelty. Adam got fourth in China, but it was fine because Reece only got fifth. In Russia the opposite happened. Both drivers seemed to be attached by some ironic cord of fate.

In between watching and fretting over F1 races, Viv had started up her fledgling business as a PR agent. She took the plunge and cold-called a bunch of semi-famous sporting personalities around the Greater London area. Only one bite so far, but the satisfaction of running her own business made up for any lack of profitability.

She missed Adam so much during those weeks, she couldn't breathe at times. And it wasn't just the physical aspect that killed her—it was his presence, the way he completed her, the way she felt more centered when she was with him, more in touch with herself. He'd become her rock, steadfast, hard as coal, brittle as ice, challenging her perception, wanting her as a real person, wanting to work things out—until she'd run away.

It was always easier to run than to let someone reach a deeper core—that uglier part of the psyche where thoughts were raw, insecure. And Adam had reached that part of her—the part that was afraid to commit, the part that shied from real conflict, the part that told her she was incapable of focusing on one thing and achieving it, the part that was unwilling to explore his darkness.

She'd let him get away with his secrets because, in truth, she'd been too chicken to demand the full story. She'd wanted nothing to destroy what they had because it was too precious, and so she'd hidden it away. But living in the real world meant taking that relationship and facing the world together, and facing each other in private, wholeheartedly. It was time to stop blaming the media for what did and didn't happen in her relationships.

"I've decided," she said to Liam the day after Reece's Brazilian win. "I'm going to Monaco. I have to be there."

"Um, Viv. Little problemo." Liam made the universal gesture for money. "Tickets?"

"No problemo. Savings." She had her last-resort savings account that was meant to be rent for when she got an apartment. Some things were more important than money.

"Well, in that case, I'm coming, too," Liam said. He went to the fridge and pulled down their calculation sheet off its magnet. "How do we stand again?"

"Two hundred fifty for Adam to 261 Reece," she said mournfully. "Do the math."

"So Adam can only get it if he wins, and if Reece …"

"Gets fourth or worse."

"Hmm. Does Adam like Monaco?"

"Nope."

...

On the verge of leaving Sao Paolo, Adam sat in the airport lounge and debated whether to send the mail twenty times before he pressed return. The reasons not to do so were numerous; the reasons to do so boiled down to a single one: to reconnect to family. Because Dad may not have much of a future left at all.

Dad,

You're surprised to hear from me. I won't labor the point.

I'm coming to Saskia's wedding on December fifth. Just so you know. She wants the family to be there. Mother will be there, too. I hope it will not be too much to ask for you to also be there, for Saskia's sake, even if I show up.

Best,

Adam

Chapter 29

Monte Carlo, Monaco

"Give me those frigging binoculars," Viv said, kicking the side of Liam's foot.

"It's my turn," Liam said, elbowing her back. "Okay, lemme see. They're on the grid now for the formation lap."

She seethed at her little brother. It had cost her a minor fortune to get these seats in Grandstand K, not to mention the last-minute flights to Nice. She'd cleared out her bank account.

She didn't know why she'd come, just that she'd *had* to come. She was worried about Adam's frame of mind for this final race. He needed to win so badly that if Reece clinched it, it would surely kill him. Kill him. And yet, Reece was starting from a much superior position in the points table. Maybe it was a ghoulish journalistic streak within her that wanted to see Adam crumble? Or maybe she wanted final proof that he wasn't relationship material.

Orange car, green car, white car—Marlowe, Fontaine, Bates. She'd seen this lineup before—in an Arabian desert, and it seemed like a lifetime ago. Her stomach twisted at the thought of the pressure on Adam to get first and to push Reece into fourth somehow. All those curves. Had he already given up in his mind? What did that look like?

"Be back soon," she said to Liam, who merely held up his hand.

She raced through the underground tunnel, squeezed past the whole row of spectators loitering around the exit. Her feet knew where to take her; she'd been here watching from the harbor area twice before. She had no press card, no VIP security pass, so she'd need some luck. She ran and ran, past spectators, security guards, race organizers.

Bruce. She saw him at the entrance to the Gatari pit area. She stuck her hand in the air to wave.

"Good Lord, it's Viv. How are ya?"

"Bruce," she sputtered, "let me come in there with you. Please."

"Well," he hesitated, glancing over at a group of race scrutineers. "Why not? If you're quiet." He held the door open and she slid inside.

"I want to talk to Adam. Before the fifteen second rule kicks in."

"Oh no, you can't do that, love. Chad only lets pit engineers—"

She booted past him. "Sorry, but I have to." She stole the Gatari cap off his head and shoved it on her own, glancing behind once to see him slack-jawed with shock.

She ducked and twisted her way around the engineers and reached Adam's car. She hunkered down to his level, just watching his profile. He stared straight ahead, his eyes tense inside that fiberglass visor. This could possibly have been the worst decision of her life.

Or the best.

Slowly he turned. His helmet flicked in a comic double take. He slammed the visor up, eyes wide, breathing heavily. He reached up to turn off his team microphone.

"Vivienne? You're here?" he yelled over the noise of the engine.

"Sure am," she yelled back.

"I thought you'd given up on me."

"Not yet."

A slow smile. "Give me two more hours, okay?"

"Come now." Bruce's arms were tight around her waist. "We all have to get off, or he'll be penalized. You don't want that."

"No." She saw that the cameras were focusing in her direction now, so she kept her head down and followed Bruce back to the garage. Yes, she'd give him two hours.

• • •

"How's the car, Adam?" came Bruce's familiar call on lap thirty-five. He could hear the emotion in his engineer's voice. He'd never made it to a final race before, and the perceived wisdom was spot on: it did feel different.

It felt dream-like, like he was going through the motions, but they didn't affect him, because he floated above it. Had he really seen Vivienne there, or was it an illusion brought on by excitement and inhuman amounts of adrenalin?

"Revs 8," Bruce said.

"You got it."

"Any oversteer, understeer?"

"None at all, she's steady," Adam replied. For the first time ever. The engineers, Marc and Olivier, had killed themselves this week working on the engine, tuning it to within a micrometer of its life. He'd never seen such dedication in the engineering team before, and neither had Bruce. He was the sole unsteady variable in the whole equation now.

Vivienne was right here! That was why it felt different. He felt different. There was so much more to life than this race. She had said it in so many subtle ways before, but now that he'd a chance to get her back, the outcome of this race was unimportant in comparison.

"You're staying on softs. Albany's two behind you. He's fine. He's holding the back. Watch Maddux behind you. He's got one stop to go as well."

Even while driving it, it was the perfect race, despite it being Monaco. The car's top form was allowing him to relax into Chad's tactical plan. There was just the little problem of Reece Bloody Marlowe sitting in front of him.

Round and round. Team messages back and forth. Another pit stop. Still two seconds behind Reece. But Reece would flag soon.

He had to. Old habits died hard, didn't they? Adam gritted his teeth.

"Oh my good God," Bruce crackled. "Reece has understeer, and he's ignoring it."

"God, the idiot."

"He's spinning! Adam, be careful, give him room if you have to. He may lose it and take you with him."

"Negative. I have Maddux on my tail."

"I know, I know. Let me think. He needs to change that front right tire. If he doesn't, he's a danger."

With only ten laps to go, Reece was never going to make a move like that. He'd race on, danger to himself and others or not. In fact, knowing him, Reece had probably switched off his team radio so he wouldn't have to listen to their advice.

"Adam, easy now," Chad called, "we want you alive."

Then Adam saw it and heard it—right in front of him. Reece flying into the bend and slipping out mid-curve, way out, spinning—a 360-degree turn. His engine screeched as he tried to right himself again.

"God," breathed Adam, jerking left then right to avoid the tip of the wing that had flown off onto the circuit. "See that?"

"Mate, are you okay?"

"Fine," Adam responded tersely. "He's out. How's Bates?"

"Yeah, Maddux had to slow down, too," Chad yelled. "But he wasn't hit. He's fine. He's five behind. Don't worry about him."

"You're all clear," Bruce said. "Take this baby home, Adam!"

"Roger that."

His engineers had already lined up in a neat row along the pits in preparation for the final lap to cheer him home. The sight of their perfect line formation in green overwhelmed him with pride and gratitude.

...

And there he stood. Viv watched him from the middle of the crowd at the podium. Formula One world champion. Waving. Smiling even. He was holding the champagne bottle. He leaned to say something to Maddux. Maddux laughed and gave him the thumbs up. What were they talking about?

She was being jostled from all sides as the crowd went mad, reaching forward for a piece—a piece of something—success, fame, glory. She pushed back viciously. They were blocking her view of his face—a rare look of unguarded pleasure.

Despite the heaving bodies, she was glad to be anonymous in this crowd after her mad stunt on the starting grid. Yes, she felt somewhat self-conscious about that. But now that he'd won, might Adam forgive her for exposing herself like that?

He had somehow procured champagne flutes from the organizers. Instead of spraying champagne everywhere, he filled the three glasses carefully and handed the bottle to a race steward. The drivers clinked glasses like old ladies at a charity rally. Viv laughed. Had he just reversed a century old trend of wasting champagne?

Then he spotted her in the crowd. His gaze locked on to her, and all motion seemed to slow down as the crowd tried to figure out what was happening. He jumped off the podium and forced his way through the masses, which parted enthusiastically, slapping him on the shoulder, on the back, even ruffling his hair. A wave of cameras switched course to follow his progress. All heads turned to see what the commotion was—where the champion was heading.

She froze. The moment had come. She could still run. Or she could make it official. F1 girlfriend, committed to a life of the driver. Could she handle this? Same again next year? And after that again?

Adam came closer, his gaze drilling into her. A tiny hint of uncertain smile tugged at his upper lip, his hair just a tad ruffled. His chest heaved under the suit. He stood before her, arms by his sides, waiting … for a signal.

Oh, what the heck.

She took a step forward so her chest made contact with his. Her arm slinked around his neck. She blinked as cameras flashed in her eyes, and then … thud. He grasped her tightly into his scorching hot body, his lips pressing down hard onto hers, familiar, warm and possessive. His hands cupped the back of her head, squashing her ears with the thick sleeves of his flame retardant suit. The crowd erupted into cheers and whistles. When he pulled back from her, Adam looked abashed but ecstatic.

She felt free. She didn't *care* how many tabloids had that kiss on the front page.

"That's the last race," he said. "It stops here."

"You don't have to decide that now."

"No, this is the end."

"Something tells me it's only just beginning," she said.

• • •

The best part was, they could go to the hotel together, hand in hand. This beat the thrill of becoming F1 champion, crazy as it sounded. All he really wanted was Vivienne. Alone. In his bed.

"Okay." She sat on the bed and looked at him, biting her bottom lip. "I know what you want. And here's the thing." Her mouth had flattened into a thin line. "You want me to back off on your family. I'll do that. I'll never mention them. I won't even ask you about them."

"You can ask me," he said. "Just don't talk in public about them."

"I'm asking you now," she said, eyes huge. "I mean, I did talk to Jacques Villiers, and I read the file Mack compiled on you, but I could never understand why you left home and why you avoid all contact with them, except with your sister. I could only … guess."

He sat down on the bed beside her and folded his arms to keep his hands from smoothing over her body as he itched for them to do. He hadn't told this story to anyone except Reece—who didn't count. It felt strange—but somehow right that she should know.

"My brother." He stopped and started again. "Eddie. There was an accident when we were kids—he was fourteen, I was sixteen. Quad bikes." He squeezed her hand. "Vivienne, everyone knows that now, but what nobody except my family—and Reece—knows is that … I was *there*. I saw it all happen."

Vivienne pressed her hand to her mouth.

"There was a gap in the rocks by the cliff face that I'd always race to with him. We'd race up to it dead even until the last moment. He knew I'd back down if I had to. I was the eldest. We were dead even again that day, but his brakes were faulty. So, coming up to the gap where he needed to slow down, he couldn't stop, and I couldn't slow down quickly enough.

"We had contact, his bike toppled and he got flung out and landed against a rock. The impact of his spine against the stone was what killed him. I heard the crack, that awful squat sound. I saw his neck at an unnatural angle, too, and that disbelieving look in his eyes that this was it, his time had come to an end.

"I swerved, stopped the engine, jumped off, honestly thinking it would be just another tumble of his, and we'd have a laugh. And then I saw his stillness. I—I screamed at him to hold on, just hold on until I got help. I didn't think it could be the end. I thought something could be done, you know? That's what I was thinking. Every second counted. But it didn't matter. He was already gone."

"God." She exhaled. Her face was pale, her eyes huge and tense like she was trying to process this. What damage was this doing to her feelings for him? Well, it was too late for that—she had to know. This was too big a part of him to hide anymore.

"It was part of who he was, or who he wanted to be—the daredevil. Evel Knievel. He tried every stupid move in the book. It was all I could do to maintain his bike in perfect order so that nothing mechanical could go wrong.

"But that week I'd just come back from a karting course and was so excited to be back with him again, and to show him some stunts I'd learned, so we decided to have a race. His brake pads were loose. I'd even checked with Dad beforehand—Dad had been driving the bike that week to inspect vines and said it was in good condition, and I was stupid … *stupid* enough to believe him."

"It was an accident." She stroked his arm, bringing him back to the present. "Not your fault, your father's, Eddie's, anyone's."

Encouraged, he continued. "I pushed him to race that day. And Dad failed him by not caring for the bike. But of course Dad only sees the blame on my side, and on the side of motor racing in any form anywhere on the planet. He's always resented my driving, which is why there's been no contact all these years."

"And why you left home at seventeen?"

He nodded. "First Mum left, six months after the accident; she couldn't stand how Dad and I fought nonstop, how Dad wouldn't back down on forbidding me to drive. Saskia went with her but came back when she realized Dad needed her more. She's actually a saint. I can't wait for you to meet her. Anyway, once Sask was back, I left. I dug my heels in even harder, and for me it became a thing of connection to Eddie. Hard to explain …"

"Try me," she said gently.

"See, driving was all Eddie had been interested in. You should have seen his bedroom, covered with posters of the greats … Senna, Proust, Schumacher, Rosberg, Hamilton. I took up his mantle. Saskia claims I was so mad at Dad for the way he handled everything that I made my career a weapon against him."

"Did you?"

"No. It was a lot more organic than that. I excelled at mechanics, even then. I'd always let Eddie dream the big-driver dream. He'd have been amazing, Vivienne, and he'd have enjoyed it. He'd have been F1's golden boy. He had that edge, and that charm. I'd have been his chassis engineer. I'd have liked that."

"You must miss him terribly."

"Eddie had such a carefree, take-no-shit attitude—the sunshine of our family, the blond, the extrovert. Always joking. Once he was gone, the color of life just drained out for me. Well, anyway, I fled to Villiers after Mum left—but you know this story, don't you? It all took on a life of its own, how I worked and worked to get up through the ranks for Formula Renault and F3. Teams took me on because of the way I could fix cars and out-do the competition. I surprised myself to get this far as a driver."

"Adam, you're a great driver. And you can let the color back into your life. Different colors, maybe, but just as vibrant."

He squeezed her fingers. "With you here now, I believe that. And I feel him, up there, saying 'we did it' to the entire world."

"You won it for him," she said softly.

He nodded. "But he's giving you the thumbs up, too."

She smiled. "And your father? Does he still resent ... everything you've done? What you've accomplished? Is it possible he was just afraid of losing another son?"

"I don't care. You're coming with me to meet them all, by the way. This darn wedding's in two weeks' time."

"I'd be delighted to, thanks."

"And bring Liam. I like the guy."

She pulled his neck down to press her lips to his. Tenderly. But the kiss that started as comfort turned hard, possessive. He tugged her into him. She surrendered, then lashed back, pressing her body against his, absorbing some of his pent up desperation. He couldn't think of the future or the past, only the sensational now.

Chapter 30

Menton, France

When the first wave of madness had all died down, they had another serious conversation in Menton, next stop down the coast from Monte Carlo, where they'd holed up in a hidden chalet for a week of glorious, private togetherness. In the soft, November, Riviera sunshine, Viv watched the haunted look of her lover's eyes ebb away, replaced by new warmth.

"You don't have to give up for my sake," she said. "I'm willing to give it a go again out there next year. I love this racing scene. The only thing I didn't love was the thought that it would tear us apart."

"It's what I want, Vivienne."

"But you're the champ now."

He held her close. "And I've found a new reason to live. Because I love you." His hands tightened their grip on her upper arms. "I don't want to endanger this life in any way. And I don't just mean the danger of driving itself."

Her heart hammered. He'd said it. And she felt it. Simple and true, like nothing before.

"I love you, too," she said.

His eyes flashed understanding, and he bent down and kissed her.

"But what will you do?" It was one thing to say it, but could he really give it all up?

"My sponsorship money's enough to settle for a moment. Wherever you want to be for your new business—as long as it's not too far from an airport, please. I'll be back and forth to help Saskia and Jeff get set up. We just have to get this wedding out of the way first."

"Can you really turn your back on F1?"

"Well, no." His expression was suddenly serious. "Chad and Bruce are testing new engines and a new driver next year, and I want to help them out—but as a consultant, tactician, decision maker. I have a feeling the team's going to be—"

"The best yet." She laughed. "Don't say it."

"That's where you might come in."

"Me?"

"The driver. He's a reclusive Finn. He needs help. PR help. And if anyone knows how to coax a driver out of his shell, it's you."

Viv smiled and trailed her finger along his fine upper lip, liking the idea of working in the same arena with Adam very much, and liking that he'd asked. "And look where it got you. You're in my shell now."

"No place I'd rather be," Adam said, catching her fingers and leaning in for another kiss.

More from This Author
(From *High Octane: Ignited*
by Rachel Cross and Ashlinn Craven)

Praise for *High Octane: Ignited*:

"I highly recommend this read for all fans of romance with scorching hot, passionate nights, kick-ass awesome fast cars and a story of love found in a world of confusion. A totally thrilling AWESOME read! I very much look forward to taking another thrilling ride with these authors"—Contemporary Romance Reviews, 5 stars

"*High Octane: Ignited* was a high energy, fast-paced novel. It starts off with a bang, and continues explosively until the end. I am looking forward to reading more stories from these two talented writers."—Cruising Susan Reviews
He'd been catching flashes of her smooth, tanned skin all night. In a conservative sea of blacks and taupes, her dress with its low-scooped back shone vibrant as a peacock's tail. But that wasn't what caught his eye. There were plenty of beautiful women at the Le Meridien hotel. What caught his attention was the way she carried herself; she didn't glide about like a model, or vamp about like an actress. Instead her posture was ramrod straight—Queen's Guard style.

He leaned against the wall, nursing his drink and watching, as she approached the bar. She gave the bartender a smile, revealing the kind of perfectly straight, perfectly white teeth that indicated extensive orthodontia or good genes—in this crowd either was likely. He studied her lips as she mouthed her order, his gaze dropping to her fingers drumming impatiently on the mahogany bar.

A man at least twenty-five years her senior, vaguely familiar, with thick salt-and-pepper hair, sidled up and stood close enough to indicate familiarity. He laid a hand on hers, preventing her from taking the drink from the counter. Her expression darkened, her mouth twisted, and she said something—something cutting judging by the pained look that crossed his face.

She strode away, leaving the older gent gazing after her with longing. Ronan suppressed a shudder. May-December relationships still made him queasy, maybe because he was the product of one. He gave his collar a tug—he loathed these things. He'd been to sponsor events like this his entire career and it never—

"Incredible job in Budapest, Mr. Hawes. The way you managed the pits was inspired. This is Pantech-Windsor's year!"

Ronan pasted on his professional smile and turned to greet the speaker. "Cheers, mate." Some tire corporation chap if he wasn't mistaken. American. They were crawling all over Formula 1 these days, thanks to Supernova Energy Drink. They'd money to burn. Supernova had brilliant engineers and brought new sponsors and fans into the mix. In fact, they had everything but a sane driver. Maddux, their lead driver, had more luck than a man deserved and occasional flashes of brilliance, but no sense of self-preservation whatsoever. Ronan shook the American's hand, received a clap on the back in return, and continued moving through the crowd.

Speaking of the maverick Texan devil, Maddux Bates made eye contact across the room, sending him a sly grin, Vivienne on his arm. Ronan froze. He nodded back, teeth clenched, and headed in search of the peacock with the military bearing. He'd do anything to avoid contact with Vivienne McCloud. The woman who had gone straight from his bed to Maddux's two races into the season, spawning such inspired tabloid headlines as "Hey You Get Off My McCloud" and "Bates Outrates Hawes."

Teal dress was alone on the edge of the room, studying an abstract modern painting on the wall. The older man was nowhere in sight. Ronan took a sip of his Pellegrino and wandered over.

She turned her head, her gaze sharp, assessing every inch.

He stared down into her heart-shaped face. Her nose was a smidgen too tip-tilted, her mouth a shade too wide, but her eyes were clear and intelligent. The dress highlighted their not-quite-green-not-quite-blue color perfectly.

"Thoughts?" he said, indicating the painting with his drink.

She blinked at him and turned around to resume her study of it. "I'm no expert where modern art is concerned, but it looks like it might be upside down." Her husky American-accented voice sent a surge of testosterone down his spine.

He extended his hand. "Ronan Hawes." He waited for the spark of delayed recognition, a comment about his season. Nothing. Then again, this Brussels event didn't house a strictly F1 crowd.

She assessed him coolly for a half a second too long, and then extended her own for a brief, firm clasp. "Cassidy Miller." She swept a lock of wavy, dark brown hair out of her face. Only ice remained in the glass she held.

"Can I get you a drink?"

"Yes, thanks. Double bourbon on the rocks." She turned back to the painting.

"Right. Double bourbon it is then." American whisky was almost as revolting as their beer.

On his approach back, he noticed that her gaze went beyond the painting and her jaw was set, the soft curve of her mouth a rigid line.

She started when he reappeared at her side.

He handed her the bourbon.

"Thanks." Her expression smoothed back into bland. "In town for the race?"

"Yes, you?"

"Mmm hmm."

"Are you a fan?"

"Of Formula 1? Not so much. But I love NASCAR."

He pressed his lips together. Americans and their precious NASCAR. "Oh?"

"I'm with someone who loves Formula One." Her lips quirked. "So I deal."

"If you enjoy racing, you'll enjoy F1."

She tilted her head, eyes wide. "You think?" She shook her head. "Formula One is so much more about the car than the driver."

"Interesting opinion, but there's the catch—the cars don't drive themselves."

"Don't they? With all that technology, isn't F1 less … I mean, aren't the NASCAR races more of a test of the driver's capability?"

His lips curved in an insincere smile, and despite his attraction to this woman, despite Vivienne across the room, he was tempted to walk away. It had been ages since he'd had to explain his sport to a novice. He'd more trouble with people toadying up to him than with them denigrating the sport. "You shouldn't even mention NASCAR in the same breath as F1. Those guys wish they had our cars."

Her wide-eyed gaze was steady on his. "Oh?"

"Formula cars are the fastest circuit racing cars on the planet. We can max them out at 350 kilometers per hour."

Her brows lifted.

"That's 220 miles per hour to you," he said. "To reach that speed you need perfection—aerodynamics, suspension, tire design, all of it."

"So it *is* the car?"

Was she having him on? No, she seemed merely curious.

"It's everything. The team, the technology, the engineering, the driver. All of it packed up and shipped out after every race to the next Grand Prix, racing on different circuits, on city streets—it's a global sport, not just for you Americans."

"Well, maybe if you came to the United States ..."

He smiled and raised his glass. "Ah but we do. Texas built us a brand new circuit in Austin. We'll be there in November."

"Texas?" She pretended to shudder. "You race in Monaco. Why not the streets of New York or San Francisco?"

"San Francisco?" A laugh escaped him as he pictured his car on one of those hills. He stepped back, readying his departure with a polite smile.

She stayed him, laying a small, fine-boned hand on his forearm. He studied it—no rings or bracelets, her fingernails clipped short and without varnish, rather like her method of chatting up. His gaze rose.

She was grinning at him. He'd been baited.

She drained her drink, threaded her arm through his, and stole his line. "Want to get out of here, Mr. Hawes?"

For more books by Ashlinn Craven, check out:
Maybe Baby

In the mood for more Crimson Romance?
Check out *His Wicked Celtic Kiss* by Karyn Gerrard at
CrimsonRomance.com.

www.ingramcontent.com/pod-product-compliance
Lightning Source LLC
Chambersburg PA
CBHW010308100726